I0687122

FRACTURED ANGEL

KEN WILLIAMS

SAKURA PUBLISHING
Hermitage, Pennsylvania
USA

FRACTURED ANGEL

KEN WILLIAMS

FRACTURED ANGEL

Copyright © 2014 by Ken Williams

All rights reserved. Published in the United States by Sakura Publishing in 2014. No part of this publication may be reproduced, distributed, or transmitted in any form or by any means, including photocopying, recording, or other electronic or mechanical methods, without the prior written permission of the publisher, except in the case of brief quotations embodied in critical reviews and certain other noncommercial uses permitted by copyright law. For permission requests, write to the publisher, addressed "Attention: Permissions Coordinator," at the address below.

Sakura Publishing
PO BOX 1681
Hermitage, PA 16148
www.sakura-publishing.com

ORDERING INFORMATION:

Quantity sales: Special discounts are available on quantity purchases by corporations, associations, and others. For details, contact the publisher at the address above. Orders by U.S. trade bookstores and wholesalers. Please contact Sakura Publishing:

Tel: (330) 360-5131; or visit
www.sakura-publishing.com.

Edited by Quentin Whitfield & Derek Vasconi | Cover Art by Rania Meng

First Edition
Printed in the United States of America

ISBN-13: 978-0-9911807-6-9
ISBN-10: 0991180763

This is a work of fiction. Names, characters, businesses, places, events and incidents are either the products of the author's imagination or used in a fictitious manner. Any resemblance to actual persons, living or dead, or actual events is purely coincidental.

DEDICATION

Dedicated to all the homeless who are mentally ill.
You will always have a home in my heart.

"I'm sure you must know that it wasn't facilitating SSI or shelter that helped the most, it was having someone care at all..."

FORMER HOMELESS WOMAN

CHAPTER ONE

Shadows danced. Living darkness surrounded her like a malevolent maelstrom. She clawed with broken nails under the oversized sweater. Dread coiled in her stomach. Lifting the sweater, she looked down at her handiwork: red and swollen welt lines had begun to ooze out blood.

Her dying fire glinted off yellow eyes, staring at her from the darkness with deadly indifference. They were already considering her dead meat, perhaps breakfast. The thought brought a brittle smile to Tracy's chapped lips. It wasn't far from the truth.

Because of the weak light, her real tormentor was banished to the shadows. This quieting knowledge allowed her to pay closer attention to the fat rat. Long whiskers twitching—its manically cruel and amoral eyes focused on her. Tracy curled her arms under her legs and drew them harder into herself, making her slight frame appear even smaller. For a fifteen year old, she hadn't filled out, or grown much since she'd been twelve. And the little weight she had gained recently was lost to a near starvation diet. Her clothes now hung loosely.

Fear dropped her body temperature. She shivered. It forced a scream that she quickly drowned with parched saliva. Her head snapped left to right. She knew *he* was there. She could *feel* his menacing presence. She knew from experience that he could reach out at any moment, raking her insides with barbed claws.

Home for Tracy was an oppressive cave, like a dwelling made of corrugated tin. In reality, it was a convergence of drainage pipes that opened up, offering refuge for her homeless clan, haphazardly formed. She shared the shelter with a rat. She also shared it with others—residing both within her mind and without. *He*, on the other hand, was a visitor, coming and going unannounced, and always unwanted. *He* didn't care for what others wanted, or their feelings. Social niceties, privacy, and so much more were absurdities. *He did*, however, thrive on discomfort, especially hers.

Tracy had to pee. But her bathroom was the trash-strewn field behind the tunnel, and *his* presence crippled her with fright. *When was the last time she had cleaned up?* Showers were one of her fantasies: *To smell soap. To feel hot water rinsing silky shampoo from her hair.* A smile came. And it rapidly broke. She knew the others had the courage to make periodic runs over to the Sally for occasional showers. But she didn't.

She scratched through a hole in her sweater at the body lice. She knew that her smell offended the others, but they were too protective of each other to boot her out. She wouldn't last long on the outside.

She was tired. Her eyes felt like lead. Wistfulness forced her gaze over to her bed, a thread worn sleeping bag that had been pushed off to the side. It hadn't always been that way.

She bolted upright. Fear hopscotched from goose bump to goose bump across her skin. She shuddered. It wasn't the presence of the rat. Anytime she thought about the changes that had come over her, it was fear that gripped her heart.

When the voices and intrusive thoughts had first begun to surface, she had thought of sharing them with her mom or others, but she was afraid of ridicule, and she was unsure if that wasn't the way of adulthood. After all, she was just a kid. How was she supposed know what normal was, and wasn't?

Sitting in almost total darkness, trepidation drew aged lines across her face. Staring hard at the rat, she watched him pawing at the dirt. *Was he about to charge her like a raging bull?* She looked around, hoping to see her companions; that is—the ones who existed independent of her mind. But, like so often recently, aloneness stared back. Cold hollowness froze her insides as if they were carved out by a scalpel. A hard shiver rolled over her. Fear registered in degrees.

Tensing her muscles, she prepared for flight. Paused. She convinced herself that it was just an ungrounded fear. She pretended that the *other* wasn't present. And, the rat was no threat. He hadn't done anything to hurt her. He hadn't even really threatened her. As was often the case, the frightening situation was made harmless once she was able to acknowledge fear and meet it head on.

She smiled. Maybe the rat could be a friend? She could use a friend. She stared down at it. *It was lonely too!* Tracy's paranoia dissipated. The insight that a fellow creature shared sadness with her opened her heart. Looking about, she found a chunk of stale bread from last night's dinner.

Slowly, she reached out her hand, holding the bread before the rat. An offering. The rat perked up with interest. With no fear, it quickly paced the few steps that separated him from breakfast. It sniffed the bread, and began to nibble. A crooked smile came upon Tracy when his long whiskers tickled her hand. Suddenly, the rat chomped down hard, yanking the bread free. She squealed with delight. Her eyes brightened, honoring the courage of the rat. *If only she had such inner strength!*

That last wish washed sadness over Tracy, sweeping the brightness from her eyes.

Tracy once again looped her arms through her legs and began rocking back and forth to the beat of a cadence, heard only by her. Humming a gentle children's lullaby, her soft voice filled the lonely void. Abruptly, she stopped. The sudden silence was first oppressive, and then terrifying. An ache swelled within her body and soul, rising like high tide before a storm. She shut her eyes. Tears broke from them. She swallowed the liquefied salt hard. A new insight: Fear had a taste. She missed her Mom. Maybe she would know what to do about the voices.

Her lips pinched hard. Her mom wasn't there. She was alone. Her only companion was a rat. It was possible that even her roommates only existed in her head. Maybe, the only reality was *Him*—the danger that lurked in the darkness. Her body locked up as she forced herself not to look about. Maybe he was simply waiting for the fire to die out, before he jumped from the blackness to devour her. Tracy rocked harder and began humming again. She ratcheted up the volume and increased the intensity. No longer was it a lullaby. It was the only trick she had left. And it did help with the voices. The dying light flickered—its will to live fleeing. Her own, was not too far behind.

CHAPTER TWO

The upscale, Spanish style house stood on a ridgeline, overlooking a harried freeway that crossed the badlands below. Inside, the day's heat was kept at bay by silently running air conditioners. In defiance, the house's windows stood wide open. It was hot. The Santa Ana winds were blowing furnace-like desert air into the L.A. Basin. Here in neighboring Orange County, the air had been scraped clean of smog particles by the howling winds.

In the old days, thousands of acres had been planted with orange trees, sweetly scenting the air. By the tens of thousands, those same trees had been bulldozed in the name of progress. Now greed was row cropped by upscale and over-the-top houses, known locally and disdainfully by many as McMansions. The few orange trees left were lonely sentinels in the backyards of ostentatious million dollar homes.

The party was heating up, with the rock band just beginning to hit their stride. They were showcasing a new song, scheduled to debut next week. It was a gathering of the beautiful people, with much exposed flesh. There were enough breast augmentations amongst them to keep a Beverly Hills surgeon busy for a year. There were also enough inflated egos to give any Hollywood production company a run for the money.

Lynne Swanson found herself hiding in the bathroom. Standing before the mirror, she tried to find the strength to face her friends, business associates and professional partygoers. As she looked up at her reflection, she briefly wondered if any of them would notice her sunken cheeks, or the black bags under her eyes. It didn't matter if they were partially camouflaged by makeup.

"Damn it, Darrell!" She cursed her ex-husband for having them buy the house in the first place. Looking about the extravagant bathroom, she blamed him for the day's event. Her head sank; she would give anything to have all her houseguests magically disappear. And if she didn't have to make the mortgage payments, so that Tracy would have a place to come home to, the guests wouldn't even be there. If she hadn't felt that her daughter didn't need the sense of continuity that the house provided after the bitter divorce, she would have sold it long ago. But now, it had become an anchor. The market had gone south, and the loan was upside down. The mortgage was an engorged monster that fed off her work like a buzzard. Her work had to go on, and the ridiculous party was part of it.

Lynne leaned forward, resting her hand on the sink. Sweat formed on her upper lip. She tried dabbing at it with tissue. It threatened to ruin her makeup. A single line of moisture threatened her whole day. She sighed heavily. She knew it wasn't fair to blame Darrell. They had both fallen in love with the house, while their own love had withered and died. He had found a young scriptwriter, and moved on. In turn, she devoted her fractured heart to her daughter.

"Shit!" Six months! Six months of living hell! Had it really only been a hand full of months since she had found the life changing note from her daughter? It was B.C. and A.D. Life before pain. Now a life *of* pain. Lynne gripped the sink bowl so hard that her knuckles turned white, when a sharp pain rolled through her stomach. During the last half of the year, her stomach had turned into an acid pit. Standing straight, she loudly sucked in some air. Only by mingling and pushing the performing band's new release could she rid the house of distracting people. Self-pity would not do. She adjusted her makeup. Picking up a small and expensive bottle of perfume, she dabbed a pinch on her wrists. No one heard the mirror shatter when she hurled the exquisite bottle at it.

Lynne Swanson stood with drink in hand, bored to death with the pretty-boy wannabe actor who had cornered her. And why wouldn't he? She *was* a looker. She was tall, and blessed with a classic beauty that always drew the attention of both sexes, especially the high income, in-the-know crowd that was her social and business circles. She was in her early forties. The black, curve-defining dress that she wore, accentuated an athletic body that played as hard at racquetball as she did at most things in life.

She glanced over to the right and caught her friend, Helen, staring back. Her eyes widened once she saw the fear painting her friend's face. Lynne was afraid to walk towards her. The feeling in her legs had fled. Looking at the agony etched on her best friend's face drove a frozen carving knife into her heart. There was a dilemma, wasn't there? How could she get all these idiots out of her house? *The mortgage be damned!* Lynne knew all too well that only news of her daughter could produce such sadness in Helen. She downed her drink. She took pretty boy's glass and did the same. "Time to go!" Everyone who heard the demand knew it was exactly that, and quickly exited.

CHAPTER THREE

Pulling up across the street from the homeless shelter, Lynne took a deep breath. She exhaled slowly and cut the engine. She found reassurance in the sound of its smooth death—a low rumbling purr. Collecting her thoughts, she sat immobile. Shaking her head slowly, she tried to dispel the image of the people she spied loitering in front of the homeless shelter. They appeared to be from a different planet.

A few teetered precariously. Why they swayed, she hadn't the faintest idea. Others slept upright against the side of the cream colored building in deep exhaustion. She was a rookie, an outsider from suburbia. She was housed, not mentally ill, a fallen-down drunk, or a strung-out addict. She was not afflicted with extreme poverty, and she had never gone hungry. In other words, she was clueless. She had no idea that some of the homeless stayed awake all night, fighting off imagined demons—a byproduct of wounded minds, while others (especially the women), dodged and hid from very real predators, who hunted them down like game.

She continued her observation. A few dug through backpacks. Even stranger, some scavenged through shopping carts, overflowing with all manner of personal stuff, all in varying states of decay.

A few sat with their feet planted in the gutter; their eyes locked into an altered reality. Again, she was too unfamiliar to ascertain what was happening to those people. They just looked creepy.

Lynne's stomach muscles tightened. She willed herself to take a closer examination at the gathered tribe, milling about aimlessly in front of the homeless shelter. Half-forgotten anthropology lectures from college kicked in. That was what they were: a collective of strange, and exotic people that formed a foreign entity that was alien to her. *But maybe not to her daughter? Was this Tracy's new foster collective? Community? Family?* That last thought, and especially that last word, dumped a shitload of acid into her stomach. Lips curled in pain. Skin whitened. She swallowed the burning sensation. *Remember*, she told herself. *Remember why she was here! Remember for whom!*

Kerry Wilson. She had called around, and it had been a consensus. He, and he alone, could find her daughter. That is, if she was to be found.

An image of her only child shot to the forefront of her consciousness. Again, she took a deep breath. Then another. When that didn't help, she dug out an antacid from her purse and popped it. Stalled. Popped another. The pain was beginning to cloud her clarity. That couldn't happen. She forced trapped air from her lungs. Lynne knew that she had to find her daughter, and everything she saw reinforced the fear that she had to find her damn fast. Her daughter didn't belong, not there, and definitely not amongst those strange people. Lynne shut her eyes when the fear turned even more painful. She gagged when bile leeched into her mouth. She was afraid of losing her to them. *Or had she already?*

She tried for a distraction. She turned her attention to the right of the shelter. There, a used car lot stood. A sign was outfitted with Christmas colored bulbs pronouncing it *Ted Tucker's A-OK used car lot*. As far as car lots went, it wasn't much. At most, fifty cars were crammed in, bumper to bumper. She had no idea how a potential customer was supposed to take one out for a test drive. *But maybe that was the idea?* If she was any judge of cars, most appeared to be in a sorry state. Lynne chuckled. Like she knew anything about cars, except when to drop hers off for its bi-weekly detailing/car wash.

Lynne's self-depreciating smile died when she noticed a man whom she assumed was *the* Ted Tucker, staring back at her. He was middle aged, and as skinny a man as she had ever seen. Even from that distance, an unhealthy aura hung about him. Maybe it was the sunken cheeks, or the caved-in chest that seemed to pull him forward. It gave him a pronounced, bent-over look. Most likely, it was the hate-filled eyes that squinted into a continuous narrow line above his small peak-like nose. He rudely locked his stare into her. Lynne suppressed a shiver. Audibly, she sucked in a lungful of courage. *It was now, or never.*

She lunged awkwardly out of the car. She slammed the door with such force that it hurled a gunshot echo down the street—very unlike any sound her well-designed car had ever made before. Hurrying, she had managed to take only a few steps before coming to a halt. Turning, she extended her hand and locked the doors. A feeling of guilt washed over her. Locking the doors was not something she typically did.

Dashing across the street, Lynne rushed passed the assemblage of wounded humanity and into the shelter, stopping abruptly once inside. The smell of cleaning disinfectant, pungent body odor, and stale urine staggered her. She brought her hand up to cover her nose. It did little good. The smell was as much a part of the building as the walls were. Over a hundred people easily occupied the large room.

A high ceiling soared to a tin roof. Two pigeons in the rafters stared down at her. Their sudden cooing, she felt, was personal. They knew she didn't belong. They were protesting her presence. Paranoia was a new feeling for her.

In flowing chaos, a multitude of mismatched chairs, couches, and card tables were scattered about. Many of the occupants slept, some so deeply that their snores contested the chitchat of others. She took careful note of the voices that were directed to non-existent partners.

Having stalled at the door, Lynne was propelled forward to the center of the extraterrestrial room, by a homeless man coming in behind her. "If it ain't too much trouble, would you mind moving your ass, lady?" The voice belonged to a middle-aged man, bent over by a heavy backpack. It wasn't that hot, yet sweat beads had broken out on his forehead. "Either that, or put a fence around and homestead it."

"Sorry," Lynne replied meekly. Moving with heavy steps, she joined a short line. She found herself standing behind a boy-man. His high-pitched voice made him sound about twenty. But there was a weariness to it that undercut his youth. He leaned forward, elbows propped up on a reception counter that was a good ten feet long. His face rested in his hands. The campfire smoke that clung to him partially masked his stale body odor.

"When did you last eat, Rusty?" the man behind the counter asked.

Lynne moved slightly to the left, to get a better look at the speaker. Surprised by his age, mid-fifties, she quickly took inventory. He stood tall, six-one, and weighed just shy of two hundred. But the body bore no hint of fat. Instead, he had the large, hard muscles of a dedicated weight lifter. This was easy to see, as he wore a cut off sweatshirt. It gave him an outlaw look, but the eyes were too soft, too big to complete the package. She found it intriguing that he never took them off of the man-boy he was talking to.

"Well? Are you going to answer me or not? I'm not just asking to hear myself talk."

"Kerry..." Rusty replied.

A partially wrapped hamburger lying before Kerry was the cause of Rusty's distraction. Lynne's new angle of sight told her as much. He was all but drooling over it.

"It's a simple question." The question was stated with impatience, but a soft voice of concern undercut it.

"I ah, don't know. Can't remember."

"Here." Kerry tried sounding tough, but his voice was too rough with weariness to carry it off. He slid the hamburger over, but unexpectedly, Rusty didn't reach for it. He continued to stare at it.

"What?" Kerry demanded, his voice sharp with exasperation.

"It's meat," Rusty replied, in a simple voice.

"You think? It's a hamburger, knucklehead."

"How do I know it's dead?"

Lynne wasn't at all sure she was hearing right. *Why would the boy ask such a strange question?* Even more important: How would Kerry react to it? Locking her knees, and tensing her leg muscles, she tried to prepare for anything. However, the next scene in this bizarre play caught her totally off guard.

Kerry brought the hamburger partially back, and hit it twice with his fist. "Is now," he said, as he pushed the now extra dead hamburger back to the man-boy.

Rusty quickly picked it up and began stuffing it into his face. Suddenly, he stopped. He was obviously very hungry, so *why did he suddenly stop eating*?

"Now what?" Kerry asked, rolling his eyes. He was just as puzzled by Rusty's reaction as Lynne was.

"No fries?"

"What? Are you nuts? Get out of my face! Next!"

With liquid legs (and unsure if it was because of fright or anger), Lynne approached the counter. "Rather crude wouldn't you say?" she asked, wondering what freak circus Kerry had escaped from.

Kerry took a step back, and cast Lynne with a frank and boldly appraising stare. His eyes were green, and Lynne could not remember ever having seen green eyes as true as his.

Kerry's lips set hard, but not thin nor cruel. "Like it's any damn business of yours!"

Quickly shattering the brief standoff of silence that ensued, he asked, "What is it that you want?" His squinting eyes told her that he wasn't really expecting a coherent answer.

Afraid that her temper would show if she said anything, Lynne tried counting into a deep breath. For sure, nothing like this had ever been covered in her Yoga classes.

"Casting call is 'bout a hundred miles south of here."

Lynne's eyes screwed down tight. Fine trench lines inched out from their corners. Kerry's statement had caught her off guard. She knew what he was referring to. She was just confused by the context of his reply.

"You know, like Hollywood." The knife, having been planted, was now twisted.

"If you're insinuating that I'm putting on some kind of an act..." Lynne began, her voice sharp with rebuke.

"I ain't insinuating nothing," came the cool response.

"Ain't?" came Lynne's fast reply, before she could stop herself. Her face flamed red after having caught the sparkle in Kerry's eyes. She was being played a fool. He was saying that her perception was ego-centered, and he was now judging whom she was...what she was. Anger shot heat into her veins. Loudly, she took a deep breath. *Calm. Stay calm.* She held her temper and refused to respond in kind.

Turning her head to buy time, she saw that she was the center of attention for more than one person, which only added to her indignation. *Who the hell did this idiot think he was? She wasn't some girl, some high school chick.*

Turning back to Kerry, she saw that the merriment that had been in his eyes had traveled to his mouth, relaxing it. She was through playing the foil for this guy. She needed to get on to business.

"I, ah, I arranged to intern with you."

"Intern? With me? Like hell you did!" Kerry bellowed, the sparkle in his eyes dying and turning into smoldering coals.

"You are Kerry Wilson, are you not?" Lynne asked in her most innocent voice. She assumed that he was the man she had been assigned to when she had made the arrangements in L.A (Sizable donations opens all kinds of doors in the non-profit world). *After all, how many men named Kerry could there possibly be? Hopefully, not any more like this man.*

"Charlene!"

"You don't need to yell! I ain't deaf you know!" The woman who belonged to the voice sat behind Kerry. She was a harried-looking, mid-thirties, African-American woman with a pained look to her eyes, like she had seen too much of the world and found it wanting. "Like the lady said, it was arranged. Got a call—same call that told us to expect Simon West later today."

Kerry's eyes opened in question, and some of the flame left his face.

"The new director? Remember?" Charlene teased.

"That's today?"

"Sometimes you're dumber than a bag of rocks," Charlene said, shaking her head in wonder.

But Kerry didn't notice it. His mood had turned reflective. Slowly, he trudged around the corner of the counter, and started for the door.

"What about me?" Lynne's question stopped Kerry in his tracks. "I presume you are Kerry Wilson?"

Instead of turning to her, he turned back to Charlene. "Do I have to?" Kerry whined, his voice strained like a little boy's.

"You have to," Charlene replied, unable to stop her face from splitting into a world-class grin.

"In that case, that would be me," Kerry replied to Lynne, in his best gruff voice, sounding like he had just gargled with razor blades. "Try to keep up, and by all means, do try and keep your mouth shut!"

CHAPTER FOUR

With a long stride, Kerry exited the shelter, walked to the curb, and stopped. He wiped the heat from his eyes. The sun was strong in the morning sky. Placing his hands on his hips, he scanned the street. It was a practice that he had brought back with him from Vietnam—an instinct to check out each horizon for danger, as well as each morning. It was a practice that continued to be reinforced during his stint in the homeless wars back home. Violence did funny things to the soul, and one's perception of life. The soft innocence of childhood could never be entertained again for those who had experienced it. Life skidded between the mayhems of what might be, and what might have been. And the reality of what violence did to human flesh and spirit for those who had experienced it. It was a warping experience. The furnaces of bloodshed had forever changed Kerry's world.

His angry mood found a target with a slow moving, red Humvee. It pulled a trailer that held two shiny jet skis. His jaws tensed. The driver was a young man with a soft face. For Kerry, it wasn't the fact that the he had *that* kind of money to spend on playthings. Nor was it the obvious spare time. No. The mistake was made when he cast a sidewise glance at the shelter. Kerry's blood boiled at seeing the detached curiosity. It reminded him of visitors at a zoo.

"SOME OF US SURE HAVE IT ROUGH!" Kerry's loud voice caught Lynne off guard as she hurried out of the shelter, all in an attempt to keep up with him. Stopping by his side, she braced him with a hard stare.

Turning her way, Kerry saw her deadly glare. "What!" he demanded.

"Exactly which rock did you crawl out from under?"

A sly smile of grudging respect escaped Kerry's hard-pressed lips. He turned his head to hide it. In doing so, he saw Ted Tucker, towering over an obviously intoxicated, homeless man. Ted's victim was older than most of the others milling around the shelter. He was sitting on the curb with his feet rooted in the gutter.

Kerry couldn't hear what was being said. Didn't really need to. He had heard the morally condemning speeches before, of those who had been fortunate enough never to have had the disease of alcoholism. And a thousand times, he had wondered where all that hate and judgment came from. Were those dying from lung cancer so cruelly condemned because they smoked? Were diabetics crucified for life-style choices that may have contributed to their disease? *Of course not!* But for some reason, alcoholism called forth the worst aspects in those not affected by it.

The poor man, who was the target of Ted Tucker's

wrath, slowly and cautiously stood. He swayed, gained his stability, and then slowly shuffled away.

"One of these days, I'm going to deck that guy."

He was caught by surprise when he turned to see what effect his anger had on his new intern. She wasn't standing beside him. Instead, she was running across the street, heedless of traffic. "Now what?" he asked, to no one but himself.

A car braked hard to avoid hitting Lynne. Another car's horn blew. A curse tossed to the wind. Kerry watched Lynne run up to Street Girl, a seventeen year old. Kerry knew her to be a runaway, now living on the streets. He saw Lynne grab her and spin her around. "Shit," he said, before darting into traffic after her.

Coming up quickly behind Lynne, he heard Street Girl say, "What's the fuckin' matter with you, lady?" Angrily, she shook off Lynne's offending hand.

"Ah, nothing. Sorry," Lynne replied, in a voice tortured with embarrassment. Street Girl continued her solitary journey down the road, muttering curses in her wake.

"You want to tell me what that was all about?" Kerry's voice was surprisingly gentle. There was something profoundly sad about the encounter he had just witnessed. His eyes squinted in concentration. He tried to find meaning in Lynne's face. The only things he found there were tight muscles and a flushed face.

"No." The reply was soft, pleading with an unspoken request: No more questions. This was a woman of many layers, some running very deep, and intense like the fast retreating tide after a surging storm. Kerry felt the need to respect Lynne's personal space, and whatever emotions the encounter with Street Girl had just given birth to.

"Okay," he finally replied, bringing a more natural shade of color to Lynne's face.

"Now what?" Lynne asked.

"Now what, what?"

'I mean, what are we going to do first? Where are we going to go?"

"Slow down. The world isn't going anywhere."

Lynne's eyes went darker. She wasn't so sure about that.

"You ever done catering?"

"Like, having a party catered?"

"No." Kerry's voice became edgier. He reminded himself what he had momentarily forgotten: That this was an upper-class yuppie chick, out for a vicarious kick. Or perhaps just a housewife, driven by boredom to seek out the thrill of the streets. To confirm his less than flattering thoughts of her, he looked down to her hand, searching for a wedding band. Eyes darkened; her finger was unencumbered.

Following Kerry's sight, Lynne's mouth turned up into a smug smile. Kerry stiffened. She probably thought that he was checking her hand for a ring, like some kind of pick up artist at a bar. She may have been pretty and she had a kick charge personality, but she was hardly his type!

"No. I mean like serving," he snarled back.

"Of course not!"

"Well, you're about to."

"I don't want to!"

"And why not? Is it beneath you?"

"No!" she squealed high in protest, which only confirmed to him that it was.

"Then what is it?"

"I want to see the homeless. See where they live. I believe you call them camps?" Her voice was firmer, like the discussion was over with.

Again, Kerry was put on guard by Lynne's impatience. Or was it despair? Panic? He stretched his neck left, then right. The tightness remained. A feeling swamped him with the notion that she was in some kind of race against time. *And, if she was...why?* Who exactly was this woman, and what did she want? He shook his head. Should he ignore his inner voice of warning? Should he simply get on with his job, and his new intern? He had learned long ago that to ignore the voice had a cost. A very high cost.

"Who do you think we cater to? The Kiwanis we aren't," he finally articulated. "And besides," he continued, in a firm voice before she could protest, "If you want to intern with me, then you do what I tell you to, when I tell you to. Think you can do that? If not..."

Kerry watched as a battle raged across Lynne's face. Her lips pulled in, and her nostrils flared. If he was trying to push his new intern into quitting, he was doing a pretty good job. *Now, to end this silly game with the coup de grace before she can recover.* "I'm the boss. We straight on this?"

Lynne swallowed her defeat, and with a gentler voice,

tried diplomacy. "Okay, but the streets..."

"Are we clear?" The challenge was clear: submit or quit; his preferred answer was obvious.

"Yes," came the meek reply.

"Besides, the homeless aren't going anywhere. They were here yesterday. They're here today, and they'll be here tomorrow. Nobody really cares. Nothing ever changes. That's the dirty little secret we all dance around."

Lynne looked up at Kerry. *How could he be so callous, so burnt out?* He looked down on her with eyes large with wonder. *How could she be so naïve? Why did the gods in heaven want to seek vengeance on him? What had he done to incur their wrath?* He worked alone. Always had. Always would. He was a lone warrior against an indifferent universe. A gunslinger matched up against a soul-destroying machine. A machine that chewed up and spit out the homeless like yesterday's useless fashions and insider stock tips. *And the one thing* he definitely was not cut out to be was a *babysitter*. No. He was not one to hold her hand while she discovered the blisters of society, or its dark underbelly.

CHAPTER FIVE

The white van Kerry drove carried its age poorly. Streams of rust spilled down from the roof. The red logo of the shelter, printed on the side, was faded, much like the hope it peddled. The back seats had been removed, to allow room for the warming ovens that did a reasonable job of keeping the food hot. However, the atmosphere inside the van was chilly. It was also heavy with tension, making measured breathing a necessity. Lynne's silent hostility was becoming too much. It was like snorting icicles.

Kerry asked, "So, what is this? A lark? Want to see how the animals live in our fair tourist town?"

Clenching her hands into hard fists, she snarled back. "Must you always be so antagonistic?"

"It's call oppositional." Kerry's voice had taken on a light conversational tone, as if commenting on the weather.

"Beg your pardon?" she asked, past the lump in her throat. She was having a hard time forcing down what was lodged there. It felt as large as Catalina Island— her pride. With dawning recognition, fueling a sense of estrangement and anger, she was beginning to understand just how sheltered her life had been up to that point, and she didn't appreciate having her nose rubbed in it.

"You know, like in psycho-babble. The politically correct term per the DSM-IV is oppositional disorder," Kerry offered.

"That would be you."

Kerry cut a quick look over to Lynne. Was she asking it as a question, or stating it as fact? He smiled. Once again, he was impressed with her nerve.

"That's right, lady. That would be me. But only to those who deserve it."

"You don't think much of the field of mental health."

"Really? Just because they play Russian roulette with those powerful drugs they call medications, and pretend they know so much more than they do...Lady, don't even start with me on this subject. I see more pain in the name of mental health than—no, *almost* more than I saw in Vietnam. But what about you? Mid-life crisis?"

With great effort, Lynne suppressed an angry reply, as she fought for a hard-pressed, neutral voice. "I'm, ah... doing a mid-career change. Going back to school to earn a Masters in Social Work. And, I'd appreciate it if you called me by my name and NOT lady! I am NOT the lead in some Disney flick."

"Whatever you say...lady."

A hard jolt rocked the van as Kerry sped over a speed bump. "Shit!" He tensed. Burning heat shot up from his sciatica. The arthritic shocks of the van were hard on the back. Slowly, his lower back muscles retreated from medieval torture. For the next several moments, the only noise inside the van was caused by a variety of loose bolts, nuts and screws, adding a chorus of chaotic music to the vehicle, every time Kerry managed to hit a pothole, or swerved a little too fast. Just as Lynne began to lower her defense:

"So? What line of work are you running from? Or is it something else?"

"Damn it, Kerry! I'm not running from anything! Why don't you try giving it a rest? It's obvious you don't like... what is it exactly? Yuppies? Upper class? Or whatever category of people you're grouping me with. Maybe I'm none of those people. Maybe I'm just me trying to..."

Looking over at Kerry, the rest of her response was left hanging in thin air. A look of determined introspection had turned his body rigid. He sat tense over the steering wheel, holding it tight in a deadly grip. *Why was she letting him get to her like this?* Clenching her teeth hard, she decided silence was the best policy.

A frozen smile, neither friendly nor unfriendly, was Kerry's immediate response. Then came his verbal one, in a haunted and hallow tone: "We're all running from something. Some of us faster and farther than the rest."

"And what are you running from?"

A shrill squeal came from metal on metal brakes. Lynne was pitched forward, and then slammed back. She grabbed onto the door handle for an anchor. "A bit touchy, aren't we?"

Holding onto the steering wheel, Kerry responded

through clenched teeth, "Let me make this as simple as I can. I'm the social worker, *and* your mentor. That makes me your boss. Got it? I do the asking. You do the telling. Questions?" When none was forthcoming, Kerry resumed driving.

"I'm in public relations," Lynne began, when Kerry pulled over, and killed the engine next to a small pocket park. Giant palms, standing like ancient demented gods carved in stone, surrounded it. The grounds themselves were evenly matched between patches of water, starved grass, and plain dirt. The irony was not lost to Kerry. Several blocks over, in a more upscale part of the city, the grass was lush and emerald green. There, walking on grass was like walking on a cloud.

"You mean were? Remember, you're a student now. At least that's the party line."

Lynne's left eye twitched—she'd been busted. Seeing her reaction, Kerry relaxed into the cracked plastic seat. "You mean you work, excuse me, *worked* for companies that sold things people didn't need. Things that make people sick like cigarettes. Not to mention that your job was to make people feel good about it."

"You are such an ass!"

"You'd have to stand in line with that judgment of me," Kerry casually tossed back.

To hide her embarrassed anger, Lynne shifted her stare towards the park. Sitting straighter, she leaned forward. Within the boundaries of the park, homeless small groups and individuals were stirring. Some were still encased in worn, wet sleeping bags, trying to shake off the night's terror, or surrendering to the waking ones. Others were propped up against trees, staring at life racing by. And still others sat in circles, drinking coffee or forty-pounders (forty ounces of bottled malt liquor). Disheartened, Lynne took in the fact that most were smoking their health away. Columns of drifting smoke spiraled skywards like mini-tornados.

"I may be an ass, but I'm also right, am I not?" Kerry replied, quietly intrigued by Lynne's reaction to the park. His sight followed hers. His forehead cringed in question. Nothing unusual was there to him. He had forgotten just how alien the culture of the homeless was to most. It was his office, a large part of his waking life, and a good chunk of his nightmares.

Chewing her lips, Lynne responded. "Okay, you're partially right. I did have a tobacco company as a client once. But it was one on a list of hundreds. Most of our clients are people whom we turn into hot property. Up and coming movie stars, sports performers..."

"Turning people into commodities—things to be traded, manipulated like cattle. Sweet. Real sweet." The door squeaked as Kerry opened it. Climbing out, he heard a soft voice cry out behind him. "Ass."

CHAPTER SIX

For the better part of an hour, they handed out small, flimsy bowls of soup, breakfast burritos, cups of bitter coffee and cartons of milk south of their expiration date. There weren't as many women and girls as Lynne had at first feared, but enough that she found it disheartening. And then shame peaked out from behind her thoughts: *Why should it be okay for men to suffer this indignity, but not women? And so many of them were obviously disabled—with both physical, and mental illnesses.* This was something that she hadn't expected.

Kerry's easy banter with the homeless helped calm her jittery nerves. It also gave her something that was in short supply: hope. Conflicted, bipolar emotions savaged her. Worry. A mother's fear tore at her like an enraged beast. Heartburn. Battery acid poured forth from the veins that fed her heart. She popped another antacid. Thoughts of her daughter living amongst the motley collection of drifters brought her to the point of tears. Her daughter was better than those deadbeats. Those losers! She turned to hide reddened eyes from Kerry. She found herself under the hard stare of an old bag lady.

Ethyl's first claim to fame was the fact that her unnaturally red hair was corrupted with gray, and matted into long dreadlocks. It obviously hadn't been washed or combed in years. Twigs and bits of unknown flotsam from the great outdoors were captured within. Her second claim was her emerald green eyes, reflecting the color of some tropical paradise's ocean. Lynne froze.

Ethyl shuffled up to her, dragging two large, overflowing, black plastic bags that defined her progress. For a heartbeat—stretching into eternity, she stood rock still, looking menacingly up into Lynne's face. Doing so accentuated just how short Ethyl was. Lynne fought the urge to scratch her head. Try as she might, she couldn't keep her stare off the offending hair. She had no idea how the tiny woman before her wasn't driven completely insane by it. She knew that she would be if that mane was hers.

"Don't forget the Hole." The softness of Ethyl's voice contrasted sharply with her physical appearance. She had expected it to be gruff, if not downright mean. This dichotomy stalled Lynne's breathing. Her stare dropped. There was concern in the woman's eyes. "And don't go alone," the old bag lady warned. *Or was it a threat?* Shame pounced. Lynne's eyes fluttered shut.

Struggling under the load of her garbage bags, Ethyl turned and slowly walked away, just as Kerry strolled up. He watched the retreating figure. Fluidity came to his facial features. He worried that her plastic bags were stretched to the breaking point, wondering protectively if anything of value was in them. Life was cheap enough on the streets. Things of little value could go a long way in getting one killed.

"What did Ethyl want?" he finally asked Lynne.

"What's the Hole?" came in reply. Lynne's eyes trailed after the flighty apparition.

"Didn't your mom ever teach you not to answer a question with a question?"

"Please!" Lynne demanded, her eyes whipping back to Kerry.

"It's our next stop."

The drive was just minutes long, all stony silence. Cutting across life experiences. The enforced quietness was easier on Kerry than Lynne. He was used to a shared existence with those lost in another reality. Interacting with clients who slipped in and out of their shared space. Even though the benefits of silence were preached in her Yoga classes, Lynne's peers always found something of importance to discuss. Usually themselves.

Santa Barbara is cleaved in two by the 101 Freeway. Ocean moves on one side, mountains frozen on the other. It is known locally as the 101. Its relentless drone added a monotone whine to the sudden silence when Kerry killed the engine of the van. Lynne looked about. Eyes cringed into narrow question marks. She saw no destination in sight. No people. "The Hole?" she asked hesitantly.

She followed Kerry's sight to the large drainage pipes that ran under the 101. Her nose wrinkled in disgust. An ocean of trash lay at the entrance. Lynne hurried to keep up when Kerry quickly exited the van, and walked to its back.

"People live in there?" Lynne inquired. Her voice was edged with disbelief. True, she didn't know Kerry all that well, but she was pretty sure his sense of humor did not encompass jokes at the expense of the homeless, or even her. She already knew him well enough to sense a loosely defined, spiritual component to his work.

Looking harder into the truncated tunnel, she half expected a troll to come lumbering out, knuckles dragging along the ground. When Kerry didn't answer, she continued: "In there?"

Kerry stopped stuffing sandwiches, apples, and cartons of milk into brown lunch bags. His eyes liquefied with harsh pain. "People do what they got to do to survive. I'm sure they're real sorry they've disappointed you. That they aren't living up to your expectations."

"I didn't mean it that way! I wish you'd quit putting meaning into my words that aren't there."

Oh, really? Then exactly what did you mean?"

"I mean..." Lynne stopped and smiled.

"Now what's so funny?"

"Do you really think this is going to scare me off?"

"Heaven forbid! Why, there's nothing out here you wouldn't find at Disneyland. Just consider all this a theme park. You know—see the homeless for a week. Come and rub elbows with the down and out. Experience the thrills of extreme poverty. Feed the mentally ill. Drink with the alchies! Talking points for your next party!"

"You are such an *ass*!"

Lynne, hands on hips, locked stares with Kerry. The blowing of a big rig's horn from the freeway finally brought the confrontation to a begrudging, if undeclared ceasefire. Kerry threw lunch bags into a backpack and handed Lynne the extra sandwiches. Putting on the backpack, he adjusted the shoulder straps and then headed for the drainage pipes. He stopped when he realized that Lynne wasn't accompanying him.

"Coming or not?" he asked, hoping against hope that he would be freed of the pest.

Lynne smiled, realizing that once again, she was being baited. She would have to keep a tighter rein on her emotions, she told herself. This man was good at using her own emotions against her.

With quick, purposeful strides, she reached and walked past Kerry, not bothering to wait for him. 'Shit," he said under his breath. He would have to remember that the woman knew how to play. He needed to adjust his strategies accordingly. He shook his head. His own long stride quickly closed the gap that separated them.

Lynne felt her resolve begin to crumble when she found herself before the entrance to the drainage pipes. She fought the weakness of fear that suddenly hobbled her feet. The pipes were five feet round. Five in a row, like silent sentries before an abyss. The bottoms of the pipes were carpeted with dried green algae. Foul, smelling water trickled out from two. They stood before the middle one. An inky blackness curtained it. She peered so hard and long inside that her eyes began to water from strain.

"Lunch is served!" Kerry's loud voice bellowed out. Startled, Lynne jumped back. It echoed off the tin sides, then it became swallowed by the empty expanse of the dark realm.

"Delivery entrance is in the back!" a disemboweled voice replied. The hairs on Lynne's arms stood on end, like the uncut weeds she had just passed. Kerry merely smiled and shook his head. He knew the voice belonged to Sam. "Next to the servants' quarters."

"Shut up, Sam!" chased the first voice. Kerry knew that would be Dorothy, Sam's longtime fiancée. "What did you bring us?"

"Sandwiches only. Lobsters made a break for it. Afraid they got away."

"Don't shoot!" the voice, again Sam's. "We're sending out the women and children. As for the rest of us—you'll never take us alive, coppers!"

"I told you to shut up. Now button it, or so help me..."

This last remark was followed by an outburst of laughter. Then rustling sounds, as something or someone made their way down the pipes. Lynne looked about, wondering who else might be witnessing her descent into madness. Finally, Dorothy emerged. She was short enough not to have to bend over, in consideration of the low ceiling. To Lynne, she looked to be in her sixties, even though she was only in her late forties.

Piercing gray eyes stood inches before Lynne. She stiffened, and quelled the impulse to move backwards. Those eyes pierced her with a rapid and well-practiced glance. Finding much to be desired, Dorothy snorted. She spat out some brown tobacco juice and moved over to Kerry. The softness that wedged onto her face gave her back five years. When she smiled at him, Lynne saw that her upper teeth were gone. The bottom, stained a dark brown.

"How you doing, Kerry?"

"You lost your teeth again!" was Kerry's reply.

"Yup!"

"Can...?" Kerry began, only to be cut off by Dorothy.

"Nope. They only gives you one set every two years. If you lose them, or they break, they expect you to go on a model's diet till then. Minus the coke, of course. Hear they're even gonna stop doing that. No dentures. No dentists. Nothing. Can you do something 'bout it?"

"Not with social services. But I know a few people. People with money who may be able to help."

"You know more than a few people! You know half the damn world."

"Yeah. The half that's poor."

"The important half," Dorothy shot back, straightening up in pride.

Sam's emergence was partnered with pungent body odor. He was whiskey seasoned with droopy, blood-shot eyes. His stomach protruded unnaturally, the first physical signs of the alcoholic's swollen liver. It would surely claim his life in the not too distant future. He looked ten years older than Dorothy. Days old whiskers added a little heft to his otherwise sunken cheeks. Short stature. But what really shocked Lynne were the bright blue eyes that sparkled with merriment, and a love of life.

"No lobsters. No deal. Won't tell you where I hid the loot. And the women stay. You can have the kids."

Kerry swallowed his laughter. The cemented worry lines around his eyes dissolved. A caring friendship was there. Taking notice of Lynne, who was standing slightly behind Kerry, Sam first smiled, then made an absurd attempt at stretching himself taller. The attempt simply made him a tall-short man. "You for me?" he asked, patting down his disheveled and badly dyed, white rooted hair.

Bright red flushed across Lynne's face. Unable to articulate a verbal response, she kept quiet. Dorothy had no such qualms. "Shut up, Sam! You're an embarrassment to the human race."

"Only your half of it."

A rustling from the pipes drew all of their attention. Lynne tensed. Dorothy and Sam exchanged worried glances. Kerry moved to the very edge of the pipe and bent down. He tensed his legs, ready to go in if need be. "That you, Jeffrey?" he called out. The question had a hard bite to it—like he already knew the answer, and he wasn't happy with it.

More rustling was heard before Kerry stepped back, and a boy of twelve emerged. He would have been a junior high, football coach's dream come true. He was hefty, without being fat. Tall enough to have to bend down considerably before he emerged. But his eyes lacked the self-confidence that athletes possessed. They were skittish and drawn inwards, like he had seen too much of the world too soon and found much to fear in it.

Kerry began to say something to Jeffrey. Thinking better of it, he directed his comments to Sam and Dorothy. "I thought he was in foster care." But it was Jeffrey who answered.

"Was. All four of them in the last six months." His voice crackled low to high, caught somewhere between that of a child, and the man that he was forced to grow into too quickly.

Jeffrey grabbed a sandwich that Lynne held listlessly in her hand, so fast that she was unable to let go in time. For a brief second, they held onto the same sandwich. A struggle given birth to by the insanity of the times they lived in. Jeffrey shot her a seasoned, wounded look. Shame. Pride crushed by circumstances. Adolescence grounded under boot. She finally let go. Embarrassment hammered at her with brass knuckles. *Would the boy or the others misinterpret her slow response?* The boy quickly unwrapped the sandwich and crammed half of it into his mouth. Now all the adults present shared Lynne's frame of mind. Their eyes fled each other for the safety of empty space.

Bile burned Lynne's throat. This was the first time she had ever seen hunger. The first time she had experienced real unadulterated hunger as a state of being. And it was with a child, a boy younger than her own daughter. She thought back to the beggars on Hollywood Blvd. who annoyed her so. They always seemed—if not well fed, at least not actually hungry. *Had hunger been present, and she simply failed to see it?* Now, twice in a matter of hours, it scarred her conscience. Suddenly, hunger had a face. *Was her daughter hungry?* Up until that point, she had been more concerned with Tracy's safety, and the condition of her mental status. Something as elemental and as terrifying as her daughter—a mere child—actually going hungry, tore chunks from Lynne's soul, and threatened to literally kick the legs out from under her.

Jeffrey suddenly stopped chewing. He looked at Kerry with guarded eyes. "If you turn me in, I'll run away again, maybe another city this time. Swear to God!" he threatened, mouth full of food. "Least this way, Mom and Sam can look out for me, and you too." Slowly, he brought the remainder of the sandwich up and crammed it into his mouth, without taking his eyes off Kerry.

Kerry began to say something. Stopped. He forced the bitter words back down. Turning, he strode back to the van with anger elongating his stride. Running, Lynne caught up to Kerry just as he was about to get into the van.

"You can't just leave him here! He's just a kid!"

"And what? You think some loving family is just waiting to take a kid like him into their home? He's already been in eleven foster homes. Make that fifteen!"

Kerry looked back. Pain bled from his eyes. Molars were in danger of shattering from the pressure of his clenched teeth. Jeffrey had already swallowed one sandwich and now he was busy tearing into another one.

"Sometimes there just aren't any good answers, only bad ones. No matter what you do, it's guaranteed to have bad consequences." Kerry's voice was so soft that Lynne found herself leaning forward in order to hear. With a start, she realized that she had never heard such pain in a grown man's voice. The next words out of Kerry's mouth quickly shattered the sympathy she felt towards him.

"Now get in, and shut the hell up!"

From within the cave-pipe, unseen eyes opened. From within, a bleeding heart cried out. But the mind was wounded, twisting hallucinations into reality. The voices—symptoms of the disease—screamed out warnings, and told her how worthless she was. They shouted in chorus that surely someone as bad as she couldn't be wanted by her own mother. That whoever was with the tall stranger must be someone out to punish her.

"But...it's Mom." Tracy's voice was barely audible. But the mere fact that she had uttered anything at all brought the tormenting voices to a raging froth of disgust.

The voices screamed louder, because she had dared question them. Every name, every curse, every insecurity, blemish, and fear she had was used against her, until she felt as worthless as the rat droppings that littered her living space. Even the looks of concern that she saw on

Sam, Dorothy and Jeffrey's faces couldn't cut through the loathing and self-hatred that the voices caused her. After all, how could they help, when the obvious love of her mother was unable to? She scooted over to a dark corner, drew up her knees, and buried her head into them. She rocked back and forth.

Crushing despair. It was so overwhelming that it twisted her gut in pain. It felt like a car had crashed into the pipe tunnel, and then into her. She crossed her hands over her stomach. A groan. The pain was so intense that her stomach muscles cramped and her lungs shut down, robbing her of breath. She wasn't sure how much more she could take. Not only were her immediate surroundings bleak. Her future was as well.

CHAPTER SEVEN

The engine coughed loudly before rattling to its death. Again, Lynne found herself across the street from the shelter, this time in the company of a lunatic. The sudden silence compounded the havoc shredding Lynne's troubled mind. A hundred thoughts and a thousand emotions clashed, demanding attention. But now was not the time.

As for Kerry, anger ate at his stomach until it was an acid pit. He tried swallowing down the pain. That only made it worse. He hadn't expected to run into Jeffrey, and regardless of what he had told Lynne, he wasn't sure leaving him there was the correct decision. It certainly wasn't right. He only knew he was correct when he had told her there weren't any right answers. He knew that to put Jeffrey back into the failed foster care system— America's deeply held secret—that was a no go. But to leave him on the streets...what was that? Lynne, clearing her throat, broke his musing.

"You ready?" he asked cautiously, sliding a sidewise glance Lynne's way.

"I, ah, sure." Lynne's brittle voice, on the edge of being

shattered by the morning's events, brought a quick look of concern from Kerry.

"You sure?"

"Said I was, didn't I?" Lynne wondered where the harsh reply came from. It wasn't like her to strike out at others. But nothing about the day had any normalcy to it.

"Yeah, you did," Kerry replied, the coldness in his voice questioning the validity of the answer.

Kerry climbed out of the van. Lynne soon joined him while they waited for a break in the traffic. Their sight was drawn down the street when a young woman turned the corner and walked their way.

It was obvious that she was homeless, from the bottom of her dirty, bare feet, to the top of her bald head. A brightly colored tattoo, of roses dripping blood down the sides of her head reigned supreme. The poncho Julie Carson wore ran riot with sharply infused reds, yellows and purples. But it was what was in her hands that drew Lynne's attention and caused Kerry's brow to fold: a dead bat.

Lynne watched in mounting horror as the girl petted it like it was a tamed house cat. She turned to say something to Kerry, who chose that instant to turn his back on the bat girl and walk into traffic, dodging cars left and right.

"What is it with you and traffic?" Lynne's question trailed empty space. The man could move like greased lightning. At other times, he was like heavy water, crippled with contemplation. Breathing in her courage, and shaking her head in confusion, she launched herself into traffic, dodging left and cutting right like a running back, making his way down a broken field of tackles. Except here, the tacklers weighed three thousand pounds.

Kerry waited for Lynne to catch up in front of the entrance to the shelter. Lynne's breathing was raspy, and not from physical exertion.

"I'll ask you again, are you sure you're ready?"

"For what?" Lynne managed to squeak out, apprehensive that he had again asked the question. Her forehead was cut with burrows, for the repeated question transformed into a warning in her mind.

"Who knows? That's the intriguing part of our job. Every day, something new." Even though his tone was lighter, the mood in his eyes had darkened several shades over the past few moments.

"From what I've seen so far, you mean a new disaster to deal with." The tightness of Lynne's voice stopped Kerry's sarcastic reply dead in its tracks. There was something at play there that went beyond mere internship. He needed to figure it out. And damn fast. Standing back, he opened the shelter door. "Ladies first."

"That's still to be determined!" Lynne snapped, and hurriedly walked through the door. Kerry smiled and followed suit.

Kerry hadn't yet shown her this part of the shelter, and it both impressed and frightened. The building went deep; seemingly a football field long, which she knew, was an exaggeration—but still that was her impression. Halfway in, a soup kitchen was located. Volunteers preparing a huge pot of soup, tons of sandwiches, and bushels of fruit, made a long serving line busy. These mostly elderly, church going types—in other words, clean cut and shaven—stood in sharp contrast to the long unkempt hair, beards, mustaches, and goatees many of the homeless sported. The long line of waiting customers answered the question as to why people hadn't been milling outside when they had pulled up. Some of them waited patiently—those who had eaten a breakfast, or at least dinner the night before. But most hadn't, staring intensely, and almost salivating as they fixated on the food being prepared.

"Hey, Bob," Kerry said to the tall man with shiny, silver hair, as they walked up to the serving line. Robert Fletcher had the air of an important self-made man; a self-assurance that had served him well as an investment banker. He had done well in life, and now in retirement, he had found another calling, one that brought him into contact with what he considered "fascinating" people.

"She a client?" Bob asked Kerry, followed by a wink.

"Potentially," Kerry responded, without a trace of a smile.

"I am not!" Lynne protested loudly, looking around to see if others thought so.

"Bob," Kerry began, a relaxing smile finally softening his hard features, "I'd like you to meet Lynne, she's, ah, like my intern."

"What do you mean, like?" She began. "I am..."

"We're ready!" Kerry yelled, loudly interrupting Lynne's protest. Snapping on thin, latex serving gloves as expertly as a surgeon, he continued: "Let 'em roll!"

The line moved forward slowly. Once the irrational fear that the food would cruelly disappear was laid to rest, those anxious to eat extended respectful and friendly greetings to the church volunteers. A warm glow embraced both sides of the line. For a brief moment of time, all too brief, the homeless lost the stigma that separated them from the other citizens of the city—those lucky enough to be housed. Smiles came easier, and shoulders relaxed. Stress lines softened, and time returned some of what it had stolen.

Lynne stood awkwardly behind Kerry, unsure what to do. She had never seen a soup kitchen before. It was something that she had read about in history books, always in the context of the *Great Depression*. Then there were the yearly *Salvation Army Thanksgiving* television advertisements that came and went with the season, barely denting her consciousness. She didn't have to think too hard to realize she had never handled one on a professional level.

"Think you could try handing out the bread without too much trouble?" The question-as-a-weapon cut through Lynne's self-musing. It added yet more guilt, and for the first time, also an element of shame. But, no way in hell was she going to give Kerry the satisfaction of seeing it. She swallowed her pride, kept her mouth shut, and moved in next to Kerry. She snapped on a pair of her own gloves and began handing out the bread.

In between handing out bread, Lynne's eyes swept the room, looking for her daughter. What she saw was over a dozen homeless on crutches, and three in wheelchairs. She saw more than one alcoholic struggle against gravity, and she wondered what torture of the soul could drive someone to drink so early in the day. But those who appeared to be suffering from mental illness captured her interest most. She saw the self-contained eyes stare inwards towards the unseen forces that ruled their lives. She heard muttered words responding to voices and sounds unheard by others. She looked hard to those souls who had been wounded by life's experiences.

Lynne was brought back to the present when a raised voice cut into her pathos:

"I don't want none of that!" it stated emphatically.

"You mean, you don't want any of that?" the elderly woman standing next to Bob Fletcher corrected him. Brown hair hung lazily on his shoulders, and a drooping goatee defined his face.

"That's what I said, I don't want none of that there. You hard of hearing, or what!"

The next man in line, a carbon copy of his partner, stepped forward. "I'll take some of that there, and some of that there," he stated, indicating a bowl of soup and bread, but no salad.

"You mean, only some of this and some of that?" the woman who served salad said, aghast that he wanted nothing of what she had to offer.

"No!' the man replied sharply. He was equally as surprised by her response as she had been by his. "Some of that there, and some of that there!" once again skipping over the salad. "Heat getting to you?"

The two men shuffled on down the line, shaking their heads. "School teacher?" Lynne asked Kerry, somehow touched by the honest and easy give and take.

"Retired," Kerry responded.

"Not so retired," Lynne offered back.

Kerry eyed Lynne for a few seconds. She was glad when she saw him relax—in fact, his mouth actually eased into a smile. The next man in line wiped the smile off Kerry's face. He was a tall African-American man with a bald head. Both hands and his head were wrapped in white bandages. He struggled with the tray. His hands were obviously painful to the touch. "Stern likes to shampoo with gasoline, paint thinner, almost anything that is caustic. Isn't that right, Stern?"

"Yeah man, that's right," came the low, rumbling reply.

Lynne took a step back and looked first at Kerry, then back to Stern when she saw that Kerry was dead serious. She looked about the large room, and took in what she could only describe as Dante's Inferno staring back: broken bodies both in and out of wheelchairs, others teetering on a miscast collection of walkers, canes and crutches stretched before her. Outside of a hospital emergency room or war, she couldn't even begin to imagine a scene with more wounded. Taking in the mentally ill, and those incapacitated by alcohol and drugs—she stepped forward, and held onto the serving table with a death grip.

She fought through the weakness that threatened to cripple her resolve for the mission at hand. She swallowed the sour tasting bile that percolated up from her stomach and coated her throat. To even think of her daughter eating amongst this crowd was gut wrenching. To imagine her daughter living amongst them was beyond her worst nightmare. No, that wasn't true. Her worst nightmare had been of her daughter being viciously beaten, possibly raped, or even dead.

Kerry followed Lynne's sight as she swept the crowd. Looking back into her eyes, the shock and pain he found in them forced him to see what really lay there. It had all become so normal, so much of his everyday existence. Now, he used Lynne's virgin eyes to reset his own. It was like he was seeing it again for the first time, as he had so many years ago.

Swinging his stare back to Lynne, he was taken further back by the anguished look that robbed her face of color. It was like Stern had thrown some of his special shampoos onto Lynne, bleaching her whiter than white. But before he could do anything about it:

"Simon West would like to see you," Charlene informed Kerry when she walked up to him. When he didn't move, she took the soup ladle from him.

"And he would be?" Kerry managed to finally ask, forcing the words past the lump in his throat.

"Your new boss."

CHAPTER EIGHT

Increments of time disappeared. Too soon for Kerry's liking, he and Lynne found themselves in a small, windowless office, which resembled a solitary cell in the max pen at Pelican Bay. The prisoner to the title, Director Simon West, sat behind a simple, functional steel desk on a simple, functional chair. He was hunched over the desk, reading a fat file. It seemed as if he was either having trouble reading the small print, or he disliked what he was reading altogether.

He was a short, middle-aged man, whose hairline was not so much in full retreat but a rout. A severe expression crossed his face like a badge of honor. His blue suit had started to shine from too many washes. Even for his small neck, the tie was obviously too tight, as flesh spilled over it. Oddly enough, his skin color was pale, sickly in fact. The only personal affect in the office was the obligatory family picture of a wife and son, atop the table.

Kerry took an interest in the picture: *Did he know them? Hadn't he seen them somewhere before?* He didn't think so. Maybe it was something else. But what was it then? Something about the picture was off. It was too bland, too Americana. A sudden sigh betrayed him. *Who was he to pass judgment?* Nothing was normal about him at all. How many people in the world surrounded their waking lives with the mentally ill? With those broken by addiction? Or those poor souls who found themselves dying in dirty gutters all alone?

Simon West looked up and caught Kerry eyeing the picture. A sharp redness flamed his face. He reached over to the picture and turned it towards him so Kerry could no longer see it. Instead of addressing Kerry, he spoke to Lynne. "You must be Lynne Swanson."

Finally dropping his cold stare from Kerry, he shifted his gaze over to Lynne. Doing so didn't bring relaxation to his face, or softness to his eyes. "I was told to expect you for your internship. Hopefully you have been accorded the proper, professional respect here." He shot a quick glance over to Kerry, as if expecting a confession that his behavior had been otherwise. When Lynne was unable or unwilling to reply, Simon's sight dropped to the file. His lips pinched tighter, until they looked like they belonged to a zombie who hadn't eaten in the last quarter of a century.

"And you must be Kerry—" he began.

"—Must be," Kerry shot back, looking around the room and seeing nobody else fitting his description.

"Quite a record," Simon West began. His grip on the file tightened until it began to tremble. "Not exactly one to be proud of. Frankly, I'm surprised you still work for us. You have trouble getting along with authority in general—the police, and the Mental Health Dept. in particular. And this says nothing of your disdain for rules and your superiors."

"I know enough of the rules to ignore the bad ones. Same goes for the higher ups," Kerry shot back. *If this gumbo thought he was just going to stand there and be insulted, he had another thing coming. Boss, or no boss.*

Simon West slammed the file that he had been holding down onto his desk. The picture frame jumped. "Things are going to change around here, starting with you. Now."

Looking hard at Simon West, Kerry came to the notion that his new boss was just trying to provoke him. He decided against taking the bait. He just shrugged.

"Starting today, we are an output oriented organization," Simon West continued, when silence poured into the office like wet cement.

"Output oriented?" Kerry questioned, when he found his voice, one dripping with insubordination. "What's that supposed to mean?"

'It means we want and need success stories. It's what our donors want to hear. It's also what the State and the Feds want to see. Everybody wants to see the difference that their money makes. They want to see these people transition into housing *and* jobs. In other words: off the streets, and out of the shelters. It also happens to be what the Downtown Business Association wants."

"Downtown Business Association? You've been a busy man. In town for only hours, and already you know the political wants of those Neanderthals."

"You're going to get nowhere with me, talking like that about the powers that be. Remember, it's *their* city."

"That's funny, I thought the city belonged to all of us."

"Why do you think they call your clients 'transients'? Because they don't belong," Simon West replied. "Here today. Gone tomorrow."

"Even if they lived here for years? Even if they're born here?"

"Even."

"And what happens if they're too sick? Too damaged by mental illness? Affected by a life of alcoholism? Or simply broken by life itself? What happens to those who don't fit into their neat little paradigms?"

"Then they're no longer their concern. Nor your concern."

"You know life isn't like that—all neat and pretty. It's messy, messy as hell."

The give and take between the two men felt like body shots to Lynne. In many ways, she agreed with Simon West. But, she was having a hard time knowing where to place the people she had met that day, and she was having an emotionally harder time figuring out where her daughter belonged. What category did she fall into? *If she was a transient and not eligible for help, then what would become of her? If Kerry couldn't, or wouldn't help, then who would?*

A deep frown creased her forehead. A chill crawled across her skin as her soul was cast into darkness. If she couldn't get Kerry to help, then who would? According to the inquiries she had made, only he had the...magical connections, as they called it. What chance would Tracy stand out there all alone? From what she had seen, not much chance at all. A shudder shook her body and soul, failing to dislodge her mask of pain. Fortunately for her, the two men were too far into their power struggle to take notice. *Please, Kerry. Shut up before you get fired.*

"From now on, only those with a proven job, or one pending are to be given services. You have thirty days to transition those that don't."

"Transition?" Kerry said, clenching his hands into tight fists behind his back. With the aid of a deep, cleansing breath, he willed them to relax. An off-centered smile slowly crept onto his face. "I get it. This is how to curtail services, cut the numbers we serve—of whom we serve. Drive them out of here, anywhere but here. Out of town preferably. Police sweeps. Hunger. Cold. Wet. Whatever it takes, as long as it makes it harder for them to exist. Just so long as we increase the pain. Anything but actually help them. That's what this is all about, isn't it?"

"Like I said," Simon West said, forcing his words through clenched teeth. "They are no longer your concern. It's a new day around here. Time moves on. We're changing, and that includes you. Do I make myself clear?" Simon West said, looking expectantly.

But before Kerry could chomp down on the bait, Lynne cut in: "Wife? Son?" To save her daughter, she knew she had to save this man from himself, and the wrath of his boss. Moving over to the desk, she picked up the picture frame and turned it. Even to her the picture seemed off, a fantasy of middle class existence. It clashed with the man sitting in front of her; tired suit and sullen face. It sure as hell clashed with the environment they were in.

A jarring transformation swept the man sitting before them. He suddenly appeared vulnerable. His face tightened, and then became fluid. To her shock, she realized that a profound sadness had swept over the man. Nodding, he reached over and took the picture from her and replaced it on the desk. Once again facing him, and not them.

"Nice," Lynne replied. This was not the reaction she had expected, but it did get Kerry beyond the immediate crisis. *Now, to extract him from this dangerous situation.* "You promised you'd show me the Cross Arms Hotel. Perhaps this would be as good a time as any."

Lynne took Kerry firmly by the hand, but before they got to the door, just five feet away, Simon West stopped them with a warning. "Another thing. We have a dress code around here. Get your new work shirts from Charlene and get on board with the new program. Either that or," and here a demonic smile broke upon his face, "I would suggest a career change. With your record here, Mental Health or police work would seem especially suitable for you."

CHAPTER NINE

Lynne rushed to keep up with Kerry. It was becoming a habit. He was a tall man with a long, purposeful stride that was always in a hurry. She never really appreciated just how long legged he was, until she tried to match him. Passing the bathroom doors, she reached out and grabbed him by the arm.

"What?" Kerry demanded, spinning around.

Lynne looked over to the bathroom door, hoping her bladder wouldn't explode.

Seeing the discomfort in her eyes, Kerry took out his pocket watch. "Hurry. Okay?" he managed to say through grinding teeth.

Walking into the bathroom, Lynne noticed a row of stalls. Startled, she stopped abruptly. She had never seen one without a door. Continuing on, she found an empty one and entered.

Moments later. "That was interesting," she quipped to Kerry upon exiting the bathroom. "No doors on the stall. It's like prison."

"We do it so junkies don't shoot up, or smoke crack

behind closed doors."

"Oh, no problem," she stated bravely, holding her head higher. "I mean, we're all women in there. Nothing none of us haven't seen before."

"Oh, really?" Kerry said through a crooked smile as two tall transvestites walked past them on their way *out* of the bathroom. They were dressed to the max with blue glitter scattered in their hair, and rouged faces. Spandex tube tops announced massive breast augmentations, but it couldn't hide the large, masculine shoulders. The red micro skirts matched nicely the color of Lynne's face. It was all Kerry could do to stop from cracking up.

Exiting the shelter, Kerry stopped, and cased the street up and down with his war weary gaze. Lynne followed suit, but he had no idea what she was looking for. "What's with you and Mental Health?" she began, trying to ease the tension between them. "Bad history of sorts?"

"Perhaps it's none of your damn business." The words were made harsher by their matter-of-fact tone.

Before Lynne could reply, she saw Kerry's body tightening up. He stood even taller now, as if prepared for fight-or-flight. She followed his stare across the street. Julie Carson still stood where she had been when they entered the shelter. She stood there quietly, petting the dead bat she cradled in her arms. She seemed lost to her delusional world, when an uneven, stroke-like smile came upon her face.

"What are you going to do about her?" Lynne finally

asked, when she found the courage to do so. She had learned quickly that asking questions of Kerry was like playing catch with a live grenade.

"You still want to see a room at the Cross Arms?" Kerry asked, answering her question with one of his own.

"I want to see every nook and cranny where the homeless live." Lynne hadn't meant to say it with so much force. Even to her own ears, her voice sounded like ground glass being walked upon with bare feet. She hoped Kerry hadn't caught the overlying emotion in her voice, but that concern was dashed when she saw his eyes narrow in concentration. Slowly, he shook his head like he was shaking off morning mist. "It's your purgatory," he replied slowly.

Kerry turned, began to cross the street and then stopped. He slowly looked back at Lynne with troubled eyes. "Actually, it's theirs." Quickly, he resumed his foolish, wrathful march across the street, being barely missed by more than one car, each in turn drawing a shouted curse from him.

Lynne's mouth dropped. Never in her life had she encountered someone so over the edge. But now was not the time to be evaluating him. She realized more than ever that in order to find her daughter, she needed his help. She reminded herself that he was, in fact, the *only* person that could help. She had too much riding on him.

Breathing in courage, she followed the mad man across an unseen barrier. A rush of emotions overtook her. Fright was expected. Unexpected was the lightness of liberation.

One world exited, and a new one entered. Like with Kerry earlier, more than one car horn added punctuation to her performance.

Braking fast and breathing hard, she joined Kerry in time to hear him ask Julie: "You still crashing over at the Cross to Bear Hotel?" Lynne assumed that was the street name for the Cross Arms. She was a fast learner.

At first, Julie looked at Kerry with confusion dancing in her liquid doe eyes. Out of nowhere they cleared, as if someone had thrown a switch. "Oh, Kerry, it's you. How you be? Did you ask something of me?"

"Where are you staying?" The soft gentleness of his voice surprised Lynne. It was like another man had asked the question.

"You know," Julie said through a little girl smile—one that forced tears to Lynne's eyes. She quickly swallowed the hard lump in her throat. The smile flooded her with memories—too many memories. "You found me the room."

Again, the unexpected rocked Lynne when Kerry, without a word, reached out and took a hold of Julie's arm. He rolled up her sleeve and inspected her arm. He repeated the maneuver with the other arm. Julie looked bored. It was a well-practiced dance between the two of them.

"Look all you want. You won't find no tracks. I ain't using."

"And the sun sets in the East." Kerry's reply was not accusatory. It was more matter-of-fact, tinged with disappointment. "Okay, let's go," he said, after he released her arm.

Halfway down the block, the three-person patrol passed a trashcan. "Ditch the bat." Again, Kerry's voice was neutral, as if it was a normal request. Nonchalantly, Julie did as requested. It was just another day in paradise.

CHAPTER TEN

If the Cross Arms Hotel wasn't much to look at from the outside, it was even more depressing on the inside. Of course, that is what Kerry would say about most things: Everything looked better from the outside, including life itself.

The corridor that led to Julie's room was dark and gloomy. Almost all of the hall lights were missing. When Kerry caught Lynne looking at the third empty light fixture, he said, "Tenants take some. The landlord won't replace missing or broken ones in their rooms."

"Pushers take the rest," Julie tossed in.

"Let's just say they don't want or *need* the spotlight of publicity."

Shaking off the doom and gloom with the fluid movement of a ballet dancer, Julie pranced over and quickly unlocked the door to her room. Stepping aside, she quaintly mimicked a bow and then ushered Lynne and Kerry in.

The room was, as expected, poorly lit, with natural sunshine struggling to seep through the torn curtains.

If that wasn't bad enough, the sunlight also had to circumvent the building towering over the hotel, dominating the view from the room's window. Maybe the curtailment of sunlight was a blessing, considering that the room was furnished in late, post-modern desolation. Lynne tried really hard not to imagine Tracy sleeping in such a dump.

As for Julie, she knew that the bed was lumpy. She knew that the "quilt," was in fact, a worn surplus Army blanket. She also knew that the dresser was ancient and bore many deep scars. In many places it was disfigured, with carvings of initials from those fearing the passing of life without anyone noticing. She knew all of this, and much more. But that was alright. This room was Julie's castle. It sure as hell beat the alley she had been sharing with an army of rats.

"I share a bathroom down the hall with half the city, but that's okay," Julie informed her captive audience. A pause in the expansion of the universe took hold of the room. The whimsical voice of the young girl forced stillness upon her abode. "I have my very own bed." The voice came from a deep, dark tunnel that neither Lynne nor Kerry wished to contemplate the origins of.

"And, I have my own dresser where I can put my clothes in, just like when I was a kid. That way nobodies can steal them." Mulling over her last statement, Julie's smile slowly died. Doubt chased her eyes into narrow canyons. "Least I think so. I mean, I think I had a dresser. Living out of a bag, a backpack...that ain't normal. Is it?

'Specially for a kid. I mean, shouldn't every child have a normal life? Sleep in a house with a bed, and have a dresser and all? Did I Kerry?"

"I don't know. I hope so," Kerry was just able to squeak out, before his throat closed painfully tight.

"Look, let me show you," Julie began, her voice pushed manically high. She had a point to prove. Which point that might be was beyond her ability to articulate, especially to herself, but she knew it was important to do so. She rushed over to Lynne, took her by the arm and dragged her over to the dresser. Even if she wanted to, Lynne wasn't sure she had the physical strength to resist.

Looking back at Lynne, with a smile brightened by pride, she opened the top drawer of the dresser. It was only when Lynne's face tightened, and her blood fled south that she turned back to the drawer. Too late did she try and shut it. Kerry was fast—too fast for her. He pushed through the two women and latched onto the drawer. In a blur, he scooped up the hip kits. He threw the syringes to the floor. The sound of breaking glass filled the void of the room as he stomped on them. Without a word, he turned, and stormed out of the room.

CHAPTER ELEVEN

Kerry stood on the curb in front of the hotel, with his arms folded across his chest. He was trying hard to breathe normally. Recalling some Yoga classes he had taken once, he tried slowing his breathing. And then, he tried to inhale longer and deeper, praying against hope that it would help. What he heard next sure as hell didn't.

"Well?"

He didn't need to turn to know who it was.

"Don't!" he barked, finding a target for his frustration and anger.

"Don't what?" Lynne asked. She was taken aback by Kerry's combative tone, but her own voice was tough as redwood. She was through with diplomacy.

"Do not ask me again what I'm going to do about it. I'm not God!" This lady was really beginning to get under his skin. The last thing Kerry needed was another conscience.

Snapping around to confront Lynne directly, Kerry spotted Susie sitting across the street, on the curb along with three homeless gents. The Breakfast Club is what the streets called this gathering, regardless of the time of day.

It had started originally when they met first thing in the morning in front of McDonald's, to hustle a few bucks for food.

Lynne felt the change in Kerry's demeanor. It was a letting go of the postponed fight that they had almost engaged in. Which was all right with her; her own emotions were churning faster than a food processor. "What's up?" she asked, pretty sure she knew the answer.

"House call," came the truncated reply, just before Kerry launched himself into traffic.

"What is it with you and jaywalking?" Lynne wistfully asked, glancing back at the empty space where Kerry had been standing just seconds before. Sucking up her courage, she quickly followed in the footsteps of his mad dash.

Susie sat on the curb, with a brown rain coat drabbed casually about her. It was immediately apparent to Kerry that she wore nothing under it. Rusty sat next to her, with his head tucked deep within the hood of his sweatshirt. Sam sat next to him, and another homeless person, whom Kerry did not recognize. "Sam. Rusty. Susie," Kerry said in greeting.

At first, nobody paid much attention to Lynne when she joined them. Finally, Sam's sight fought through the raging hangover, caused by the forty-pounders he'd had as dinner the night before. "You sure she ain't for me?" he asked Kerry, casting an appreciative eye to Lynne and remembering their encounter at the Hole.

"Keep it clean," Kerry responded.

Sam huffed and pulled out a *King Cobra* from the inside of his coat. "You gotta admit, she's easy on the eyes," he replied, before taking a deadly swig of the rotgut liquor. Looking up at Kerry with eyes made bright with defiance, he continued, "Easier on them than your ugly mug!"

Susie pulled a small plastic baggie of grass from her coat pocket and began to roll a joint. Her hands moved with an expert's dexterity.

Lynne was no prude. She had seen coke sniffed at a few parties before, but this was different. They were sitting in the middle of a city in broad daylight, and rolling a joint as if it was the most natural thing in the universe. She looked with small, troubled eyes to Kerry. Sighing, she registered the fact that he seemed to care less; one-way or the other.

"How are you doing, Susie?" Kerry finally asked, with the gentleness of a poet.

Instead of answering, or as an answer in its own right, Susie lit up the joint. Taking a deeply troubling hit, she tried passing it to Kerry. He waved it off.

With nervous, twitchy eyes, Lynne looked up and down the street, expecting the traffic to come to an abrupt halt. The universe—her universe, was tilting, and she expected some telltale sign, some recognition of that fact. But there was nothing. Life simply went on. This was normal in this part of town, in this time.

Looking back to Sam, Kerry and Rusty, with guilt darkening her eyes, Lynne was brought up short.

Nobody had paid her disquiet any attention. Instead, all three men were looking at Susie with deeply troubled and caring eyes. She found this—their collective compassion—deeply moving. If that feeling were a color, the street would have been bathed in morning blue.

"That's what I want to..." Sam began in answer to a question Kerry had asked, one that Lynne had missed due to her self-musing, but Rusty quickly cut in.

"We."

"Okay! Okay! We! Don't make a federal case out of it! We need to talk to you. Susie needs help."

"Lots of help," Rusty chimed in. The kind of help only you can give her. We can't."

"I can't help her." Kerry's reply was slow and drawn out, like it was physically painful to talk. "I can't help her that way."

"Sure you can," Rusty said.

"She'd go if you took her," Sam insisted.

"No, she won't!" Kerry stated emphatically, looking at Susie with guilt-ridden eyes.

"Yes, she will!" Rusty stated.

"She will," Sam said, adding his weight to the argument.

"Won't!" Kerry insisted.

"Will!" Rusty challenged back.

"Will you?" Lynne asked, her voice torn with exasperation. As far as she was concerned, the argument sounded like one amongst children. She was also confused, and mad at Kerry's reluctance to helping Susie.

It was readily apparent that Kerry cared for Susie, but he was refusing to help her all the same.

"Will you?" Kerry asked reluctantly, obvious to all but Susie, that he hoped her answer would be no.

"Whatever you say," she responded, matter-of-factly.

"Meet me tomorrow morning at the shelter. I'll give you a lift." The words were clipped. His voice was stern. His jaws clenched. Susie answered by taking another draw on the joint.

"We'll make sure," Rusty said, speaking on behalf of the Breakfast Club.

"Let's go," Kerry said to Lynne. He turned and began to walk back to the shelter. Lynne hesitated, wanting some kind of closure.

"Best hurry," Rusty said.

"He'll leave you in the dust," Sam added.

"For sure," Susie concurred.

Laughter from the Breakfast Club followed Kerry and Lynne down the street.

CHAPTER TWELVE

A severe shiver jolted her. She probed the darkness with frightened eyes. Tracy knew he was hiding in the shadows. Even before Sam and Dorothy had left to go dumpster diving, and Jeffrey had wandered off, she had felt his cold presence. His deathly, yet strangely seductive existence could be felt all throughout the cave. A shudder rolled over her. His biting chill was like icicle claws strumming her soul. Blackness, like she had never felt before, wrapped itself around her heart, squeezing. She shivered to no avail. She tried not to look his way, straining her neck muscles in resistance. She even contemplated begging Dorothy and Sam to stay. But without words, he had warned her against that.

Whoever he was—and she had an inkling as to his identity; he was powerful, in fact, omnipotent, if her hunch was right. His persona, his presence, expanded until her steel home became a claustrophobic cell. She worried that it might explode, unable to contain the overpowering force of his being. Still, his essence expanded even further, forcing the air from her lungs.

Then, she perceived a change in the ambiance of the tunnel. At first she was perplexed, but then it dawned on her. He was pleased with her discomfort, with her sucking in the air that brought lightheadedness.

An offensive smell struck, like a fist to her head. Sulfur, the smell of rotten eggs, invaded her nostrils. It soaked her tongue when she tried to bypass the sickening odor, by breathing with her mouth open. She gagged. She was thankful there was no food in her stomach, for she would have certainly vomited. She tried shaking her head, but nothing seemed to change. Of course that was the purpose of it all—to make her feel defenseless and alone before him. It was all designed to make her surrender and kneel before the Dark Prince. She knew! She knew!

Looking around, her eyes crinkled when she realized the absence of Sam and Dorothy. *Had they announced their departure? Had they said goodbye? Had she merely spaced out? Dumpster diving? Was it them who had mentioned it to her? Or was it all made up?* Confusion ruled. Like so much of her life of late, what was real and not played havoc with her mind, her sense of being.

"Momma." The word came out soft and weak, frightening her. She hadn't meant to speak the endearment out loud. In fact, at first she was unsure if she was the speaker.

"No!" His command reverberated off the steel walls, threatening to shatter her eardrums. She dug her hands into her ears, but his next command was not muffled at all. It was as clear and commanding a voice as she had ever heard. "You will never utter those words, again. Is that clear?"

"Yes," came her detached voice, stretched thin.

"You know what will happen if you do? Don't you?"

Not trusting her voice, she shook her head no.

"She will die." The voice was no longer angry, but rather matter-of-fact.

"Please don't," came her weak, if heartfelt response.

"Then, you don't."

"Okay."

She could hear rustling in the unforgiving shadows as he settled in. He was making himself comfortable for a long stay.

"Do you know how this works? Or must I explain it to you like the dumb ass you are?"

"How what works?"

"Just as I figured. As dumb as the day you were born. As dumb as a sack of shit. Useless! You're a total waste of the very air that you breathe!"

"I'm sorry."

"You know it's all up to you."

"What's up to me?"

"Who lives and who dies. Whoever you bring into your life—be it a friend, rescuer, or even a lover—they will die. That's about as simple as I can make it."

"But, why?"

"Because you're no good." Exasperation began to harden the voice. "Never have been. Never will be. Is that simple enough for a stupid girl such as yourself?"

"I guess."

"Do you need proof?"

When Tracy didn't answer, the voice in the corner continued. "Remember Muffin? That pathetic thing you called a dog? You must had been six when he died."

A picture of the curly haired mutt that had been her best friend came to her mind. A smile started to soften upon her lips, but then she froze when she heard the evilness speak. "She was running away from you when she ran into the path of that vehicle. She knew you were no good. She knew you for the poison that you were. The poison that you still are. So I sent the truck to put her out of her misery. I was doing her a favor."

"Why would you do that?!" Tracy said through tears, her voice torn with pain.

"Because of you—*you,* she died. Don't you see? You gave me no choice."

Tracy bolted upright. She could feel the Dark One's hand stroking her face, freezing the skin under his touch. A loud whimper came up from the deepest recesses of her soul. She brought her hand up to remove his, but nothing was there.

"The same way I can take out your mom, or anyone else," the voice said, ignoring her question. There was haughtiness, and a cruel roughness to it that caused Tracy to curl into a ball. She tucked her hands under her legs, and then pulled them into her chest. "But, like I said, it's all up to you. You target who will pay for the despicable thing that you are."

"Why are you torturing me? Why!" Tracy screamed out.

"Because that's what I do! Because of who you are: Filthy. Despicable. Rotten."

Tracy cut a quick glance over to the black corner. She wanted to know—needed to know—if he really had a pitchfork, if he was red, had a tail, and the head of a goat. Only the blackness stared back. But it was more than the mere absence of light. The blackness was a force, a negative power that sucked in energy, light, and finally life itself, taking it to another dimension—one found only within the deepest reaches of the nightmare mind. It was like the black holes she had studied in astronomy, sucking everything in and letting nothing escape. It was also the place where mental illness met evil, and the life of a young girl hung in the balance.

CHAPTER THIRTEEN

Lynne tensed. An uneasy feeling swelled within her constricted organs. She was standing in front of the shelter with Kerry. She had finally caught up with him a few blocks back, and she had even managed to match his stride. But the thick ice of hostility was another matter altogether. It felt as if it weighed a ton, both pressing down on her and curiously—connecting them. Either way, she was not happy about it.

"You had enough?" Kerry finally asked, sticking his hands into his pockets, to prevent him from crossing his arms across his chest. He knew that was a particularly belligerent stance. Others had told him often enough in the past, and he was determined to avoid that outward sign of Lynne getting to him at all costs.

"You talking about tomorrow?"

"Of course I'm talking about tomorrow," he barked, pulling his hands out and crossing his arms. *After all, why should he care what she thought of his reactions to her?*

"No. I'll see you tomorrow." Lynne's voice was cool, a sharp contrast to the volcanic emotions boiling within.

The day's experiences had convinced her more than ever of the need to find her daughter, and extract her from the craziness of the streets.

"It's your call," was Kerry's simple reply.

Silence. The kind that entombs, trapped them. Neither made any attempt at calling the day a draw by walking away. Lynne cleared her voice, making sure it wouldn't break if she spoke. Finally she asked, "How come you didn't want to help that girl back there?"

"Help? Help who? Susie? Julie?"

"Susie," Lynne replied in a small voice. Had she already regulated Julie to the ranks of the lost? Or had she just plain forgotten about her? Either way, her conscience was busy, raking her over the proverbial coals. Shame was a new emotion for her.

"And how am I supposed to help?" Kerry's voice was piano wire tight, his eyes smoldering with unsuppressed anger.

"I don't know. Surely your city has a mental health department."

"Those idiots!" Kerry lashed out. A wounded laughter that caused goose bumps followed. Lynne prepared to take a step back. A more demented laugh would be hard to imagine. "Those morons! What makes you think they will help! And it's the county, not the city. Dear God, give me a break from the clueless!"

"That would be me, I suppose?"

"I suppose," Kerry replied, dragging his voice down several octaves.

Lynne's eyes pinched to slits. Her lips quivered. The wound that Kerry had inflicted made him feel about as bad as he had in a long time. It wasn't like him to hurt others. He had no idea why he was letting this woman get under his skin. An inkling of insight told him it just wasn't her. It was all of them: Susie, Julie, and of course the one he couldn't even bring himself to name, buried within the deepest recesses of his mind. Also, he was an ass. It was as simple as that, he reminded himself. Still, he would try and make a small gesture of amends.

"Look, this is what we'll do. Tomorrow, we'll give her a ride out to the County. But once we're there, it's up to her. Fair warning though, you shouldn't expect too much. They won't help."

"Why are you so bitter? What have the Mental Health done to you?"

"I told you once. I won't tell you again," Kerry began. His throat was dry, like he had been sucking on a salt tab. Pain had transformed his anger until his voice crackled, threatening to break. "Do not question my tactics or motives. You are here simply to observe until you get tired of whatever game you are playing. Then, you can run back to your yuppie friends, and tell them tall tales of the dark side at your cocktail parties." *So much for making amends,* flashed through his mind.

Turning his back to Lynne, he started for the door and then stopped. "I start early. If you can't manage to get here by seven...don't bother."

CHAPTER FOURTEEN

Fever pitched sweat. The white cotton tee shirt that she slept in felt glued to her skin. Panic wrapped hands around her throat and squeezed. The sensation of suffocation was overwhelming. Wet cotton dreams had entombed Lynne in a straightjacket of terror all night long. Now, she had inhaled it. The sensation of not being able to breathe threatened to drive her mad. Try as she might, she couldn't wake from the nightmares. Even the soft chimes of her meditational alarm clock couldn't help. She slept through the first set. It was only when they came closer together, and louder—intruding into her troubled sleep, did her dream mind give way to consciousness.

"Shit!" She bolted upright, waking with a start. She was surprised to feel her heart racing fast. It beat hard. *Did heart attacks begin this way?* A tickling sensation brought her hand to her chest. She looked down at the moistened hand. It was then that she realized that a sweaty sheen covered her body.

She staggered to the shower. Hot water pounded her

while she tried to dig through the fog befuddling her waking mind. Fractured images of troubling dreams enslaved her consciousness: Fleeting impressions of her daughter; age six, maybe seven, with large chocolate eyes—accusing ones, that drilled their unblinking sight into hers. *Had the mental illness been present even then? Did her failure to detect it mean that she was a failure as a mother?* She leaned her head against the shower door. Was her daughter even mentally ill? Or was it something else entirely—like drugs that could explain her changed behavior? Or was she—Lynne, being punished for some transgression? Would God be so cruel? Could he be?

Shaking her head violently, water splashed hard against the glass door of the shower with dull thuds. With a loud groan, Lynne reached out and turned off the water.

Kerry didn't dream. At least he didn't remember them if he did. It was his old friend, tequila, which did the trick. He had drunk enough to fill a swimming pool. Unfortunately, the pain that pounded his head was the price to pay for amnesia. Of course, when he was shaving, the nightmares forced their way to the forefront of his hangover. If they couldn't extract their due in the nighttime, then they would do so in his waking life. The universe had to be balanced. Guilt demanded blood, one way or another.

Voices bounced inside the confines of Tracy Swanson's head. It was as if they were ricocheting off the tin pipes of her shelter: "You're no good!" they screeched. "You're scum! You'd be better off dead. Everybody would be better off if you were dead. Nobody will miss you." Finally, they unified in a chorus chant. "Kill yourself! Kill yourself! Kill yourself!"

The last exhortation brought her to the realm of the living, if one could be so generous with that term. To Tracy, it was all hell. Waking or sleeping, it was all one—the continuation of pain and aloneness. She was having a harder time differentiating between sleep and being awake lately. One bled into the other, until the wall separating them was more like a child's top rotating; hallucinations, nightmares and consciousness merely being different sides.

Rolling over in her sleeping bag, the filtered early morning sun revealed that she was in fact, alone. Had the dreams in the night scared the others away? Had they abandoned her like her mother had? The thought that it was she who had run away percolated up, only to have the voices shout it down. It was important for them to isolate her. They needed to make her even more vulnerable, if they were going to succeed in driving her mad. To hurtle her towards the final solution that too many of the mentally ill often succumbed to.

CHAPTER FIFTEEN

The usual crowd of tired homeless greeted them as they both pulled up to the shelter. They stood like defeated sentries, heads tucked into bent shoulders. Listless. A handful slept on the sidewalk, or against the front of the building. Kerry's body suddenly stiffened. Searching for the reason, Lynne looked closer at the twenty plus people before them. That's when her own body followed suit. Standing off to one side was Simon West, arms folded across his chest, and looking like he had spent his morning sucking lemons. To say he looked displeased would be a huge understatement.

"Morning," Kerry offered cautiously, as they stopped before him.

"I want you to disperse these people." The words were clipped, and spat through teeth clenched so tight that Lynne thought they might be wired shut.

Kerry looked about, his face locked down with confusion. "But, they aren't doing anything."

"Duh! You think? That's the point!" In an attempt to rein in his emotions, Simon West tried breathing. It didn't help. "They should be out looking for work. Or, and I know that it's a real shocker for you, actually working."

"But, most of these people are disabled—broken by life."

"Like I said before," Simon West stated behind a harsh sigh, "we only service those who have a job. We help them save money, give them job counseling, things that move them on. As for the others—send them to another shelter, even the streets as far as I'm concerned."

"Anywhere, but here," Kerry spat out.

"Precisely," Simon West stated firmly, embracing his arrogance in Kerry's eyes. The man in the shiny, over worn business suit, abruptly turned and walked back into the shelter.

"Shit," Kerry said quietly.

"That's one unhappy man." Lynne was surprised by her assessment, and even more surprised that she had articulated it. Kerry looked at her hard, wondering where that judgment came from. The slight relaxing of his hard-pressed lips acknowledged the truth of the man that had evaded him. Then, they set even harder.

"You heard the man!" his loud voice barked out. "Take it over to the Sally, or the Rescue Mission. Come on. Let's move it." The words were like slashes from a cat-o-nine whip against his soul. This was not who he was, what he was. He was unsure if he had ever uttered harsher words in his life. And he had just done so to *those people*—his people. But before anyone could move, another voice, thousands of times more abrasive, broke the morning air.

"Call the cops. Damn you all to hell!" Ted Tucker, the owner of the car lot next to the shelter, shouted out to one and all. One of his sales men dared to lock stares with him.

"Why are you just standing there? You stupid, or just retarded? Go call the cops!" Ted Tucker next swept the slowly departing crowd in front of the shelter, with hate-enlarged eyes. For a moment, Lynne worried about a heart attack—so red was the man's face. Then, she became concerned about survival, as Ted Tucker's sight fell on her and Kerry. He began storming over.

"Problem?" Kerry asked, quickly placing himself between Ted Tucker and Lynne.

"Problem? Problem?! Yes, you're the problem!" Ted's words were literally sprayed with spittle.

"You mean generally, or something specific?" Kerry responded with a measured voice.

If hate had a smell, then it was draped about Ted Tucker like harsh aftershave.

"You!" Again he spat out the words, confused by Kerry's restrained response.

"Why me? And I know I'm going to be sorry for asking, but here it goes. Is it something I've done, or just who I am?" Kerry inquired.

"You! I mean, your name. It's all over my business. I mean the wall, that's why!"

"His name?" Lynne dared to ask, looking about for a graffiti scarred building. "What wall?"

Ted Tucker turned and began a rapid stride over to

his lot. He stopped when he noticed that no one had followed. "Come on. I'll show you."

The front panel glass of Ted Tucker's office had been shattered. Kerry looked about for the weapon that had caused the destruction, but nothing out of the ordinary was to be found amongst the shards of glass littering the ground. He looked at Ted Tucker, who was glaring back at him.

"You still don't get it, do you!?" Ted asked him.

"Get what? What exactly am I supposed to get?"

"Inside," Ted said, and he marched through the front door that was likewise shattered, crunching glass underfoot as he did so. The tingling of falling glass followed Ted Tucker before Kerry and Lynne did.

Inside, it was readily apparent why no weapon had been found. From the amount of smeared blood on the wall and droplets on the floor, Kerry guessed that the perpetrator had used bare hands to gain entry. It was also apparent that the breaking of the glass was incidental, and not the focus. Bizarre messages on the wall glared back at them. Enough blood had been used that it laced the air with its sickening sweat odor. A smell that quickly rolled Lynne's stomach. A smell so powerful that it threatened Kerry with flashbacks to a time he wished to forget.

Some of the wording was misspelled. A lot of it was in another language entirely. Kerry knew that it existed nowhere else in the world, except in one person's highly delusional mind. But one word liberally sprinkled throughout the text screamed out for attention: KERRY.

Ted Tucker stood with hands on his hips, and a smug arrogance stamped on his face. "And what?" Kerry finally asked the man, against his better judgment.

"And? And!" Ted Tucker sputtered. "It—this obviously belongs to a psycho! And you know every psycho out there! They're all yours! This is all your fault!"

"My fault?" A weary smile came to Kerry. He slowly shook his head. As for Lynne, a look of concern turned her lips thin. She tightened her eyes. None of which sat well with Ted Tucker.

"Yes, your fault. You're like their Godfather!"

"I don't see..." Kerry began. His reply was cut short by a police car pulling up in front of the used car lot. A tall, thin cop came out of the driver's side of the car, and he beckoned Kerry to join him. Kerry immediately made his way over. Lynne hesitated. Then she followed sluggishly behind. It was like her feet had a reluctant mind all their own. Unanswerable questions slowed her pace even further.

"Bob," Kerry began in greeting. "Problem?"

"You might call it that. I'm taking her to the E.R." the cop said, pointing to the rear of his car with his sharp chin. "But I thought you might want to have a few words with her first. You know, grease the skids as it were. Try and give her some comfort. A little encouragement wouldn't hurt." The cop looked over to Ted Tucker, who stood with his skinny arms folded across his equally skinny chest. "Depending on what he does, she may be locked up for a while."

Fearing the worst, Kerry's eyes clouded over. A bitter taste of burnt almonds washed over his tongue. His eyes stayed glued to the cop as he opened the back passenger door. A pale looking Julie sat there. Her white blouse was heavily stained with blood. Her hands were encased in bloody bandages. Kerry knew that the cop had broken half a dozen departmental regulations by not handcuffing her. He silently tipped his head in acknowledgment of this simple, but deeply humane gesture.

Julie's guilt-evading stare stayed locked to the back of the seat in front of her. "Are you okay?" Kerry asked. Julie remained mute.

"She should be okay," Bob replied, when it became obvious that Julie was not going to answer. "She'll need stitches, but none of the cuts appear to be too deep. Most of the bleeding has stopped."

"Why, Julie? Why did you do this?"

"She said you did it," the cop began. "That it was you who broke the glass and wrote on the wall with your own blood." Fighting common sense, Kerry, Lynne and Bob threw their collective stares to Kerry's hands. The beginning of a smile curled Bob's lips when he realized what they were doing. Kerry knelt.

"Why?" He asked Julie again.

"You took my spikes away. Without them, the dope doesn't work so well." Her attempt at gallows humor failed to find an audience. The cop, Kerry and Lynne felt their faces go fluid with the pain and confusion they felt for the young girl. "After you left, I just sat there staring at the stomped kits, and..." and here she looked up into Kerry's eyes with her own, remembering the terror that quickly followed. "The voices. They came back. And then the gray men in the folds of the drapes came out looking for me. Because of you, I had to run—I ended up walking the streets all night. I came looking for you, but they said you went home. How come you get to go home, and I have to run? I ain't got no home. Nope. It ain't fair. The gray men, they didn't go home. They followed me—even here, yelling at me, saying horrible things. I'm not as bad as they say I am. And I didn't do those things they said I did either! You're supposed to be here for us—for me.

"How come you broke my needles? Did you want the gray men to get me?" Her response was so low that Kerry found himself leaning forward to hear what she was saying. Julie shook more vigorously. Left, then right, shrugging off the confession. Her voice became firmer and louder: "You did it. Yup. It was you. Don't try to put this on me." Following Kerry's line of sight, she looked down at her hands. A severe crease caved in her forehead, and what little color that she had left her face. Kerry had the distinct impression that she was seeing her bloody hands for the first time.

"Well, I best get her to the E.R," the cop said, with a fatherly voice that was both firm and gentle.

"Do what you can," Kerry softly pleaded. Turning, his forward progress was stopped cold when he saw tears streaming down Lynne's face. They were heavy with agony. Thrown for a loop by her strong reaction, and unsure what to do about it, he resumed his trek over to the shelter. His footsteps felt heavy. Guilt encased them in cement. While this wasn't the first time he had been blamed, for the onset of delusional battery against someone with mental illness, it still cut him deep. He just couldn't stop caring. Maybe he cared too much. He just didn't know how to cut his heart off from the people he cared about most in the world. He was as much a part of them, as they were of him.

CHAPTER SIXTEEN

In the end, and unbeknownst to them, it was the concern for her fellow campers that forced Tracy out of her corrugated steel crypt, and into the unknown. The inner voices, Tracy's unseen but very real other-worlders, were threatened by the show of friendship. They reacted accordingly. A cruel and unforgiving disease concocted vengeful plans. They warned her of her new friends' false feelings towards her. They cautioned her of her surrogate family's real agenda. The more her friends tried to help, the crueler her tormentors raged against them. The more they showed their concern and love for her, the more threatening the voices captured within her mind became.

Finally, they had convinced her that Dorothy, Sam, and even Jeffrey, were part of the vast conspiracy out to harm her. These inner dimensional terrorists told her that her so-called friends' job was to keep her in the steel tomb, until the police could find the time to come and take her away. The voices told her of the living hell that a mental ward would be. In explicit and gory detail, they told her how the mental health professionals would forcibly medicate her. Fry her mind with electricity. Slice and dice her brain with a lobotomy. In the end, they convinced her that the white coats would steal her soul. And in the unlikely event that her replacement family actually did care for her, there was the ever present and all-consuming warning from the devil. He would kill anyone who was careless enough to befriend her. Either way, she was damned if she did, and they were damned if she didn't.

She jammed a fist into her mouth, to prevent yet another anguished cry. Her intestines were on fire. A parched throat made swallowing painful. Were her new friends betraying her? Were they out to harm her? Or, if they really were her friends, and they were in fact trying to help, would they be killed for the effort?

Confusion reigned. A vicious headache delivered unbearable pain. Her eyes crunched shut, but dehydration made tears impossible. Confusion was everywhere. *Everywhere.* Her mind reeled with uncertainty. Simple existence was becoming harder by the day. She knew that she had to leave the tunnel. She was hungry. She had already turned down Dorothy's offer of a stale sandwich because the voices told her it was laced with rat poison. As for water, she couldn't remember the last time that luxury had passed her chapped lips. Same warning. Same reason. Same result.

Time lapsed without measurement. Days? Hours? Minutes? Regardless, it was too soon when she found herself on State Street, jostling with the tourist and shopping crowd, like a drowning swimmer caught in a vicious riptide. Business people, emptying out from the Spanish themed offices that lined State, would soon join the tidal movement. High noon threatened to overwhelm her with humanity. But Tracy had knowledge neither of the time, nor the day of the week. Or even how long the walk from her cave, to where she presently found herself had taken. Time had become another casualty of her disease. It was an abstraction that merely added confusion into her life. It was simply another uncertainty. People stared. She assumed they gawked at her, because of how pale she looked. She hadn't stepped foot from the steel tomb since she had first arrived in town weeks before. Harsh white light was a physical presence. The unfiltered sun poured molten lead into her eyes. Squinting helped a little—very little. And still no tears.

It never crossed Tracy's mind that her dirty and uncombed hair, the filth encased on her clothes, and her obvious lack of bathing were drawing the interest of some. Sadly, all looked past her. Those fine citizens of the city who had trained themselves to ignore the pain of the disabled homeless, grew ever more numerous. And when the people of the city did stop to think about them, it was with questions and hard feelings, as to why the cops didn't simply run them off.

There were too many people. Too much movement. Feeling like a fish trapped in an ever closing net, Tracy knew that what was left of her sanity depended on her getting off the main thoroughfare. The El Paso, an upscale outdoor mall, brought Tracy a measure of relief. Her breathing slowed; the sense of overwhelming panic retreated. She soon found herself in front of a small boutique that sold exotic sandwiches and epicurean salads. Her mouth watered from the smell of freshly baked bread. She looked through the window, and watched customers being served. It came as a shock to her when she realized that she hadn't eaten produce of any kind since coming to the city, this from a girl who loved salads above everything else. Looking down, embarrassment added color to her face. What she saw was the poundage that her carb heavy diet of left over breads, donuts and pizzas had added to her body. What she did not see was the concentrated, innate thinness that her near starvation diet had inflicted upon her slight frame.

Peaking inside, she saw girls her own age eagerly lined up at the counter. Of course, she didn't question why they weren't in school. Such mundane affairs of the world no longer interested her. A pang of envy kicked her tender stomach. Ubiquitous white earphones dangled from their ears. That was another thing on her list of have-nots since her arrival in Santa Barbara. She hadn't listened to music on her iPhone in what seemed like decades. Frowning, she remembered a time when she couldn't live without her sounds. Now, sounds of a different kind dominated her life, seldom leaving her in peace.

Other kind memories tumbled forth. The dam had been breached. A gentle smile relaxed some of the granite hardness of her eyes and mouth. Youthful innocence radiated. She couldn't hear the giggles, but she saw their innocent laughter when an inside joke was shared amongst the girls. Tracy's smile died. Discomfort descended on her when she noticed the fashionable clothes that they wore—the same kind she used to wear. Looking down, again, shame physically pained her. Their clothes—her clothes of old, were so unlike the tattered ones that she currently wore. Hunger came to her rescue, when it forced all her mental energies to focus on the sandwiches she could see being prepared. Moisture starved saliva tortured her parched mouth. A loud gurgle rolled her stomach. Not only was she hungry, but thirsty as well.

Luck strolled out the door, when a hurried tourist tossed a half-eaten bagel into a trashcan and walked away. It took all Tracy had to stop herself from running over to the trash bin. A loud groan came. Looking into the bin, she saw that it was mostly empty. Standing on her tiptoes, she tipped herself into the trash bin. Stretching, she was just able to reach the bottom. She grabbed the bagel. A predatory smile announced victory. The bagel was covered in cheese and jalapeños.

Tracy stuffed the bagel into her mouth. Her cheeks popped out like a chipmunk. She had never tasted anything so exquisite in her life. It was only when she looked back that she saw that the girls her age had exited the eatery. They stood off to one side. Their collective stare welded onto her. Her inner voices told her that their giggles were directed at her, mocking her, savaging her in their condemnation. The voices robbed her of sight, so she didn't see the shock and sadness that pulled at the girls' eyes, aging them a decade in a matter of seconds.

The voices shrieked louder, demanding that she turn and flee back to her entombment, where they would have her alone, to once again terrorize her without witnesses to offer her comfort. After all, Dorothy, Sam and Jeffrey were usually gone during the day, and frequently at night as well; besides, they—the voices, had already done a good job discrediting them. It wouldn't be long now until Tracy would be all theirs.

In her haste to flee, Tracy stumbled into a bench that lined the outdoor mall. An exposed rod cut through her pants and into her shin. She corrected her line of escape and ran like hell. She hadn't seen that one of the girls had held out a drink towards her. She didn't see that another girl had broken into sobs, and yet another one had left her uneaten sandwich on the top of the trashcan, in hope that Tracy would return. She didn't experience the humanity of the girls, as she surrendered to the hideous terror of mental illness, of the aloneness: the cruelest symptom. Tracy ran like the devil was clipping her heals, leaving questions and hard learned truths in her wake. Rescue would have to wait another day. That is, if it came at all.

CHAPTER SEVENTEEN

Kerry kept looking over to Lynne. Her eyes were swollen and red; not yet recovered from the tears that he had seen in them earlier. He was in unfamiliar territory here. Regardless of his gruff exterior, he had never consciously set out to hurt anyone. He was unsure what he had said, or done to do so. Guilt. It was something he had in overabundance from the war. He didn't want any more. Probably couldn't handle more. And to add insult to injury, tears were something that he had no idea how to respond to. They drove him nuts.

He cut a quick glance over to Charlene, who had kept herself busy ever since they had entered the shelter. She knew Kerry well enough to give him a wide berth whenever he inadvertently hurt someone. He may have the poet's gentle soul, if one took the time to look past his grumpy exterior persona, but he was also in possession of the lion's ferocious roar.

Just when Kerry couldn't take the maddening quiet any longer, and he was about to confront Lynne, the front door of the shelter was hesitantly pushed open. Before it closed, the foul odor of someone having soiled him or herself, sent the few homeless sitting in the front of the shelter scurrying away. A stinging pain came to Lynne's eyes, caused by an odor that no amount of blinking could erase. Her hand flew up to her nose to pinch it shut.

"Can I help you?" Kerry asked, his voice constricted as he tried hard to shallow his breath.

The woman before him was somewhere in her late sixties, or early seventies. Her white hair was cut professionally to frame her angular face. It was no hack job from the streets or shelters. While her clothes were obviously soiled, she had attempted to keep them otherwise clean. Likewise, she had combed her hair. Her face and hands had been washed in the recent past.

Everything about her spoke of class, and not necessarily the kind that money bought. She held her head high with dignity, regardless of circumstances. "I am aware that my body is emitting vapors," she said. Her eyes lowered with shame.

Swallowing the lump in his throat, and keeping his nostrils closed while he spoke was one mean feat, but Kerry managed. "And you were wondering if you could shower?"

"Yes. That was the question I was about to articulate. Also, if you might be kind enough to give an old woman some clothes? My attire is a bit 'under the weather' as they say." The woman's voice was firmer, and growing in strength. Raising her eyes off the counter, she threw her shoulders back and locked stares with Kerry. In spite of being shamed by her current situation, pride demanded that she not look away—that she confronted what others thought of her head on. "I'm afraid I can't pay for the articles requested. I have no money."

Before Charlene could state the new policy, Kerry reached under the counter and pulled out a drying towel. Smiling, he handed it to the woman. "How about if I make you something to eat? From the look of things, it's been a while. Besides, a hot shower always makes me hungry." A twinkle came to his eyes. It was obvious that he found the feistiness of the woman enticing. Regardless of the trying and humiliating circumstances that she found herself in, she fought through it to carry herself with pride. She was a fighter, and one with class.

Her light brown eyes came alive with gratitude. Her surprisingly clear stare reached to the depths of his soul. "I'm beyond that now." The voice was stronger. It was laced with a tough acceptance of what is. To Kerry, the matter-of-fact tone added to his esteem of the woman.

"Beyond eating?" The words slipped out from Lynne's lips, before she could self-censor.

"The showers are down the hall to the left," Kerry began. "I'll see if I can rustle you up some clean clothes."

The woman made no move, but stood expectedly.

"Is there something else I can help you with?" Kerry asked.

"Don't you want me to sign in? Places like this always do."

"No. Maybe this one time we can skip the formality."

"But...you need names. Names give you your stats."

"Not to worry. Besides, stats can be made to say whatever you want them to."

"Thank you," the woman said to Kerry, before turning away. Lowering her head once again in shame, she slowly and reluctantly shuffled into the bowels of the shelter. The battle for self-dignity was taxing, and it seesawed between victory and defeat on a radically swinging pendulum. It was enough to give the casual observer whiplash.

"What did she mean? Beyond what? Eating?" Lynne asked.

Kerry and Charlene ignored her.

"Boss man ain't gonna like that none," Charlene told Kerry.

Kerry's attention was once again dragged to the opening front door, when Susie entered. Unlike the old lady, her entrance was bold. She cast her sight neither left nor right, never hesitating for even a single step. She was all business, and her trajectory was a straight line to Kerry. "They said I'm supposed to go with you."

"Yeah, right," Kerry replied with a rough voice. "Up for a ride?" he asked, turning to Lynne, eyeing her with a cold stare. *This is all your fault*, was stamped into his hard green eyes, and rode on the back of his stern voice.

"Sure," Lynne replied, feeling guilty, but unsure why.

Starting for the front door, Kerry froze when Simon West walked in from the back of the shelter. He shot a quick glance to Charlene. Her eyes twitched nervously. "I just passed the showers," Simon West stated, without a greeting of any kind.

"And?" Kerry asked, thinking that the man could use some training in the pleasantries of human interactions.

"And? Like who's in it? It's past the allocated time for showers. Remember?" His voice was tight, like a teacher repeating a lesson to a group of kids who should know better. "Showers are restricted to post dinner hours and before lights out. Did you not read my memo?"

"I'm waiting for the paperback edition," Kerry shot back.

"What?" Simon West barked.

Charlene groaned.

Lynne thought she was going to die.

"I want answers," Simon West replied, folding his arms across his chest, and waiting impatiently for an explanation.

"Well, it's like this. The client has an interview for a job, and it couldn't wait. I'm sorry, but I thought..." Kerry's lie trailed off, hoping against hope that Simon West would buy it.

Pain ticked by as lost seconds. All waited for Simon's verdict. Finally, an ever so slight smile softened the man's lips. "Maybe I misjudged you."

Before turning to leave, Simon West took in Susie with a suspicious glance and looked back to Kerry.

"I'm taking her to enroll in business school." Kerry thought he might as well press his advantage, for he knew the first lie would not stand long unexposed. *Two lies for the price of one. It was the American way.*

"Dressed like that?"

"Of course not! We're going to stop by the thrift store

first. Get her a few things, dress her appropriately."

"Is she going with you?" Simon West asked, looking over to Lynne. Her lips were pressed tightly together. She hated being referred to in the third person. He could ask her directly.

"Yes," was Kerry's simple reply.

"Very good then," Simon West said, rising his chin and trying to stretch taller. "I like your new attitude. It's a good beginning. I might even add, refreshing."

"You do? I mean it is," Kerry quickly added, when he saw Charlene ever so slightly shake her head no.

For a moment, Simon West looked out onto the street through the large plate glass windows. A stern look came to him, as if he were administering corporal punishment to a child. "It really is for their own good."

With effort, Kerry stopped himself from laughing. He imagined how badly Simon West would react when he found out the truth. Kerry knew he wouldn't see the humanity in his lie. He would simply see that he had been played.

Once Simon West had left the reception desk, all sighed an audible relief. "Let's go before the man finds his mind," Kerry stated.

CHAPTER EIGHTEEN

Few people inhabited the streets during their drive to the County's Mental Health Dept. Kerry and Susie were quiet with familiarity. And Lynne was simply a third wheel. Without distractions, she had the time to reflect on just how much she had been subjected to in such a short period of time. It was still very early in the morning—before most businesses opened. Gazing at the closed shops, her mind wandered further down that road. She felt like she had done a month's worth of work in the brief time she had been with Kerry. She shot a quick look over to the man. It was a new one—a look softened with respect. With surprise, she questioned: *How did he...how does he do what he does year after year without breaking?* The only sound in the confines of the truck cab was Susie chewing the hell out of a wad of gum, blowing bubbles like a child. And *why shouldn't she*, Lynne asked herself. After all, she was almost a child herself, barely older than her own daughter.

"So here's the script." Kerry's started, his voice finally breaking the monotony of the ride. "I'll drop you off in front of Mental Health Services. You go in. Go up to the front desk, and ask them for help. Look me up later. Let me know what they say. You know how to catch the bus?"

"I know," was the reply. Bored. Indifferent.

"Shouldn't you go in with her?" Lynne asked.

"Butt out!"

Lynne replied to the harshness of Kerry's reply with stony silence. She drilled him with a hard stare.

"Kerry don't like Mental Health none," Susie offered. Her voice was all business. It was cut with a matter-of-fact attitude. She pulled out one end of the gum and held the other end with her teeth while she twirled it. "Ain't that right." There was no question in her voice. It was flat. Bored with certainty.

"You got I.D.? They won't see you without I.D."

Susie opened her purse and began to rummage through it. Glancing sideways, Kerry spotted a sandwich bag full of grass. The vehicle swerved left, when he took his right hand off the steering wheel and grabbed the bag. In a neat stroke, he threw the bag out of the window.

Seeing what was unfolding, Lynne turned backwards just in time to see the bag land at the curb, where three homeless men were sitting with their feet planted firmly in the gutter, watching their lives speed by. Hitting the street hard, the sandwich bag splattered grass everywhere. Christmas was early this year. The three men scrambled for their gifts.

Kerry turned the ignition off as the truck rumbled in

protest. Then it died. He climbed down from the truck, but made no other move. His hateful stare tore into the cold concrete building that held so many nightmares of his. Without saying a word, Susie got out of the truck and walked into the building. Kerry got back in and started the truck. It roared to life, belching sweet smelling gray smoke when he gave it too much gas.

"How can you just turn her loose like that? What kind of man are you?"

In reply, Kerry laid seven feet of rubber on the pavement. If he was trying to outrun living nightmares, it was a waste of gas.

CHAPTER NINETEEN

A cemetery was the last place that she thought Kerry would take her, but here she was, walking alongside him, on grass glistening with morning dew that dampened her feet. The sweet smell of freshly cut grass filled the air. It reminded her of her childhood, when her father would cut the family lawn every other Sunday. She shook her head slightly. She knew that she had to lose the memories. She needed to steel herself for whatever awaited her, and for whatever drama Kerry was about to unleash upon her.

They approached a small, plain headstone on a slight rise. They stopped before it. Her legs turned wooden. "What, pray tell, are we doing here?" Lynne was finally able to ask.

Kerry said nothing at first. His gaze was trapped by the headstone. His eyes pinched in obvious pain. Rolling his gaze upwards, he looked at her like no explanation was needed. When he realized it was, and he found the courage to explain himself, he began, "You wanted to know what kind of man I am."

Lynne shook her head yes. She was afraid her voice

might betray her, should she attempt a verbal response. She felt that she was on a psychological safari; one with no road map or reference points.

"I'm the kind of man who doesn't forget," Kerry responded slowly. His eyes opened wider, probing Lynne's with an intense questioning gaze. As if finding the answer that he was looking for, they dropped to the headstone. Lynne followed suit.

"She was only seventeen," Lynne said, with a tight voice, having read the date of birth. The words caught in her throat. It was as if glass shards had suddenly materialized in her mouth.

"Mental Health said she didn't fit their criteria for help. That she wasn't 'target population.' Whatever the hell that's supposed to mean."

"What happened?" Lynne was barely able to push the question past the painful lump in her throat. As it was, her voice was wobbly.

"She was a cutter," Kerry began, not having registered her shaky voice. He was too far into memory for that. "She just kept on cutting, regardless of what I said or did—no matter how hard I pleaded or begged. She kept cutting away until one day she didn't stop. Only criteria she fit then was dead." The words were bitter. The voice was broken and jagged with pain.

The battle against the weakness that coursed through Lynne's legs was lost. With an audible groan, she slumped to the ground. In alarm, Kerry kneeled down next to her.

"Just leave me here, please. Leave me alone."

"What's going on? What's the matter? I just wanted to explain..."

"Please!" Lynne pleaded, her hair falling over her face, hiding the avalanche of tears. "Just leave."

"But..." Kerry began, only to stop. He looked around for help, not knowing what he had done wrong. "I can't just leave you like this."

"LEAVE!!! GODDAMN YOU!!! LEAVE!!! NOW!!!"

With his knees cracking in protest, he slowly stood. Looking down, he saw wet grass stains on his pants. Off in the near distance, grounds keepers were busy doing gardening work. Life went on. But it had suddenly changed.

Kerry made his way over to his truck. Standing next to it, he hesitated. What should he do? Nervously, he played with his keys. He didn't want to leave her without a ride. Looking over to Lynne, he saw that she was holding onto her purse as if her life depended upon it. He knew her cell phone was in it. She could simply call for a cab.

As he drove away, he had the distinct impression that he was seeing Lynne for the last time. Most curious of all, he was saddened by that fact.

CHAPTER TWENTY

Later that day, Kerry was back at the homeless shelter. Sitting behind the counter, he sniffed the fried chicken that was before him. Someone had dropped off the remains from a party the day before, as a donation. A scowl rolled his face. From the questionable smell, he knew why. Rusty rolled up and looked expectedly at the chicken, and then him.

"You eaten today?" Kerry asked.

"Nope."

"You don't want this," Kerry said shaking his head. He rolled his eyes for added emphasis.

"Why?"

"Looks kinda funny. And it smells."

"So?"

"Well. Guess I've eaten worse," Kerry said, without much conviction.

"Yeah. I guess you have."

"Rusty, you're as funny as a heart attack."

Kerry sensed Simon West's entrance behind him by Rusty's sudden, tense reaction. Quickly reaching over,

Rusty grabbed the chicken and the brown bag that it had come in, and rushed out the door. Kerry turned to witness a furious Simon West blowing in from the rear of the shelter.

"Did you really think you'd get away with it?"

"Get away with what?" Kerry asked in false innocence.

She...she...that woman that you let shower!" he stammered. His face glowed red, and the words came forth with the benefit of a shower of spittle. "'For a job interview, no less! I saw her when she exited the bathroom after you had already left. Did you take me for such a fool?"

The gleam in his eyes was all the answer that Simon West needed. His anger was now tenfold. "I had to pay someone to scrub the showers down when she left, and you can still smell her in there!"

Simon West took a deep breath, and the bright red glow that was his face slowed to pink. A weak smile came forth. Slowing down, he began again. "I warned you last time. Apparently, you didn't listen. So, now, I'm telling you again. This is straight from headquarters. In other words, I have their approval. You do something this stupid—if you continue to be so defiant—your services will no longer be needed here. This is as official as it gets. Next step is...you get the picture."

Kerry was past the point of caring. Simon West was merely articulating the obvious. His career with the shelter was quickly drawing to a close. Still, thirty years of service was making its bittersweet feelings felt.

That was a long time—a time that spanned most of his adulthood.

Simon West started for the front door and stopped. "You will of course be docked, for the money that headquarters had to pay to scrub down the showers.

"Also," he continued, when Kerry shrugged off his loss of pay, "I want you to start preparing the dorms upstairs for the emergency winter shelter. We open in a week. Hopefully it's the last time we have to offer that particular service."

Simon passed Lynne just as she was entering the shelter. His anger had too much of a hold on him to pay her any attention. She was simply another warm body utilizing the services of his shelter.

Lynne's eyes were puffy. They no longer bled tears. She had obviously used something on them to take the red out. "You okay?" Kerry asked. But before she could answer, the door swung open and a young man—nineteen at most, entered. He was in a wheelchair. At first, the yellow plastic bag that he held in his lap perplexed Lynne. Then the overpowering smell of urine answered the question for her. It was a urinal bag that had apparently sprung a leak. It also explained his wet pants.

"Jesus, Ed. You smell like something crawled up inside of you and died," Kerry stated, with a voice absent of rancor.

The jest was taken as such, and Ed smiled a little boy's smile. Lynne began to appreciate how Kerry used humor to break the ice of any, *and she meant any* awkward situation. It was like the homeless waited for his wise cracks, just so they could tell them that whatever embarrassing or painful situation they found themselves in, it was simply run of the mill, life happens stuff; nothing to get too upset about. "Nothing meant nothing," as she had heard him say more than once.

She also began to appreciate just how important smell was to his job. It was a sense that she had never paid particular attention to before. Now, it conveyed states of health, sickness and a proximity to death. It told Kerry, and now her, as much important information as any other sense could.

Ed's little boy laugh soon turned boisterous. So manic in intensity that it told her of his state of mental health.

"Well?" Lynne finally asked, when Kerry began to read a sheet of paper in front of him.

"Well, what?"

"Aren't you going to tell him to shower?"

A slow, sly smile came to Kerry as he looked from Lynne to Ed, and then back again. "So, now you're the social worker?" He turned back to Ed. "You know where it is. I'll have Charlene find you a pair of dry pants. You can throw those away."

Louder maniacal laughter followed Ed when he made his way into the interior of the shelter.

"But..." Charlene began, once Ed was out of hearing.

"Not now. Okay?" Kerry's voice was strained. A loud exhale of breath followed.

Charlene simply shook her head.

"I'd best be getting out of here," he said, a little stronger.

"You best," Charlene agreed. Both ignored the quizzical look that played on Lynne's face.

"What just happened?" she asked, when Kerry began to walk for the door.

"Come on. We need to go someplace," Kerry urged.

They walked out the door. They stood in front of the shelter and watched Simon West driving away in his old Volvo. "There's a story with that man that I'm not getting," Kerry stated.

"What do you mean?"

"I just got a feeling about him."

"A feeling? Like what?"

"Like—I don't know. Just a feeling. I'm sure we'll find out in time."

CHAPTER TWENTY ONE

Lynne's hands rolled into tightly clenched fists. They were in Santa Barbara's Eastside. True, this was a part of town she had not seen before. Small shops lined the street, with many of the signs in Spanish. But that wasn't why her hands were tensed.

They stood at a stoplight, waiting for red to turn green. Standing across the street from them was an old lady, weighed down with life. The stoop to her back was severe. It was like gravity had opened a hole under her, and it was threatening to pull her into the underworld. Her heavily wrinkled face was sucked cruelly inwards without the structural support of teeth. Painfully, Lynne swallowed. She tried hard not to envision her mother in such a predicament. Then she vaguely remembered that Medicare had dropped dental coverage. She tried to remember what she had thought of that news when she had read it. Nothing. Now, that reality stood in condemnation before her. A heavy sigh escaped her compressed lips.

Lynne looked over to see if Kerry knew the woman.

Or more importantly, if he had seen her own emotional reactions. No. His gaze was cast down the block. Following his line of sight, Lynne spotted a modern day wagon train, approaching from the other side of the street. Five homeless men, each pushing a shopping cart walked in line. Like their forbearers before them, they traversed hostile territory, with all their worldly belongings contained in their wagons. With car traffic being absent, the only sound was that of clanking wheels—never meant to suffer such punishment.

Looking back to Kerry, Lynne saw the hurt that punished his face. These homeless men were not abstractions to him she realized, but friends wandering the wilds of modern day America. Like their forbearers, many would not survive the trek. Unlike their ancestors, they did not engage in genocide along the way.

The sound of the old lady, coughing up phlegm and spitting it like a drunken sailor, broke the spell. Looking up, Kerry realized that red had turned to green and was now blinking with the threat of going back. He stepped smartly off the curb, followed closely by Lynne. Loud, honking horns from the next intersection, which was a busy one, quickly drew their attention. There, in the middle of the street, stopping the effective flow of traffic, stood Susie; naked as the day she came into life. Kerry smiled. *She had the choreography of a traffic cop down pretty damn well.* Lynne frowned. *How could mental health not help her?*

"Well? Lynne asked. Her voice was rough with hostility.

There was also a slight wobble to it, as she was unsure where to direct the anger.

"Well what?"

"What are you going to do? You just can't..."

"Can't what?!" Kerry shot back, his voice raw with anger. "I've already tried more than once. Don't you get it? Society doesn't want to be bothered with someone like her. Mental Health sure as hell doesn't.

"Look, it's not like she's going to hurt someone. To many in the community she's even vaguely entertaining— almost like a pet."

Vertigo slammed into Lynne. The ground rolled under her feet. Her equilibrium did not so much fade as rapidly flee. *If that was so, then what chance did her daughter stand?*

Reading her mind, Kerry said, "This is the way of the streets. It's not what I want. It is what it is. If I waste my capital and my trust with her by calling the cops, she won't turn to me for help in the future...when she may really need it. Besides, she's high profile. This type of acting out brings with it its own temporary solutions."

"And if she should die like your friend back at the cemetery?"

Kerry's responded with icy silence. He grimaced like a professional mugger had just delivered a sharp body punch to his liver.

"'What kind of man are you,' you once asked. I'm the kind that looks for truly lost causes before I become engaged."

As if on cue, a cop on a bike stopped close to Susie, who in turn, took off fast. Sighing heavily, Kerry turned down the street, then hesitated when Lynne failed to follow suit.

"Are you coming?" To his surprise, he hoped that the answer would be yes.

Also unexpectedly, and for the first time, Lynne was unsure what to do. She had assumed she would find her daughter. And after finding her, she would take her home and deal with whatever problems had to be dealt with. *But now?* A whole other world had been introduced to her—one with many potential tragic outcomes. Like most middle and upper class people, she had always assumed a safety net existed for those in need. The brutality of absolute poverty, of unmet medical needs, and mental health problems, was a crushing eye opener.

In the end, she followed Kerry. No longer out of hope, but a sense of duty. Regardless of the condition she would find Tracy in, she knew she would need her mom more than ever. And Lynne was determined to be there for her.

CHAPTER TWENTY TWO

If Lynne thought that the walk over was fraught with anxiety and fear, their destination was downright scary. It was the type of seedy motel that she had passed a thousand times in L.A. But she had always been in a car, and she never once questioned who lived in them, or why. Now she would find out.

As they entered the uneven and pockmarked blacktop parking lot, they encountered a card table with two folding chairs. Surrounding the perimeter were forty rooms that fed directly into the lot, and another forty on each of the next two floors. From one room, Lynne noticed a curtain blowing lazily outwards from a torn screen.

Kerry's attention was riveted to the two men—career type criminals who occupied the chairs. Lynne's breath caught in her throat when one of them rose in challenge. He, like his partner in crime, wore white, wife beater tee shirts to better accentuate their muscular physique. Courtesy of the joint were crude Nazi tattoos on their arms, and double lightning bolts on their necks, signifying membership in either the *ABs*, the Aryan Brotherhood, or the *NLR*, the Nazi Low Riders. Kerry hadn't seen their types lately, but like all good things, their absence had to come to an end.

"What the fuck do you want?" the first man snarled, as he confronted them.

"You want to run her?" his partner asked, leering up from his chair at Lynne. Instead of turning red from embarrassment, she turned deadly white. Never had Lynne been so frightened by fellow human beings in her life. And she definitely did not want to imagine how the man had lost most of his upper teeth, leaving him with the scariest smile she had ever seen. Just the mere knowledge that people like those two actually existed outside of a Hollywood set, was more than she could fathom.

"If you ain't buying, you're in big trouble, the both of you," the first man stated. Then to add effect, he cracked the knuckles of both hands so loud that it sounded like artillery sounding off. Pop. Pop. Pop.

Kerry swallowed hard, and his eyes narrowed. He hadn't counted on trouble. After all, who in their right mind would expect to see dope dealers in a parking lot, selling their wares? *Where was a cop when you needed one? Now what?* And then there was Lynne. In another situation he might have been surprised, and maybe even slightly embarrassed by the surge of male instinctual protection that washed over him. Now he was merely trying to figure out how he could extradite them from the situation without either one of them getting hurt.

An answer his prayer came from Stacey, a young hooker

who came bouncing out of one of the rooms. Looking past the hard age in her eyes, Lynne realized she wasn't much older than her daughter.

"I know you'd come!" Stacey said. She threw her arms around Kerry and squeezed hard. Kerry did his best to ignore the swell of her breasts pressed into his chest. Letting go, Stacey smiled when she caught the discomfort that flushed across Kerry's cheeks. Her attempt to pull down the short, high riding blouse was to no avail.

"Heard on the streets that you were looking for me," Kerry replied. He cast a weary glance to thug number one. "Is Gloria here?" he continued. He looked over towards the rooms directly behind Stacey, from which she had come from. Anywhere was preferable than being in the presence of the two men who threatened him. "How's she doing?" he asked, addressing the worried look that made Stacey's eyes narrow.

"Oh, Kerry. I ain't never seen someone die from AIDS before."

Thug number one beat a hasty and undignified retreat back to the table. For once, Kerry was glad for the misperceptions of AIDS. It was obvious that the man thought that his very proximity to them could transfer the infection to him. Maybe Kerry should follow up. *Like walk over and cough on him?* He decided otherwise. Even Kerry didn't have that much of a death wish. Still, the mere thought brought a smile to his lips. Then it quickly died as he mulled over Stacey's words.

"No. It isn't pretty," he said to her.

"What is?" Stacey asked wistfully, looking around, and then giving the thugs a hard stare. Snapping out of it, she draped her arm through Kerry's and began walking him to a ground floor room. Lynne wasted no time in following them.

CHAPTER TWENTY THREE

The overwhelming darkness of the room was heightened in comparison to the sun drenched parking lot from which they came from. The air smelled of sickness and death. Body sweat. Leaking body fluids. Decay in general was baked to a high degree within the confines of the small room. Stagnant air. Lynne was close to losing her breakfast.

Kerry walked over to the couch, where a rail thin Gloria hid under a pile of tired blankets. In spite of the sweat rolling down her face, she shivered violently. He knelt down, being careful to avoid the small mountain of bloody tissues lying beside the couch. Looking over to a table, he saw a junkie's kit hidden behind moldy green bread. His face was set hard. His knees popped loud when he stood.

Walking over to the curtains, he grabbed them. Violently, he tore them down. Startled, Lynne jumped back. Stacey smiled. Kerry forced open both windows. A forceful breeze of fresh air poured in. The pungent smell of death's perfume retreated.

He then walked over to the kitchen sink. Picking up

a drying towel, he wet it and made his way back to the couch. He knelt down. Gently, he washed Gloria's face free of sweat and grime. The despair registered there was another matter. Shut eyes pried open. There was a groan, followed by a small, fleeting smile. "Knew you'd come." Her voice was hoarse, like she had gargled with razor blades.

"How are you feeling?"

"The way you told me I would if I didn't stop using."

"Sorry, kiddo," Kerry said. A wild strand of hair fell into Gloria's eyes. Lovingly, he brushed it back.

"Not as sorry as I am," Gloria responded weakly, giving him a smile. A thin smile acknowledged her attempt at humor.

Kerry's stare drifted to the table. There, amongst the paraphernalia of a junkie's life, was a pile of ugly brown rocks. His frown forced Gloria's sight to the table.

"Your Grandma?" Kerry asked.

"How'd you guess?"

"I talked to her. She told me."

"Ain't that some shit!" Slowly, her smile died. "I called her? Did I ask her to send rocks?" she questioned in shame. Her voice was as thin as her emaciated body. A groan followed. She struggled to gather the strength to ask: "There's more, ain't there?"

Standing again, Kerry's knees cracked with thunder. "She'll be on the five-fifteen. She's coming to take you home."

"It's too late." Gloria's voice was fading fast. Lost hope

drained it.

"It's not too late to die with your family around you, is it?" Kerry gently inquired.

"But..." Gloria began. Kerry cut her off with a wave of his hand.

"No buts. It's time to go home. Go home to those who love you. Not only for yourself, but for their sake as well."

Gloria reached out. She took Kerry's hand. It was not only cold; it was stick thin. Reminiscent of a starving survivor in a horror flick. Her wrists were badly swollen. "Thank you," she replied. Her throat was constricted, giving her voice a childlike quality. *And why shouldn't it sound as such? She was all of twenty-three,* Kerry reflected sadly.

"She's coming by Greyhound," he began directing his comments to Stacey. "Could you...?" he trailed off.

"You've done your part. Now, let me do mine," Stacey replied. Hand in hand, she guided Kerry to the door and ushered him out.

Kerry stood fast, frozen in time by the door. His gaze shifted upwards, captured by another dimension. With the anger of the unknown giving her strength, Lynne roughly spun him around. "What was that about?"

"She's got AIDS. She only has..."

"You think!" Lynne yelped, interrupting him. Seeing that her raised voice had drawn the attention of the two thugs, she lowered it as she continued, "I mean, what about the rocks?"

"She's a crack addict," Kerry began, giving her a soft smile. "She called her grandma who raised her. Grandma lives on a farm in Oklahoma. In a delusional state, she asked her to send rocks. Of course, Gloria meant rock cocaine..."

"So she sent her real rocks from the land," Lynne stated. Her voice rose high, being built on a platform of awe.

"So she sent her real rocks," Kerry concurred. "Her grandmother's too innocent. Too pure for our times."

The scratching of chair legs against blacktop. One of the two thugs having slid it back, stood to his feet. Their attention riveted onto him. He started a slow, menacing walk.

"What do you say we not press our luck with those two," Kerry said. He reached for Lynne's hand.

"Let's not," Lynne agreed.

Kerry felt his heart shift into overdrive with the feel of Lynne's hand within his. And he was very aware that she allowed him to keep it there as they exited the parking lot. It was with great reluctance that he let go once they reached the street.

Lynne immediately picked up on the time lapse. She was surprised by Kerry's hesitancy. She was even more surprised by her own reluctance. It forced her to question something that, up to now, had been an easy answer to the intensity of her feelings towards him. Her eyelids lowered. Had her assumption of hostility to the man hidden other emotions? He was so unlike anyone she had ever met before, unlike any other man she had ever known. He was macho. Hard-edged. She was used to more refined men. Kerry was anything but.

CHAPTER TWENTY FOUR

A uniformed man stood in front of the shelter. Feet planted firmly apart. Hands hooked defiantly into a web belt. Mace hung belligerently. Kerry cast the man in the uniform a scalding stare. He and Lynne walked past him without greetings. They entered the shelter. Kerry slowly rolled back his bewildered anger. The guard was too small, simply too mousey to hold a grudge against. Besides, he was also comical looking, captured within the confines of an overly large gray shirt, and oversized black pants. A hat also rode low, reaching his ears.

"What's up with the guard?" Kerry asked, upon approaching Charlene. She sat behind the counter. She was busy filling out end-of-month stats—the curse of every non-profit employee in the land.

"Boss man's idea." She didn't bother looking up. "Says we need protection. You know, a law and order thing." She shifted her sight from the forms before her to Kerry. Her large, soulful eyes told it all: She had seen a lot of crazy shit in her life, heard even more, but this...

"With that?" Kerry tossed, looking back through the

plate glass at the guard. He stood awkward. Self-conscious.

Charlene's eyes fell back to the seemingly reproducing forms and gave out a helpless groan.

"Why not?" Lynne questioned. The hard voice announced she was looking for a fight. "I think it's a good idea. A little order around here would certainly improve the ambiance."

"Ambiance?" Charlene questioned. Again she looked up from the stack of forms before her. She looked over to Kerry. Kerry smiled. It was his first genuine, mouth-relaxing smile of the day. Hell, of the week.

"If I ever lost you..." he started. He left the remaining words unsaid. But their shared sentiment was clearly etched on his face for all to see.

"You should have such luck," Charlene replied softly.

"I know I would lose it around here," he replied, finishing his thought. He turned to confront Lynne. "Because order is usually the last thing uniforms bring."

If he thought his words would melt Lynne's hostile mood, he was sorely mistaken. She was not one to be intimidated by mere words. Especially when she was covering up feelings that were both confusing and infuriating at the same time.

"I thought you wanted to help these people," he said to Lynne, his voice softer. "You've been breaking my chops enough about it."

"Don't take my concern for a few as condoning this lifestyle. I don't like wasting tax monies on these..."

"Losers?" Kerry interrupted. Her flushed cheeks told

him that he had, in fact, finished her thought. "You're no different than most of the good citizens in this city. Help a few if you must. Those right in your face. Otherwise, screw the rest. How do you think most got where they are now?"

"I don't know! I didn't put them there! It's their own fault. A life style they chose, not me. They made the decision to live out there. I didn't force her. No. You can't blame me. It's not my fault." Lynne's face flushed redder. Eyes tight with anger.

"Her?" Kerry asked reeling in some, but not all of his anger. Internal signals were popping off like trip flares, just before a fire support base was hit by an enemy assault. But his emotional state refused him respite. No time to allow his cool intellect to look for the cause and effect.

"What? Her?" Lynne questioned, her voice ragged, spent with exasperation.

"Don't play games with me! You said, 'her.' So who is her, I mean, she?" Kerry challenged, confused as hell.

Charlene threw Kerry a shirt, breaking the confrontation. She'd seen enough. Heard too much. She didn't want any more of it.

He held up the shirt before him and scowled. It was a typical short-sleeved polo shirt. The shelter logo was over the heart. A disgusted look came next.

"New work clothes. Uniform if you like," Charlene responded to a questioning look from Kerry. "Boss man says we're to wear them from now on."

"Boss man also says he's deducting you a day's pay," a voice replied. All eyes turned. Simon West slid into the reception area. His pencil thin lips spoke volumes of barely suppressed anger.

"Did you really think that you'd get away with it a second time? Do you take me for such a fool?"

"You mean the shower thing?" Kerry questioned.

"*You mean the shower thing?*" Simon's voice was twisted with mockery and spite. His small eyes withdrew further into his face. They threatened to disappear altogether. "You really are a moron!" he spat out. "The one good thing out of this incident of insubordination, besides docking you a day's pay, is that it is your last warning.

"I checked with L.A. Apparently I need to give you two warnings. So I was mistaken last time, but not this time. This is official. According to our agency's personnel policies, next time you defy my direct orders, I get to fire you." A caustic smile came forth. "Please, don't make it too long."

"Hot damn." Muttered only for Kerry, but spoken loud enough for all to hear.

"What did you say?" Simon demanded.

Kerry shrugged, and asked, "Anything else?"

"Yes. We've signed a new contract with the V.A. They've agreed to pay us to provide beds to homeless vets. They— the homeless vets, must have their DD 214s with them to access this service."

"And if we don't have enough vets to fill the beds? Do they remain empty?"

"They stay empty. At least until the emergency winter shelter opens. I wish we didn't need the money the feds pay us to run it. Goes against our new policies. Glad it's only for a few months." It was a drifting voice, conspiratorial in nature.

"A whole lot of people depend on those beds to survive the winter." Kerry's voice was cut sharp with dread. He didn't have to look too far down the calendar to see a time when the homeless in Santa Barbara would be without the lifesaving winter shelter, especially if the Boss man got his way. *Maybe then enough of them would die. Presto! Homeless problem solved. Good for business. Good for the city's image.*

"Speaking of which," Simon said. "I want you to open up and air out the two overflow dorms. Also, I want you to make the beds up."

"You want me to make them up?" Kerry questioned.

"Why not?" Simon asked through a smirk. "Surely making up a few beds isn't beneath a social worker? Or is it?"

His smile expansive, Simon turned to leave.

"Those vets? What happens if they don't have their DD 214s? That was the first thing I ditched when I got home."

"Then they stay homeless."

"And thanks for your service to God and Country." Kerry responded in savage sarcasm to Simon West's back. The Boss man didn't bother to turn around. As in Vietnam and Afghanistan, Kerry knew that Marines were expendable, even on the streets.

"Do me a favor, Kerry," Simon West stated. He still didn't bother turning around to address his target directly. "Don't make your next transgression too far down the road. Time's money. And you're wasting the agency's."

CHAPTER TWENTY FIVE

Kerry took Lynne to the second floor of the shelter after Simon West slunk back to his office. No words were exchanged. Making beds was next on the agenda. No rocket science here. It was something that Lynne did at home every morning—half-assed. She simply threw the quilt back on the bed. Bi-weekly maid service did the real work.

Kerry had withdrawn into himself after the confrontation with Simon. He was still in that *quiet* mood. They stood motionless before a closed door. Impatient, Lynne shifted her stance from foot to foot. Finally running out, she stated, "Come on, Kerry, what could possibly be so hard about making a few beds? It's not exactly what I imagined social work would be, but what the hell."

Kerry groaned. He gave Lynne a strained look.

"How long could it possibly take?" Lynne insisted. She didn't know when to leave well enough alone.

Kerry smiled. He unlocked the door. He stood back. Bowing slightly at the waist, he extended his hand, inviting Lynne to walk through the door before him. In a huff, she took him up on his invitation.

She immediately came to a halt, forcing Kerry to do likewise. "Holy shit!" she exclaimed.

Easily a hundred and fifty bunks stretched out before her. Piles of folded sheets were off to one side. Blankets and pillows on the other. Kerry walked over to the pillows. He picked one up and threw it playfully to Lynne. She caught it. His smile acknowledged her shock. "Shall we?" Kerry teased. "After all. What could possibly be so hard?"

Four hours later. Lynne was convinced she was twenty pounds lighter from the exertion. But all the beds were finally made. Standing in the second bay, she wiped sweat from her brow. Her arms ached. A slow burn smoldered in her lower back. She prayed to God that she hadn't pulled a muscle. She couldn't remember having worked that hard in a very long time. How did the maids in the swanky hotels she stayed in, do such backbreaking work day after day? A greater appreciation of their work flickered to life. Then she smiled. She had caught Kerry staring.

"Never say that I don't take you to the finest places," Kerry teased.

"A date with you is always an adventure." The term 'date' cast an awkward spell, only broken by Simon West's entrance.

"Now that wasn't so bad was it?"

"Are you here for a reason? Or to simply check up on me?" Kerry inquired with a stern voice. He was tired. He was also mentally exhausted.

A smirk worked its way onto Simon's face. He walked over to a bunk and ran his hand over it. The blanket was taut as barbwire. Regardless of his best effort, a measure of respect snuck into his voice. "Not bad."

"Guess there are some things you learn in the Marines that you never forget." A haunting tone to the voice drew Lynne's stare to Kerry. Her stare drove deeper into Kerry's eyes, but Simon's biting sarcasm quickly shut the door to the pain.

"That's right; you're one of those poor, pitiful Vietnam Vets. The ones that can't leave the war behind. Get over it. It's history."

Kerry's jaws tightened. His hands became fists. Without taking one step forward, he managed to force Simon back simply by his furnace like gaze. A fine line of diamond sweat beads appeared across his forehead.

"Kerry," Lynne said, to little effect. He stood rigid with anger. She began chewing her bottom lip. Kerry's eyes were unfocused. Unknown to her, he was staring down a thousand yard time tunnel.

"Kerry!" She stated louder, unsure if he had heard her. She had never really known any Vietnam vets. And she had always been uneasy with all the myths that Hollywood propagated about them. Then again, how was she to know if they were merely myths? How much did she really know about them? Or for that matter, of the man who stood transfixed before her?

"Kerry." She lowered her voice, pleading.

Slowly, Kerry's eyes regained focus. He swung his attention to her. A weary smile softened his mouth. "It don't mean nothin'," he said, more to himself than to her. "Don't mean nothin'," he repeated.

Inching his way along the wall in retreat, Simon West said, "No. It won't be long now." The door closed with a soft hush. Echoes of time were reverberating.

Moments later, Kerry and Lynne exited the shelter. The last thing Kerry expected was to have a shotgun stuck in his face. But, that was exactly what a man wearing black body amour and a facemask did. "What the hell?" was the only thing he could articulate before being thrown roughly to the ground. Looking frantically upwards, he twisted to the sound of a soft cry. He assumed it was Lynne's.

Then another voice demanded attention. It was harsher. It was also brittle with fear. "You move, and I'll blow your fuckin' head off!"

CHAPTER TWENTY SIX

Kerry sat on the curb, his feet in the gutter. He was holding a towel wrapped around a chunk of ice, which he pressed into the back of his head. Thankfully, there was no blood. He was more ashamed about walking into the SWAT team than anything else. *What had happened to his street honed attentiveness to his surroundings?* He knew. If only he hadn't let Simon West get to him. Then he would have been more vigilant, and the whole mess could have been avoided. Yet again, Vietnam had reared its ugly head, like some kind of grotesque python.

He cast a quick glance over to a sergeant. The cop seemed to be in charge. He was talking to a puffed up and officious looking Simon West. Looking over, he saw Kerry's burning stare. Reluctantly, he moved over to him.

"All of this is because that—that moronic security guard. The one that you hired called in a terrorist threat!" Kerry challenged.

"It's not that simple. There's more to it than..." Simon began his defense. Kerry angrily cut him off.

"Jesus Christ, what did he tell them?! They never come

that fast when I call."

"He, ah..."Simon began, only to be cut off again.

"I know. I know," Kerry snapped, having been told the gist of the threat by Charlene. "A spatula? A fucking spatula! And a rubber one at that!"

Simon West shrugged. What was the point in making excuses? Kerry would simply interrupt him again. Besides what could he say?

"A spatula," Kerry repeated. He was incapable of believing the chain of events. He could visualize his headstone: *Here rests a Vietnam Vet. He survived the war only to be done in because of a fucking spatula!*

"We all make mistakes," Simon offered weakly. He raised his hands in mock surrender.

"And then some," Kerry added. He felt Lynne's hand softly brush his shoulder. She was warning him that he had pushed the issue about as far as he should. Well, maybe in her book. Not his. He had this thing about guns. He had seen what damage they were capable of doing.

"Don't make a federal case out of it!" Simon snapped. He was tired of Kerry's theatrics.

Kerry looked up, his face open wide in amazement. "That's easy for you to say. You weren't the one stretched out on the ground with a rifle barrel planted in your ear, now were you?" He stood and threw the ice and towel into the gutter, barely missing Simon's penny loafers.

Steam rose from Simon's head. Looking around helplessly, he realized there was nothing that he could do to retrieve the situation. He did the only thing possible.

He retreated to the sanctuary of the shelter, leaving his employee and intern at the center of puzzled looks from suited up SWAT members, and homeless alike.

CHAPTER TWENTY SEVEN

It wasn't long before Lynne and Kerry had the stage all to themselves. Nothing cleared the streets faster than a police presence. As for the police, they were more than happy to join the homeless and desert the scene after such a farce.

"So? What do you do for fun around here?" Lynne's bold question caught her off guard, as it did Kerry.

"Fun?" Kerry questioned.

"Yes. You know fun? How do you release the tensions of the day? Especially a day like this? Even for you, this must have been a particular trying one."

A childlike smile was Kerry's first response. "You live around here?" he questioned.

"Yes. The hotel I'm staying at is not too far from here."

"Got a bathing suit?"

"Of course I do."

"I mean, with you."

"Yes."

Kerry suddenly bolted across the street. A gold colored Mustang with vanity plates barely missed him. "Well?

What are you waiting for?" he yelled back. Lynne was still glued to the spot he had left her at.

CHAPTER TWENTY EIGHT

Kerry refused Lynne's repeated request to tell her where he was taking her. He simply reiterated that she change into a swimsuit when they stopped at her hotel. The ride to the beach at Campus Point was conducted mostly in silence. Located at the University of California at Santa Barbara, it was twelve miles north of the city.

Once at the beach, Kerry grabbed the two body-boards that he kept in the back of his truck, in case the surf was up, and he could steal time from work.

The air was refreshing and alive, with salt added as a chaser. The sand was warm on their feet from baking in the sun's rays all day. The water was another matter. It was cold! Yet, after the initial shock wore off, it wasn't so bad. Or was it because they were frozen and couldn't feel the pain...

Lynne had never body-boarded before, and she wasn't sure if she was up for a new adventure. She had also never gone swimming in the ocean so close to sunset.

But she caught on fast, and she ended up riding several waves. She felt the surfer's exhilaration of the speed and power of a wave. Like them, she became intoxicated by it. The trick was letting go. Becoming part of the ocean. Going wherever the waves wanted to take you. For some odd reason, acknowledging that she had no power was extremely liberating. She was awed by the experience, and pleasantly surprised when she felt the tension of the day wash away. Impressed by Kerry's childlike, animal cries whenever he caught a particular good ride, she smiled. For a quiet man, he had a loud voice.

Too soon did the sun begin it final plunge into the ocean. Doing so, it skipped radiant rays across the water, like an ancient god flinging stones across the surface. Reluctantly, they exited the ocean. In awe, they looked back to watch dolphins darting through the waves. These magnificent sea creatures were enjoying themselves as much as they had. Kerry picked up floating seaweed and tossed it playfully to Lynne. She smiled. Lynne cast a wistful look again back over her shoulder. "That was—I don't know what that was. I've never been..."

"Body-boarding before?"

"Yes. Body-boarding. It's really quite exhilarating!"

"So? What's the real story with you, Ms. Lynne of PR?"

"What do you mean?" she replied. Trying for a dodge, she could tell from Kerry's frown that she was less than successful. She looked wistfully about, as the bent rays of the sun began to cast everything in soft reds and warm yellows. *How could life be this beautiful when pain gnawed at her soul?*

"You aren't kidding anybody, but yourself. You aren't

doing this for school."

"Yes I am." Lynne's low voice betrayed the truth. Her breath caught sharp. She was being torn between heaven and hell. *If she could just hold onto the peace of a moment ago, for even a handful of minutes...*

They looked deep into each other eyes. Kerry was trying to bridge degrees of separation. He replied as gentle as he could: "Your heart isn't in this. Yet it is. Something, or someone, is driving you."

Lynne wanted to open up. She wanted desperately to share with Kerry the tragic story of her daughter and her hunt for her. But she was afraid. Afraid of the pain that might overwhelm her should she drop her defenses. It was unchartered territory. She was frightened of letting go—of losing control. She hadn't done that with anyone. She was a successful businesswoman, who took pride in the fact that she needed no one. That was no longer true. Maybe it had never been true. She realized now that she had needed her daughter before all this had happened. And now? She needed Tracy even more. And she needed Kerry's help in finding her.

As for the stirring emotions for Kerry that washed over her, she couldn't surrender to them. She couldn't become distracted. She just couldn't! She couldn't share with him her need for his help. What would happen if he said no? Perhaps if she had been truthful in the beginning... but now?

"And then there's the question of that little incident at the cemetery. Don't think I've forgotten that." Kerry said. Swallowing was hard. Breathing was labored. He felt shitty. It was he who had had caused the pain and confusion that tore at Lynne's eyes. But he was an expert at running away from the problems of life. And he knew that was a no-win solution. Besides, if he was going to help Lynne, he needed to know the story behind her quest. And he could feel just how close she was to a breaking point. He couldn't let that happen without a fight.

Before his eyes, the tension evaporated from Lynne's body. But Lynne's moment of truth, of catharsis, was trapped within when a young surfer girl, board in hand, came running up to Kerry. The tight fitting, powder blue wetsuit accentuated her lithe body. Her smoldering eyes betrayed the interest she had in Kerry. She held the long board easily, with a firm grip. "Hi, Kerry," she said.

But of course, her voice would be husky, Lynne thought. It added a sexual undertone to her greeting.

"Oh, hey," Kerry awkwardly replied. His sight jumped from Surfer girl to Lynne, then back again.

"You said you'd call," Surfer girl replied. Her voice was lowered in faux hurt. Real disappointment.

"Oh, sorry. I got busy. I mean, that's why, ah...why I..."

"That's okay. It's not too late, you know. Not for you. Call me." Her voice turned haughty. "I'm sure you remember the number." She leaned over and planted a hard kiss on Kerry's lips. Then she departed.

Lynne was surprised to feel a little envious. *Why should she care?* The fire burned out.

"Your daughter?" she asked Kerry.

"Cute. Real cute," Kerry said through his embarrassment.

They stood timid, unsure how to retrieve the magical spell of the moment before. Playing off Kerry's soft sigh, Lynne asked, "So? Where tomorrow? What time?"

CHAPTER TWENTY NINE

"She's late again. I don't have all day!" Kerry looked at his pocket watch. His frown deepened. "Tell her..." he began, only to be cut off by Charlene.

"I'm not telling her nothing. She's almost as ornery as you are. I'm not going to get yelled at this early in the morning. Nope. Not me."

"But..." Kerry began to plead.

"Hush!" Charlene snapped. She put her finger over her lips for added emphasis.

The front door to the shelter squeaked open. A young girl hesitantly slid in. She stood sideways, looking in. Kerry saw the beginning of a shiner around her eye. No small feat, considering how much dirt was caked on her face. Already it was partially swollen shut.

"Dear God Almighty," Charlene whispered.

"How can I help you," Kerry offered in his softest voice.

"I, ah," the girl began. Her hand drifted to her torn blouse. The white bra underneath it was exposed.

"How about we start with a cold cloth for that eye. If we don't get something on it, it'll swell all the way shut." Kerry moved from behind the counter. He put on the friendliest smile he could muster, under the circumstances. Walking very slowly, he approached the girl. "Let's go sit in the dining area. Charlene, could you..."

"Consider it done." Charlene thanked God for the miracle that kept her voice from breaking.

Taking the young girl gently by the arm, Kerry led her into the interior of the shelter.

Seconds later, Kerry directed the girl to chairs at the end of a long table. The smell of coffee warmed the air. Hot oatmeal was being prepared for breakfast. Its reassuring odor drifted over from the kitchen. Charlene brought Kerry a damp, cold wash cloth. She gave the young girl an encouraging smile before returning to the reception desk.

"This might sting a bit," Kerry warned the girl. Tilting her head slightly back for a better look, he said, "It doesn't look too bad. But for safety's sake, we should take you..."

"No!" the girl interrupted. Her response was swift and hard. "No doctors."

Then let me call the police. Someone did this..."

"No!" The girl's answer was even more emphatic. Her chair scooted back from Kerry; she was poised for flight.

"Okay! Okay. Just calm down." Kerry moved cautiously towards the girl. Gingerly, he washed the rest of her face. He sighed in relief. No real damage had been done. At least on the outside. *What kind of a man would do this to a girl?* The question tore at his soul. "Name? Could you at least give me that?" he asked, as he held the wash cloth to the girl's eye.

Shoulders slumped. The girl's response was a general relaxation of her posture.

"So, what are you? Fifteen? Sixteen?"

A dark shadow crept over the girl's exposed eye. It looked to Kerry like she was working hard at something. What? An answer as to her age? Or, as he was beginning to suspect, was she listening to internal stimuli?

"Why do you care?" The question caught Kerry off guard.

"Come again?" he asked.

"I went to this other shelter. They told me I couldn't stay without I.D."

"Which you don't have." Bitterness coated Kerry's words before he was able to self-censor. He darkly reminded himself that most shelters, including his own, had more rules to regulate the homeless than one could shake a stick at.

"Then, they told me it didn't really matter as I was probably too young to stay there anyway. So how come?"

"How come what?"

"Care. How come you care?"

"Maybe it's not about choice. What I mean is, I don't see where I really have a choice here. I see a girl in trouble, in need of help. What else can I do?"

"What the others do."

"And what's that?"

"Pretend."

"Pretend what?"

"You know. Just pretend. Then walk away."

"Pretend? Right. Do you want to stay here?"

"Do you ever hear things?" she asked.

"You mean voices?"

"Voices. Noises—things that aren't there. You know they're like real—but aren't there." The girl held the washcloth tightly to her eye. She focused her good one onto Kerry, looking for honesty.

"I don't know. Sometimes I guess. I talk to myself. Or more accurately, I talk to someone—or something. Other times I hear voices, explosions, rifle-fire from the war." An ironic smile. "I even argue with God sometimes. It's something I used to do a lot when I first got back. You ever done that?"

The girl looked on in awe. *If he could talk to God and live a normal life, why couldn't the devil communicate with her without crippling her mind?*

He didn't know why, but Kerry knew that it was very important not to lie to this girl. Besides, he felt that she needed to understand that the world didn't end just because she heard things. That hallucination was a symptom of a disease, not a definition of who she was.

"What do the voices say?" Kerry asked.

"Why do you argue with God?" the girl replied.

"How can I not? How can he, or she, if you will, allow all this suffering? War. Disease. Mental illness."

"I've been thinking about war a lot." The girl's voice was whispery.

"At your age?" Kerry questioned.

"Why not?" she asked, prying into his soul with her good eye.

"Any particular one?"

"War in general. As an invention. An institution."

"Yeah, me too." Kerry's reply was slow in coming.

"Why was it invented? Why is it the one thing all cultures embrace? And every generation throughout history. With a great deal of enthusiasm I might add!" A pause in the conversation told each that this issue weighed heavily on their souls.

Finally, Kerry offered, "I don't know, but I can assure you that God and I have gone to the mat on it."

"Do you think that I'm a bad person?" The girl lowered the cloth, staring hard and fast at Kerry.

"I don't really know you. But no, I don't think you are. I'm a pretty good judge of character. You just don't fit the bill of a bad person. Sorry."

"Then why do they say that I am?"

"You mean the voices? The ones in your head?"

"Yes."

"Why don't we go and talk to some people. Maybe they can help you with the voices."

Silence dragged by. The girl was being played by her inner demons. She fingered the tear in her blouse. Looking down, she noticed it for the first time. She frowned. "I can't go like this."

Rapidly getting up with hope, Kerry replied, "I can fix that. I'll go get you a shirt. Don't go anywhere. I'll be right back."

Exiting the clothing closet, Kerry ran into Charlene. A feeling of hope lifted his heart. "Hold the fort down, will you? I got to take our young friend into mental health services. Imagine *me* wanting to take someone to those headhunters!" He should have paid more attention to her drawn lips.

"No, Kerry. You don't have to."

"She left?" His voice was deflated.

"She left."

"Why didn't you stop her?!" He regretted saying it as soon as the words had slipped from his mouth.

"And exactly how would you propose I do that? She came running out from the back like the devil was after her. Short of tackling her and tying her up, there wasn't much I could do."

"Sorry," Kerry replied. It was easy to hear the pain and frustration cut into Charlene like a blade. He also knew where the blame lay. *How did you not see the play? How stupid could he possibly be!*

Tracy's lungs felt like she had inhaled white-hot coals. She bent over, gasping. Along with the excruciating pain, she was extremely short of breath. Blinding stars swam before her eyes. Gulping air like a dehydrated person would drink water, finally eased her discomfort.

Frightened pedestrians kept their distance. Judging stares were cast her way. If they verbalized their fear, her own breathing was too loud for her to hear them. Staggering over to a trashcan, she leaned on it for support. Recovery would take time. Looking down, she saw a partially empty bottle of bourbon that a cop had taken from a homeless person earlier. *Maybe the booze would cut the hunger pains*, she reasoned. Had it been hours? Days? Maybe forever. At least since the incident at the boutique café. Had she eaten then? Or was it all part of her imagination? Her delusional world? And why had she been stupid enough to go to the shelter? *And open up to a stranger like that?* Hadn't the voices warned her?

At least she was able to understand when they told her the stranger had gone to call the police; that they wanted to lock her up. Beat her. Rape her. Only then would the real bad stuff begin.

Reaching into the trashcan, she snagged the bottle. The only reality that was certain anymore was pain. In this case, the pain in her gut. She had gone too long without food. The hunger was all encompassing. But as primitive as the pain was, at least it was real. In fact, it was the only reality that she could count on.

Since time was illusionary, she had no real idea of when she had last eaten—days, weeks, maybe even months. *How long could one live without food?* The very concept of time now gave her a pounding headache. A twisted smile corrupted her lips.

The amber liquor burned her throat. She gagged.

Within moments, a sense of calmness came over her. The voices in her head dulled. While they were still there, they weren't quite as angry as before. And the fear and memory of the beating and attempted rape, lessened its hold on her. She took another hit, beginning the journey of treating her mental illness with drugs. It was simply another tragedy in a long list to suffer alone.

She tucked the bottle under her arm. Ignoring startled stares, Tracy launched herself down the street in search of her fate.

CHAPTER THIRTY

After the encounter with the girl, Kerry decided to wait for Lynne outside. If he was hoping that fresh air would improve his state of mind, he could keep on hoping.

The morning was cut with the first chill of late autumn, reminding Kerry that the hard cold weather, at least for California, was just around the corner. It was that time of year he called the season of death. Every year, twenty-five to thirty of his homeless clients died in those few months. They died from the cold, and diseased livers, from weakened hearts and damaged lungs, from a variety of cancers, and suicide. But mostly, they simply gave up.

Kerry was bitterly aware that for many, the spirit to live had left their bodies long before Death was ready for them. The struggle for survival—day in, and day out—year after year, just became too much, for too many of his clients. The will to live was crushed by the indifferent sands of time.

Just then, Lynne came hurrying around the corner. Kerry tried to breathe his anger away, as he watched her purposeful stride make haste of the last several yards that separated them. "Nice of you to join me." Regardless of his best intentions, it came out brittle and small.

"Don't even start!" If he had expected contrition of any kind on her part, he was sorely mistaken. Her clipped and forced speech left little to the imagination.

"Stock market open a wee bit late?" Kerry took satisfaction that his voice was more neutral now, than the spiteful tone of seconds before. He was winning the internal battle for control.

"I got a ticket," Lynne stated, with a quiet voice. Her cheeks reddened.

"A ticket?" Kerry questioned, his voice rich in awe. "What kind of ticket?"

"The kind you have to pay a fine for!" Lynne took a deep breath. "So what's the day's agenda? What's next on the schedule?" she inquired.

Kerry smiled. A little boy's enjoyment at teasing sparkled in his eyes. They were like drops of moisture in a spider web, caught in the sunlight. "Ever visited an elf?"

Graceful, eucalyptus trees stretched upwards with open, outstretched arms to the heavens, like worshippers at a revival. Weary, gnarly oaks bent low with age. They scraped the ground with their branches like old men, stooping towards the gravity of age. The air was heavy with the sweet smelling oil of the eucalyptus trees. The oaks contributed a frothy earthy scent. The enchanted forest lay just west of UCSB, bordering what had at one time been an outdoor corral. Now it was covered with waist high and fire dry chaparral. Salt laden, cool ocean breezes gently swept in from the other side of thirty-foot high sand dunes that separated the magical forest from the Pacific.

Lynne couldn't remember when more life affirming odors had satiated her surroundings, and caressed her mind with a sense of wellbeing.

"Elves you said?" she asked. But Kerry ignored her. Instead, he walked over to a large oak tree, with a line of 2x4s nailed crookedly into it. Realizing it was an impromptu ladder, she gawked in amazement.

She walked over to Kerry. Lynne followed his gaze upwards into the tree. Hidden within the twisting branches was a tree house. Turning back to Kerry, she asked: "What are we supposed to do?"

"Well... seeing as the elevator is out of service, I suggest that we climb."

Once she was up and in the tree house, Kerry followed.

Lynne sat quietly with her feet tucked. She watched Kerry intently. His movement was slow. She realized that they were constricted with respect, as if he was in someone's home. Daunting insight came in a flash. That was exactly where they were: in someone's humble, yet ever so noble, abode.

Kerry picked up a crumpled Taco Bell bag. Opening it, he sniffed. A slow frown. "Looks like we're too late."

"Late? Too late for what?"

"Got a report of a runaway kid living here."

Color fled her face. She felt her muscles turn to spaghetti. A sharp chill shimmered up her spine. Lynne was grateful that she was already sitting. Now if she could simply will her lungs to function, she would be fine.

"Here?" she asked. With dreaded insight, she looked around with new eyes. Soiled papers. Yellow urine stains. Rotten food of unknown origins. A rust-red spot. Blood? "How? Why?" Her voice was small, like a child afraid of the dark.

"Why?" Kerry asked, his voice weak. "Why!" he repeated. His voice raised in anger. He threw down the bag. "Because she was a throwaway. Her parents were too busy to take care of her. Vacations in France...or maybe business trips across country. Whatever the circumstances, it was easier for her to live like this than without love at home."

"That's a cruel thing to say! You don't know that for sure. You... You don't know what you're talking about."

"I don't?" Kerry challenged. He spun around, towering over Lynne. Unfortunately, he didn't hear the pain ripping Lynne's vocal cords to shreds. Nor did he see the tears threatening to burst free. "You have any idea how many throwaway kids I've dealt with in my career?"

"You just think that you know it all. But you don't! How about burnt out war vets!" Lynne hurled. She was having a hard time standing.

"What about them?" Kerry's voice downshifted. He was entering territory he usually avoided with others.

"How many of them have you dealt with? How many

vets find it easier to cut themselves off from others, from the real world, rather than deal with their own psychological issues? Well guess what? There are many with trauma in their lives. And they don't make others pay for it."

Kerry moved over to the edge of the tree house. Looking down, his sight drifted to that other time, that other place. "You don't know what you're talking about." If he had thought about it, he would have found it ironic that he was repeating Lynne's statement from just moments before.

"Oh, don't I?" She asked, her voice registering high. "How much longer are you going to continue to hide amongst the homeless? You don't have to continue to work the streets. With your intelligence, your experience, you could easily be running the shelter. But you'd rather hide behind your cut-off shirts and bad ass attitude!"

"And what?" Kerry's raised voice startled a bird into flight. He turned back to look at her. "Be like Simon West? Be like you?!" He regretted it as soon as the words left his mouth. He knew he was lashing out in anger, to dodge his own pain. He was unsuccessful. He succeeded merely in adding a layer of guilt to the pain that was already lashing at his heart.

Lynne's shoulders slumped. God, she was tired. "You're right," she began. "It's much better to sit in judgment of the world from your throne. Even if it's just a street gutter. But God damn you! You don't know shit!" Lynne rushed the ladder. Beginning the descent, she was just barely secured a firm grip, to stop from tumbling to the ground below.

The barely missed stumble sent trembles through Kerry. Daring to peek over the edge of the tree house, he only breathed when she set foot on the forest floor. She stood, with both hands on her hips. Legs planted apart, and defiant as hell. Smiling, he told the tree, "Lady's got guts. I've got to give her that."

CHAPTER THIRTY ONE

The creaky springs of the truck's bench seat groaned loudly in protest, mostly from the punishment they were taking from the badly maintained streets. The lack of functional shock absorbers in Kerry's battered mode of transportation also had something to do with it. Street noise was loud. The road was thick with congested traffic. Smog turned Kerry's eyes red. Lynne's own were likewise, albeit for a different reason.

"How long does it take?" she asked, after clearing the blockage in her throat. She sat with hands under her, in a vain attempt to warm them. She was also trying to stop them from shaking.

Kerry cut a quick glance her way. "What?"

Again, she found it necessary to clear her throat before proceeding. "The cemetery? The girl that you blame Mental Health Services for her death?"

His next glance was longer. He searched her face for the source of the question, of the pain that hung heavily in the cab of the truck. But before he could ask, something else caught his sight and claimed priority.

Lynne pitched forward when he slammed on the brakes. Then she was smashed backwards in whiplash. The seatbelt shoulder harness was overwhelmed with the erratic and sudden braking.

"Now what?" The question came out more as a plea than a real inquiry. She followed Kerry's line of sight. Susie stood on the street corner. She looked different. Lynne hardly recognized her. It was a hooker outfit: short skirt, midriff-baring red blouse, and high stiletto heels. Susie was also no longer in possession of her carefree airs. Her face was drawn. It looked haggard. How could it look otherwise, being heavily painted with garish make-up? She watched as Susie's eyes jumped from car to car, from driver to driver, judging, evaluating: Who was in need of quick morning sex?

Kerry slowly edged the truck over to the curb and stopped. Susie noticed them. She hurried over, looking anxiously over her shoulder, as if the devil was on her tail. Kerry knew she was soaring high on something. She didn't even recognize his truck. She climbed in as Lynne scooted to the middle.

"Want to party?" Susie asked. She kept her eyes on a magical spot twelve inches in front of her. "I'm good. Real good. For a few bucks more, I'll do you both."

Kerry gunned the truck. He laid feet of rubber on the blacktop and roared into traffic. All three were thrown back. "Susie," Kerry began, "it's me. Me and Lynne?"

Susie blinked hard, forcing her delusions into retreat. She shot a look of recognition over to Kerry. To no avail, she tried shrinking into the seat. "Shit!"

Before anyone could say anything further, Kerry dragged the steering wheel hard right and again slid the truck over to the curb. Turning off the ignition, the engine rumbled to its death. He looked over to the corner. Rusty stood there like a defiant *James Dean*, hands buried deep into his pants pocket. When Rusty saw the truck, he nonchalantly meandered on over, as if he had neither a worry, nor a care in the world.

"What are ya up to?" Kerry asked Rusty, when he stuck his head into the passenger side widow.

"What?" Rusty replied. His face was drawn tight in confusion.

"Yeah, what?"

"I, ah, don't know. I guess I'm looking for a man."

"Why are you looking for him?"

"I don't really know."

"Then you wouldn't mind doing me a little favor?" Kerry's voice had dropped to a barely audible level of gentleness.

"What's in it for me?" Even though Rusty tried to sound tough, his voice came through like one that belonged to a fractured angel.

"How about Karma."

"Karma!" Now his voiced skyrocketed. His eyes narrowed in anger. "Only Karma—is bad Karma." Rusty spat the words out like they were cured in hot sauce.

"Just do it for me. Please. We'll debate the nature of Karma at another time."

"Yeah," Rusty replied. His voice was otherworldly. He pitched his sight upwards into a strung out dimension. "That I can do." Softening his voice even further, he continued, "I could use some good Karma. I really could."

Kerry looked from Rusty to Susie. Then over to Lynne, and finally back to Rusty. He was dealing with a Rolodex of pain. He wasn't quite sure how he had gotten there. Sucking in his courage with an audible intake of air, he said, "I want you to take Susie here somewhere nice." He dug out a twenty from his pocket and handed it to Rusty.

"Nice?" Rusty asked in wonder. "I don't think I know any places like that."

Susie looked at Rusty. The realization of the depth of pain she saw in him sliced through her delusions, and quieted her need for self-medicating drugs. Her body relaxed. She released the tension her body had been holding in. Realization of the hurt found in others— especially in her friend—forced her out of herself.

"Least, not since I've been back." Rusty's voice had a muffled, fog like quality.

"How 'bout the park? Or maybe the beach? Hell. Take in a movie. I don't really care where. I just want you to take good care of her. Be nice to her."

"Nice? That I can do."

"Be nice to yourself also."

"I don't need nobody to take care of me!" Susie protested, but not too strenuously. It had been a long time since anyone had been nice to her.

"Then you take care of Rusty!" The hardness spilled

out before Kerry could stop himself. His attempt to exhale tension was only partially successful. He continued in a more measured voice. "If I see you out here on these streets again—today, I'll call in a 5150. Not something you want."

"You wouldn't dare!" Susie snapped. She wheeled about to confront Kerry. *Was he serious?* When she saw that he was, she backed off. "I know what happened last time you tried to 5150 someone!" Susie said, her voice raised in righteous attack. *Nobody was going to hospitalize her again. Not now, not ever!*

"Susie, don't," Rusty gently implored. But she was too far into the cycle of pain and despair to hold back. *After all, why should she be the only one to feel pain?*

"She died. Didn't she?! Cut herself up like a slab of beef. Was she your party girl? Or wasn't she kinky enough for you?"

"Stop it!" Rusty beseeched. He pulled the door of the truck open.

Susie recoiled backwards, like she had been slapped. The harshness of her words had finally broken through her psychosis. Her face contorted in pain. *What kind of monster was she?*

"Don't force me." Kerry's threat was unconvincing. His voice was too brittle. It was apparent to all that Susie's weapon of choice had found its target.

"You know he will," Rusty added. He was trying hard to do his part.

Susie climbed down from the truck. Her shoulders

slumped forward in shame. If there had been anything sexy about her movements before, there certainly weren't any now. She had easily aged a decade in the last few minutes. Her eyes were crestfallen. A shadow had fallen over them, claiming her soul.

"Not to worry. I'll take good care of her," Rusty reassured Kerry with words, and Susie, with a firm, yet gentle hand placed on her arm.

"Like hell you will!" Susie protested.

"Like hell I will! I promise, I'll fight for you. " Rusty poured his caring sight into her soul, giving battle to the dark forces found there. He knew all too well the hold darkness could have on someone.

Resistance fled. She allowed Rusty to guide her up the street.

CHAPTER THIRTY TWO

Mid-morning. The sidewalks were agitated with business suits and office clerks, rushing for their second or third Lattes of the day. Lynne looked suspiciously about. She had not been there before. That is, not with Kerry. This was Montecito—the Village, as it was known locally. It also happened to be one of the most expensive prime real estate locations in the country. The world. The surrounding homes went for millions of dollars. Oprah Winfrey's dig was minutes away. Local folklore had it that she paid a cool fifty million. Along the street, coffee shops, boutiques, and real estate offices were housed in quaint buildings. Her look turned to one of questioning confusion. "What are we doing? There aren't any of your people here."

"Want to bet?" Kerry asked. He parked the truck and killed the engine. He opened the door and exited.

Lynne grumbled as she hurried to keep up. Just when she was sure that she was being tricked somehow, she noticed the foot traffic up the block, parting like water flowing around a rock. The answer as to why: Charlie

Klaus. He was a large man in his mid-forties. He sat cross-legged on a dirty and well-worn blanket. His pants were indecently split open. Silver duct tape was wrapped around his feet in lieu of shoes. A long, wild beard spilled down his chest, and he had shoulder length brown hair that had begun to gray. Approaching the man, she knew that he was their destination.

"Hi, Charlie," Kerry offered in greeting. He nonchalantly ignored the gawking looks of others. Their addition to the scene added confusion to the passing herd.

"Won't do you any good!"

Lynne thought the man's voice was decidedly high pitched for his somatic body type.

"I'm not here to have you taken in," Kerry said. "If that's what you're thinking."

"Oh. Okay then," Charlie replied, relaxing his vocal cords.

"But if you'd like a place to stay? A referral to a shelter? Perhaps a ride to a soup kitchen for a meal?"

"No!" Charlie exclaimed emphatically. "I gave up food months ago. Don't sleep no more either. Don't need it. Waste of time. It's a crime to waste time. No time to waste time. I work for the C.I.A. now. My uncle is ambassador to the Soviet Union. Besides, sleeping reminds me of death. I'm not dead, am I?" He looked up to Kerry with a wounded child's look. Lynne's heart threatened to break.

"No. You're not dead," Kerry reassured the man, his voice soft with kindness

"Then I'd better call the Soviet Union!"

"It's Russia now."

"Yeah! My uncle's the ambassador for them too!"

Kerry looked over to Lynne. The first hint of tears sparkled in her eyes. "Couldn't we, you know, give him some money for food?" she asked. Her voice low and conspiratorial.

"You're a big girl. Do what you think is best," was not the reply she was expecting.

"You're such an ass," was not exactly what Kerry expected in return. Digging through her purse, she found three ones and a five and handed them down to Charlie. He greedily grabbed them and shot up. His pants fell down. He scooped them up and held them up with one hand. Waving off traffic with the other, he madly dashed across the street. Her jaw slackened in surprise when she saw him enter a hobby shop.

"Now what?"

"Just watch," Kerry replied.

Within moments, Charlie exited the store, and made his way over to a nearby bench and sat.

"Come on," Kerry said. Together they crossed the street. Soon they were standing next to Charlie. He had bought a balsa wood, paper airplane. It was the kind that one could assemble and fly in minutes. He tore open the package and began making a paper airplane from the instructions that came with it.

"I don't really need no sleep. It's a waste of time. Besides, that's when they come for me. If I don't sleep, then they can't get me. No, they can't get me. Besides it's a waste of time. Don't have time to waste time. No

I don't." The monologue was unabated while Charlie worked intensely.

In no time, the paper airplane was completed and Charlie launched it. It sailed gracefully into traffic. It brought a little boy's chuckle to the man who eagerly began to construct his next one.

A softening to Lynne's eyes told of her own childlike pleasure, in the acknowledgement that she had brought such joy to another being; even if she had done so inadvertently. Even if it was for a man who inhabited a make believe world so alien from hers. On deeper reflection, she was no longer so sure of that proposition. Kerry's world—the world of the homeless and the mentally ill—was becoming ever more her own.

Had it only been days since she left the soft confines of her sanitized world? And if she was now closer to the world that the mentally ill lived in, was she also closer to the hidden world of her daughter? She had existed in it for how many months? How many years? How long? How lonely— so very lonely, it must had been for her.

That insight brought a whole new level of pain and guilt. But it also redoubled her determination to find her daughter at all costs. And to be there for her. Her hope of finding her help was no longer certain. Nor so narrowly defined. She had begun to see the world through Kerry's eyes: That maybe there would be little professional help that could right the world of her mentally ill daughter. But that didn't mean one couldn't be there both as a friend, and her mother.

Lynne shuddered. She realized just how fearful her daughter must have felt going through her mental breakdown. And that she had struggled all alone with such a hideous disease. How had she missed it? Lynne berated herself. If only she could relive the past.

CHAPTER THIRTY THREE

It was early afternoon. Kerry and Lynne pulled up in front of the shelter. Kerry began to exit the truck. Then he stopped. He sensed Lynne was making no move to follow. Easing back into his seat, he focused his stare on the streets. Unspoken questions poisoned the air between them. Time crawled by.

"Well?" Lynne finally said.

"Well, what?" Kerry replied. He was venturing cautiously. Red flags were popping up all over the place.

"Aren't you going to tell me I told you so? Or lesson learned? Or say something about how naïve I was?"

"Did you see the smile you brought him? Feel the joy that he felt?" Kerry placed his hand on her shoulder.

"Yes. But I gave him money for food. He was supposed to get something to eat." She had decided to follow this safe line of thought, being too ashamed to bring up her earlier insight; her sense of guilt about her daughter. It was like an animal trapped inside her, clawing at her gut with sharp talons.

"Maybe you gave him something more precious than

food. Anytime you can bring somebody like him, in his condition, a smile, a moment of happiness, you've done a good day's work. No. I'm not going to reprimand you. You did good today."

The air inside the truck was thick and uncomfortable, reminding Kerry of the heavy moistened atmosphere of Vietnam. But this time, the cause was the recognition by both of them that Kerry's hand lingered on her shoulder. Looking down, Lynne made no effort to remove it. As for Kerry, there was neither the willpower, nor the desire to do so. As if their lips were magnets, Kerry found himself being pulled into Lynne. Her eyes were at half-mast. Her lips moistened. At the last possible moment, a rude and persistent rapping on the passenger side window crashed the spell. Kerry jerked back. Lynne's checks reddened.

Kerry prepared to tell the intruder to back off, to give him a minute to compose himself. But the man standing at Lynne's window was definitely not homeless. He was in his mid-forties and clean-shaven. He wore an expensive haircut with pride. It was the type that forbid, upon pain of death, even one hair to fall out of place. His tan was deep and golden bronze. The kind purchased on the beaches of Mexico, or the Caribbean. His eyes were electric blue. He was a real woman's draw, Kerry surmised. Of course his clothes had to follow suit: A nice light tan jacket, open silk shirt and casual, but expensive pants. Kerry could just bet the man's leather shoes had those funny little tassels on them, the kind that annoyed him to no end.

Before Kerry could react, Lynne shot out of the truck, like an addict fleeing detox. Following a low groan of exasperation, Kerry did likewise. He slouched over to witness Lynne giving the man a quick peck on the lips. Kerry's blood pressure began jumping jacks.

"I was hoping for a little more passion!" the man said in faux pain to Lynne, while expertly casting a quick, evaluating glance over Kerry.

Kerry became acutely self-aware that his faded blue jeans, scuffled boots, and blue work shirt, stood in poor contrast to the model from *Gentleman's Quarterly*. And of course, the man had to have more than a touch of expensive aftershave lotion about him; a particular male trait that Kerry hated. Still, though it was expensive, it did smell good.

"And this would be?" the man asked, before either Lynne or Kerry had recovered enough to say anything.

"Excuse me," Lynne began. She was clearly flustered. "It's just, well, you caught me by surprise."

"Name? Does your friend have a name?" The man's voice strived for neutrality, but it was edgy with hostility.

Again Lynne's cheeks flamed red, but this time there was a healthy element of anger. "Forgive me. This is Kerry..."

"I'm a social worker. Lynne's interning with me."

"A social worker! Don't believe I've ever met one before."

"We don't bite."

"Name's Duncan Smithe, with an e."

Kerry didn't care much for the limp handshake of the

187

man. He quickly withdrew his hand. He had to struggle not to wipe it on his jeans.

"A social worker," Duncan Smithe repeated. "No. Never have had the pleasure to meet someone of your profession." Duncan's smile was artificial. It conveyed hostility more than warmth.

"Like I said, we don't bite." Kerry's tone slipped down a notch.

"I wouldn't be so sure of that if I were you."

"You wouldn't?" Kerry asked in return. "And why wouldn't you?"

"Nothing against you personally."

"But of course not. Still, what is it?" Kerry's voice was smooth. But it was also heavy, like black oil fouling the ocean.

"Not only are you killing this country with taxes to support dubious social experiments, but you encourage this..." Duncan Smithe began. He looked around at the permanent fixtures that the walking wounded had made into their shelters. It would be a waste of time to tell the man that these homeless—with their variety of disabilities, had no other place to go. That nobody wanted them, especially during the day. They were bad for business. They looked different. Some smelled funny. Bringing reinforcements to his sneer, his lips pinched tightly together. The man resembled a pit bull sucking lemons.

"Come again?" Kerry replied. He was inching towards meltdown.

"Duncan has an issue about too much money being wasted on social programs by the government," Lynne stated hastily. She was trying desperately to diffuse a rapidly deteriorating situation.

"Issue?" Kerry stated, his voice artificially raised high. "Mustn't do anything to aggravate an issue! No. Heaven forbid that their pain, or death, get in the way of his tranquil life. No. It just wouldn't do." Looking around at the casualties of the war against the weak and poor, Kerry suddenly grunted.

Thinking it would be better to address Lynne, and try to salvage a situation that had careened dangerously, Duncan Smithe with an "e" began, "It's not just me, honey. That is, if my memory serves me right. You yourself were quite adamant about this issue, as were most of our friends. Not to mention our business associates."

When neither Kerry nor Lynne said anything, Duncan Smithe continued. This time, his voice was a little shakier. A little less under control. "Unless you've changed. I know how much stress you've been under. The shock with..."

"This isn't the time!" Lynne stated sharply. Her voice came out louder than she'd meant.

"Shock? What kind of shock?" Kerry asked. He sensed an opening and moved rapidly to exploit it.

"Didn't I say this wasn't the time?! You deaf or something?"

Duncan Smithe cleared his throat.

"How come you didn't call? I have my cell with me. 24/7," Lynne asked. She was a smart woman. She knew that a good offense was the best kind of defense.

"I thought I'd surprise you," Duncan Smithe stated. He cast a dark glare Kerry's way. "Maybe that wasn't such a good idea," he continued. His voice deflated.

"How did you know where to find me?"

Kerry shifted his attention onto Lynne. While her voice was not downright hostile, it was still less than friendly. Kerry was beginning to appreciate that this woman had a strong sense of self. Of boundaries crossed at one's own risk.

"You did call the agency. Told them where you were staying. Even told them about this shelter. But you never mentioned anything about an internship."

"Let's go," Lynne stated firmly. She began to walk briskly over to a red Ferrari parked down the street.

"Did you find her?" Duncan Smithe's barely audible question caused a slight stumble to Lynne's forward motion.

"Her? Find her?" Kerry stated quietly to himself. He intently watched the couple walk down the street. From their body language, it was obvious that a sharp exchange of words were taking place. Kerry smiled. He was pleased with that knowledge.

CHAPTER THIRTY FOUR

The next morning broke with overcast gray clouds. It added another layer of gloominess to Kerry's mood. Of course the liquor that he had pounded down the night before didn't help either. He had started his drinking innocently enough. One shot glass at a time. Then images of Vietnam slipped in past the day-to-day filler of his life: Scenes of a hospital ship that held the horrors of war. The deadly skill of the NVA—North Vietnamese Army mortar crews. And Marines that bled to death quietly. Those that screamed for their mothers as they died. Vietnam was just a bunch of foul memories that pushed his drinking hard at times.

He looked into the rearview mirror, playing for time before getting out of his truck. His green eyes were set deeper than usual this morning. He tried scraping the bitter aftertaste of the binge from his tongue with his teeth. With a grunt of surrender, he climbed down from the truck. In a hopeless attempt, not to inflame his pounding headache, he walked gingerly across the street. Entering the shelter, he tried very hard to prevent his timid footsteps from sending a hurricane of painful sounds blowing into his skull.

Charlene and Lynne manned the counter. If he was hoping for sympathy from them, he was greatly disappointed. Without so much as a greeting, Charlene thrust a paper into his hands.

"What's this?" Kerry's voice was scratchy. Whiskey rough.

"A do's and don'ts list," Charlene offered cautiously. She cut a worried look over to Lynne.

"What the hell is a, 'do's and don'ts list?'"

"Rules to live by."

"Come again?"

"Rules. You know rules. Rules that the Boss man wants us to implement. You know, on the proper way to run the shelter."

"Client conduct rules," Lynne offered.

"Like?" Kerry asked. He was afraid to trust his hung over eyes. He was also having a hard time believing what he was hearing. He took a quick glance down the paper in his hand. Sure enough, all he saw was blurry print.

"Like no loitering. No more food giveaways. Shelter doors close at 9:00," Charlene replied.

"9:00? In the evening?" Kerry asked. He ran his hand over his head. He tried reading the memo again, expecting that it was all a bad joke. No luck. Blurriness still played him.

"Like in the morning."

"Close the doors? Then what?"

"Well. First, we kick everyone out. Then we close and lock the doors."

"But this is a homeless shelter! You can't run an empty building. You can't schedule homelessness, emergencies—hunger!"

"According to the Boss man, you can. We now run this operation by the clock. Says too many homies hanging around all day long. Looks bad."

"You mean too many complaints from our *friend* next door."

"What about the soup kitchen?" Lynn asked tentatively.

Kerry's eyes came off the worthless paper. "*That*, we open at 11:00. But even then, all must be out by 12:30. No exceptions. And if we haven't fed everyone by then?" It was the rhetorical question that was on all their minds. He knew the answer. They all did. But if he needed the answer to be verbalized, he got his wish.

"Then they go hungry," Simon West stated, as he walked briskly in from the back of the shelter.

Uneasy silence tortured the three before Simon West continued. His voice was condescending. "No one is going to die if they skip a meal. In fact, it will probably do some of them some good."

"Yeah! Right! Especially if it's their only meal of the day. Starvation diet does wonders for the complexion." When he had finished his sarcasm, Kerry found himself under the gun stare of Simon West. The man's slow boil was no longer so slow.

"I don't need, nor appreciate, your so called witticism."

"And they don't need this bullshit, especially coming from us. We're supposed to care. Remember?"

The tense atmosphere was heavy enough to sink a battleship. The two men present were drawn into a hard stare down. The two women were busy trying to figure out how to end the standoff before Kerry lost his job.

"Weren't you going to show me some more of the streets?" Lynne cautiously asked. She wasn't surprised that her motivation wasn't exclusively on losing an avenue in finding her daughter. Her concern was also for Kerry, and what losing his job would mean for him. She knew him well enough now to know it would kill him.

"That reminds me," Charlene quickly added, bringing reinforcements to Lynne's gamble. "The hospital called. Someone by the name Skitty is there. She's askin' for you."

As if choreographed, Simon West did a smart about face and exited. Kerry followed the retreating figure with a bitter stare before snapping out of his mood. Turning to Charlene, he stated, "I don't know anyone that goes by the name, Skitty. Do I?"

"You do now," Charlene replied.

CHAPTER THIRTY FIVE

The ride over to the hospital was reflective and silent. Thankfully, it only took ten minutes. That was the thing about Santa Barbara. Within miles, sometimes just a few blocks, neighborhoods switched from homeless camps to palaces going for millions.

During this enforced solitude, both Lynne and Kerry were very careful not to bring up Duncan Smithe, or his role in her life. Which was not to say that his presence didn't weigh heavily on them.

The receiving room of the E.R. was quiet. Only two nurses were present. One was middle-aged. Kerry thought she had incredibly bright eyes for such an early morning. *How could anyone greet the morning with anything other than apprehension?* The other one was much younger.

"Skitty?" Kerry began. You got anyone here going by that name?" He had addressed his question to the younger nurse. A mistake.

"Skitty?" The nurse's voice was full of uncertainty. "Would that be a first name, or a last name?"

"How the hell am I supposed to know?" Kerry barked.

"Just Skitty. This is your E.R. Not mine."

"Well, if you don't know, then how...?" the young nurse began her reply. She stuttered to a stop. She looked back over her shoulder to the older nurse. Her panicky eyes pleaded for rescue. The other nurse moved alongside her wayward companion. She smiled. It told the world that there was nothing she hadn't encountered before: Meth freaks cycling high. Dopers crashing. Bleed outs. Perhaps most tragic of all: The loss of hope and the will to live. She'd seen it all. And nothing this side of hell was beyond her capacity to handle. She would make everything all right. "Can I help you?"

"Skitty?" Kerry replied. His voice was stressed. Body tense. He knew the morning's bad start wasn't the nurses' fault. But hell, it wasn't his fault either. "Someone by that name called me from here. Beyond that, I don't know." His voice trailed off.

"I tried to tell him," the first nurse began.

Waving off her companion with a wayward motion of her hand, the second nurse replied, "You're that social worker from the shelter."

"That'd be me." Kerry's eyebrows drifted lower. Was that a good or bad thing in this nurse's world?

"Half the transients that come through here list you as next of kin."

Kerry smiled. It was a thin, ironic one. "Yeah. I'm down with the rich and powerful. We're tight. Real tight. And for your information, they're not transients. Not all of them. Not even most of them. Many have lived here for years. More than a few their entire lives."

This was a pet peeve of Kerry's. No matter how long a homeless person lived in Santa Barbara, they were always referred to as transients. Like they somehow didn't belong in their fair city. It was especially bitter to him when their deaths were announced in that context in the local media. That is, if they bothered to publish that fact at all. Sometimes, he felt that a homeless death was simply an inconvenience to many in his city. But that wasn't fair. It wasn't the total picture. More than once, a good citizen of the community had stepped forward upon his request to help cover burial costs, when no other funds were available.

"Of course. Sorry," the nurse replied to her credit. "We admitted a homeless woman this morning. Perhaps she is this...Skitty."

"Good! Now we're getting somewhere." Then his voice turned down in suspicion. "Skitty's a she?"

The nurse smiled. One that reminded Kerry of a cat that had just eaten a mouse.

"Where can I find her?"

"She's in the I.C.U. Go down this corridor. Turn right. Then the first right after that."

Kerry and Lynne turned to exit. They were stopped by a cold message enveloped in a warm, caring voice. "Be forward. She's only got hours left—days at most. Stage four cancer." A cold wind chilled Kerry and Lynne. They turned to each other with recognition in their eyes.

"The smell?" Lynne asked. There was an edge to her voice.

"The smell," Kerry confirmed. *How could he have been so stupid?* A thousand times he had used smell as an all-important warning system. Death had an odor all its own: A rotting, sweetened stench. There was no other smell in the world like it. He had first detected this unique odor in Vietnam. Since then, a hundred times over. And still, it had evaded him.

CHAPTER THIRTY SIX

Their stance shifted awkwardly. They stood outside the electronically locked doors. Kerry hated waiting. Lynne hated hospitals. Then there was the matter of what was behind the locked doors. They were waiting for clearance from the head I.C.U. nurse, who needed to beep them in. A man who sat alone, with his head in his hands, collected their stares. Undoubtedly trying to make sense of the uncertainties, the cruel twists and turns of life. *Or, more likely*, Kerry thought, *of its certainty*. No one got out of it alive. The one certainty that all religions and philosophers started and ended with was the fact that all life ended in death, and the only question was how we dealt with that fact.

Obviously, this man was dealing with it in a great deal of pain. Kerry jumped when the buzzer announced that the door was open.

They walked into the room. The patient in question was in the first bed. "You, Skitty?" Kerry asked. It was a rhetorical question. The woman before them was the highly educated one from before, who had come to the shelter in shame. She was the unique person he had allowed to shower against the rules. Having done so, he had betrayed the ever-evolving new policies that viewed all homeless as statistical fodder. Saving living souls was not the end game. It was all about collecting the right statistics.

"One of the many names I've gone by, during my brief existence here on planet Earth." The crackly voice cut into Kerry's musings. She tried lifting her head. The effort was too taxing. With a soft groan, she lowered it back onto the pillow.

She looked worse than the last time they had laid eyes on her. Her skin was so thin that it was translucent. It was highlighted with bluish veins streaking down her neck. A film of death clouded her eyes. And still, the smell of decay lingered. Kerry knew that no matter how hard one tried, or how much soap one used, that smell would still be there—forever. But the intensity of her stare stood in sharp contrast. And it was drilled into Kerry. As far as she was concerned, Lynne didn't even exist.

"You were most kind to me the other day. It meant a lot."

Kerry was not the kind of man to take a compliment easily. He grunted hard and shifted his weight from one foot to the other.

Skitty smiled softly. "Word on the street is that your boss was not happy with what you did for me."

"That is one unhappy man. Somewhere on down the

line he woke up on the wrong side of life. Besides, I didn't do all that much."

"On the contrary. You gave a dying woman one last wish. Even if that wish was to simply be allowed to bathe. Even if one is homeless, one must maintain certain standards."

"I don't know you all that well, but something tells me you maintain standards no matter where you are. That nobody could ever take them from you."

"You are too kind."

"You're not necessarily going to die," Lynne blurted out. The statement was weak. It was more along the lines of a plea, than a statement of fact.

"No?" Skitty asked. Her voice and eyes both rose in disbelief. "You're a very bad fabricator of the truth."

"That would be you," Kerry said to Lynne. A small, conspiratorial smile was shared with Skitty, like a private joke between two old friends. Try as she might, Lynne could hold neither his, nor Skitty's stares. It just wasn't right that this kind old lady was homeless. Nor that she should die like that. Bolting images of her mother again flashed through her mind.

"I know you by reputation," Skitty began, shifting her attention back to Kerry. "We have no need to lie to each other."

"No we don't," Kerry replied. He knew exactly where this was going.

"Death is our old friend. He is someone to hate—perhaps you more than me. But someone to fear? I think not. Correct?"

Kerry looked off. Troubled. As more than one homie had told him on the streets: He was tight with Death.

Death had followed him home from Vietnam. He was a familiar presence on the streets, and sadly, Kerry's constant companion.

"I have one final favor," Skitty began. Her voice cut into Kerry's musings. She reached out and took his hand into hers. The coldness of the limp grip did not surprise him. It simply confirmed the nurse's grim prognosis. It was a coldness that hijacked the synaptic train straight to his heart, causing it to misfire.

"What is it?" Lynne asked, when it became apparent that Kerry had lost his voice, along with the recognition to all present that he wasn't as tough as he liked to pretend.

"When I die..." Skitty stopped to wave off Lynne's protest. She no longer had the energy to speak and move at the same time. Still, her radiant eyes had the strength to pin Lynne into silence with a deadly stare. "When I die, I want your assurance that my remains will be cremated." Having hushed Lynne, she turned her full attention onto Kerry. "The thought of being encased in all that darkness—all that dampness, is not something that settles easily within."

"And?" Lynne asked. It became uncomfortably clear that she had more to say, *and* that Kerry, for a variety of reasons, had lost his voice.

"And," Skitty continued. Her voice was hallowed with pain. Slowed by fatigue. "I want Kerry to promise me that he will spread my ashes over the ocean. Not only do I not

want to be confined within a casket underground, I
don't wish to spend eternity within a jar on someone's
fireplace mantel."

With dying effort, Skitty searched Kerry's eyes, until
she was convinced that he understood. Sinking further
into her pillow, her voice was broken and distant. "I want
to be free. Free of all this pain. Free as the ocean. Can you
do that? Can you give me my freedom?"

CHAPTER
THIRTY
SEVEN

A faraway look clouded Kerry's eyes as he leaned on the wall outside the I.C.U. with his hands in his pockets. *What was it with men and that particular stance?* Lynne wondered. She stood apart. She was not sure what to say. What to do. Finally she did what she always did in such situations. She just started talking. "What the hell's the matter with you?"

"Now what are you talking about?" Kerry's eyes shifted back to the living.

"Why didn't you tell that sweet old lady you'd grant her wish?"

"Because, I don't do death." Kerry's reply came as a slow draw.

"You don't do death?" Lynne's voice vacillated: low with mockery, high in disbelief. "What is that supposed to mean?"

Lynne watched intensely. War raged across Kerry's face. She was unsure if he would reply or simply storm away.

Kerry came off his leaning stance. "Let me try to put in a way that even you'll understand. To you, death is spelled with a small d. For me, it's spelled with a capital D."

Lynne felt hammered under his intense stare. It had invaded the deepest reaches of her soul. The hard gaze had a physical element to it. This was new territory. She found this intensity too much to bear. She broke eye contact. Looking off, she quietly stated, "I don't understand. I don't understand the meaning. I guess what I really mean is, that I don't understand you." Her voice was meek. Her eyes went back on him, searching.

"Of course you don't." Kerry's reply was neither sarcastic nor a put down. It was merely a statement of fact. Life had taught him the truth about Death. "You weren't there. You couldn't possibly understand unless you were. Nor can you understand that he followed me home. That he stalks these streets looking for more victims. His appetite is unquenchable. Timeless."

Lynne involuntarily shuddered. It was like someone had opened a freezer door. Iced air reached out, bruising her soul. If Kerry really believed those words, what did that say about his sanity? Was hanging around him such a good idea? She realized she wasn't concerned about her safety with him, but with Death. If what Kerry said was true, could Death look her way? Tracy's?

Weakness punched the backs of her knees. She reached out to the wall for stability. She questioned her own sanity. *How could Death be personalized to such a degree? Was Death, in fact, an entity? And if so, then where did she stand in a relationship with him? Where did her daughter?*

Kerry's voice brought Lynne back to the present. "You

asked what I had against Mental Health. The same thing I had against the war machine. And now, apparently, the shelter. Through neglect and indifference, people die. Playing by the rules until the rules become more important than people, we allow Death to enter.

"He feeds off the vulnerable, Lynne. I refuse to play that game with him. When we cherry pick who deserves our help, we do his work for him. I won't play by those rules. I don't do Death. Not anymore."

"Vietnam was a long time ago."

"Oh, really? So that excuses millions of deaths? Millions wounded and maimed—thousands of children born deformed by Agent Orange, Agent White? And what excuses do we have for the way we treat the homeless and the mentally ill? Is that also in the past?"

Another wave of vertigo hit Lynne. Her vision became restricted to Kerry. Everything beyond him was an inky darkness. Breathing was hard. It was also pain.

"You know, right now, *he* prowls the streets, looking for some homie to claim."

Lynne faltered. She reached out to Kerry for balance. "Please. Don't," she begged. Kerry brought her within his caring embrace. Against her wishes, she felt protected with her head against his chest. This was so unlike her. She didn't need a man to protect her. But maybe that was the whole point. It wasn't necessarily a woman needing a man for comfort.

It was one human being to another, reaching out in a time of need. With dawning recognition, she saw the truth of the words: *We are not alone in this world.* We need one another for comfort, for strength. Also in times of sadness. Weakness was when we shut ourselves off from others. Courage is the sharing of pain. It is opening up our vulnerabilities to others. That took great strength. Real courage. But that was not how she had lived her life, at least up to that moment.

"You've been hiding something from me from day one." Kerry's gentle voice floated to her. "What is it? Let me help you."

Lynne looked up into his green eyes. She had never seen such eyes before in her life. Looking off to the side, her sight fell on the closed door. "You're right. But I can't. Not here. Can you accept that?"

Kerry cupped her chin with his hand. He looked deep into her eyes. This time, she did not feel awkward. Instead she held his gaze, sharing something precious and fragile. Finding what he was looking for in her eyes, he replied, "Okay. But soon."

"Soon. I promise."

"You know, it's sad, but true. Some of my people have a better death than a life," Kerry said, looking past Lynne to the door they had just exited.

"You have to keep that promise," Lynne said.

"But, I didn't promise," Kerry protested.

"Yes you did," Lynne replied. She placed her hand over his heart. "Yes you did," she repeated. "It's important. Not only for her, but also you."

"We'll see. We'll see."

CHAPTER THIRTY EIGHT

For once, the quiet drive to the shelter felt natural. The absence of noise was healing. The quietness also gave space, allowing chaos' acceptance. Nothing needed to be forced, nor controlled. Life was simply what it was. Walking up to the front of the shelter, Lynne was suddenly hit with an overpowering scent of aftershave lotion. Looking askew at Kerry, Lynne asked, "You wearing aftershave?" She was unsure how she had not detected it before.

"What do you think? Isn't exactly my style now, is it?"

"Then who?"

Looking a few yards down the street, Kerry spotted Mr. Sandoval, an elderly Mexican-American man with long, snowy white hair. He had a long white beard that contrasted nicely with his deep brown, leathery skin. He sat on a folding beach chair, facing the traffic and watching the end of his life sprint by. A backpack rested at his feet. With Lynne in tow, Kerry walked over to the old man.

The distance was quickly closed. Lynne bent over.

Sniffed. Even more quickly, she recoiled backwards. The smell was overpowering. *How could someone put that much aftershave on?* She sniffed again, sure she was wrong. In response, Mr. Sandoval sniffed back. Again, she jumped backwards. Kerry smiled and laughed.

Bending down. Kerry dug through Mr. Sandoval's backpack. The elderly gentleman made no attempt to stop him, as if the two men had danced this tune many times before.

Kerry's face darkened as he withdrew and began lining up several green and blue bottles of aftershave. He placed them on the curb: A small army of deadly friends. Some full. Some empty.

"I've warned you a thousand times!" Kerry's voice was rough, like his throat had been sandpapered.

In response, Mr. Sandoval gave Kerry a proud smile. He attempted to stand; unsuccessful. He was too intoxicated for such a complicated move. He collapsed noisily, back into his mobile seat. It threatened to tip it over.

"If you weren't so old, I'd eighty-six you from the shelter in a minute." Kerry's voice was low.

"What do you mean, 'eight-six?" Lynne asked, no longer able to contain herself.

Kerry smiled. She had misheard the phrase. "You mean, eighty-six, don't you?"

"Ah, okay," Lynne stammered. "What I mean is—oh never mind." She turned. Then she turned back. Her face was rigid with question. "I mean about all that—I mean this." She was not familiar with finding herself in a sea of the absurd without a life preserver. She was doing the best she could. Unfortunately, that was not nearly good enough. She tried again. "What did that old man do that was so wrong? Assuming *eighty-six* is a bad outcome?" Lynne was trying really hard to recover some sense of saneness *and* control over her life. "And what's all this got to do with those bottles of aftershave?"

"Where have you been all your life? I don't think I've ever meant anyone as..." Kerry began, but then he stopped.

"Go ahead! Say it! Naïve! What's so great about knowing what you know? That people live like this? Die like this!" Tears began a silent rush down Lynne's face. *Dear God, how could her daughter possibly survive this crazy world?*

"He drinks it." Kerry's voice could barely be heard. *Why had he pushed her? This world, all this craziness and pain was not her fault. Why had he let her get to him?*

"What!" Lynne's cry of anguish wasn't just for Mr. Sandoval. It was for her daughter. And for all the people she had met in the last few days. Maybe even for her.

Mr. Sandoval burped and smiled. The sickening sweet smell of aftershave wafted upwards.

"I think it's time we had that talk," Kerry stated. Taking Lynne gently by the arm, he guided her down the street.

After they were several yards away from the shelter, he said, "Step into my office." Stiffly, he sat on the curb. With great exaggeration, he pretended to sweep the area next to him clean. "Office hours are now open. And you know what?"

Lynne's answered with a sniffle. He smiled.

"You happen to be the first in line."

CHAPTER THIRTY NINE

Slowly, Lynne sat next to Kerry. She knew the conversation that Kerry wanted. *But like this?* She looked around. A settling stillness descended over her. *Why not?* After all, this was his office. She had heard more pain spoken; more hard truths told on the streets than she had ever experienced in years of counseling.

"So? What's going on, Lynne?" Kerry's voice cut into her self-reflection, forcing her to turn to face him. "Who is it?"

"Who's what?" One more time, a defense was mounted. It was by now a conditioned reflex. But, it was weaker. Her heart was no longer in it.

"Who are you looking for? Who's cutting such pain into your heart? Whose name is tattooed on your soul?"

"Tracy. She's my daughter." Even though the words were softly spoken, her voice had all the subtlety of a jackhammer inside a house of mirrors.

"Go on," Kerry encouraged.

"She's fifteen. Everything was fine through the early years. We were close, as close as a mother and daughter can be. She was gifted and sweet. Tracy excelled at everything she tried: Piano. Dance. School. Everything always came easy. Always tested in the top five percent."

"But then Nirvana crashed?"

"Yes," Lynne concurred. Her voice was still low. A voice directed inwards. "Kerry, you have to believe me. It was subtle at first; so insidiously subtle that I didn't see it. Or, maybe I did. Maybe I simply didn't want to believe it. She was always shy. She always had a hard time making friends. But that began to change in high school. Of course, I was happy for her. Kids need friends."

"Her friends? Were they good kids?"

Lynne inched back to get a better look at Kerry.

"I'm not judging you," he reassured her.

"Yes. At first I thought they—I thought they were good kids. But now? Looking back, I'm not so sure. I mean, I always tried to get to know them, but they seemed to always have an excuse for not hanging around, for not coming over."

"And? What else changed?" Kerry had been here before, a thousand times. The child that was given birth to and raised, suddenly transformed into a stranger in the house. The family, and especially the parents, torn apart. Blame assigned. Hearts broken, all because mental illness snuck in like a thief in the night, robbing the child of its mind. It was a form of kidnapping. One where the victim was never to return. Cruelly, ransom was irrelevant. The sweet memories of childhood were suddenly replaced with the terror of losing the child you loved.

"Like I said, subtle changes. Our time together became less and less. She spent more time out, and when she was home, it was behind closed doors, plugged into music. And I guess I made false assumptions. Excuses. That this was the way of teen hood.

"You know nobody gives you an instruction manual when they're born. You walk into the hospital pregnant— and single in my case. You walk out a parent—a unit, and it's like you're supposed to know what to do. What to expect. Being a parent doesn't necessarily come naturally. It's something that you learn as you go along. It's a day-by-day thing, mostly trial and error. I wish to God someone had given me an instruction manual. Like they do when you buy an appliance. A TV. Even a telephone…

"Sorry, I digress. After she ran away, I learned she began cutting school during her freshman year. Her grades began to slip. Then, they crashed into D's and F's. She began to sneak out at night. And then she didn't come home."

Lynne paused. A soft, unfocused look came to her eyes. It was like the hypnotic sound of flowing traffic had lulled her into an alternate space, one defined with emotional memories. Emotional pain.

"And?" Kerry said, gently prodding her.

"And?" Lynne's voice was small as she tried to come back to the land of the living. "I did what any red blooded American would do. I went through her room."

"And?" Kerry asked again. He was trying desperately to keep the conversation, the confessional flowing.

"I found a bag of grass."

Lynne's gaze became intense. Kerry followed her line of sight. Across the street, a young boy of sixteen, maybe seventeen, was digging through a trashcan. He was looking for something to eat. He was skinny as hell. Dressed all in black, with a white skull on his black tee shirt. A badly cut Mohawk added a childish tone to the boy. Finding a partially eaten sandwich, he tore off the rotten part, and had at it.

Despair flooded Lynne's voice. "It all fell into place. So easy. Of course, too easy. The grass I mean. It was something concrete. An easy answer. I ended up sending her to one of those tough love wilderness camps. I thought that with a little detox, a little drug therapy, a little discipline, everything would be okay."

"But it wasn't."

Lynne slowly turned her gaze to Kerry. Even though it was tough to hold, he knew it was important not to look away. "Being around you. Being around all of this, I now know—I can admit that she was mentally ill. Who knows? Maybe I knew it back then. Maybe it was just too hard to acknowledge it. This is all so different." Lynne shifted her gaze. Once again, drifting back to the boy who had resumed his dumpster diving antics. "It's all so weird."

"How so?"

"It was easier to accept my daughter strung out on drugs," Lynne said after a deep sigh. "How can that be?" she asked, turning to Kerry. "And, for God's sakes, it was only pot that I found! It wasn't even a hard drug! But it was an answer. Even if it was a cruel one."

"What do you mean, cruel?"

"Because the answer—that answer, was a lie. But anything was better than the truth."

"Mental illness?"

"How could I be in such denial?"

Kerry fought down the urge, the instinct to take her into his arms. To tell Lynne pleasant platitudes, and try somehow to lessen the pain that bled from her soul.

"We're in denial because of our prejudices. Ones created and conditioned by Hollywood. Think who our role models are for the mentally ill: Jason. Psycho. Freddy Krueger. The list is endless. Of course, they seldom mention that Abe Lincoln and others like him suffered from mental illness, now do they? That many creative and great people have not only overcome their illness, but just maybe they are who they are because of it."

"Did that make me a bad mother?" A second of eternity ticked by before Kerry could swallow the lump in his throat to respond. She added stiffness to her backbone. Judgment day was at hand.

"No. Like you said, there's no instruction manual that comes with any of this. Not when your daughter was born. Not when mental illness struck. How were you to know? As for all of this," Kerry stated, his voice strained with bitterness, "none of these people asked to be born this way. That boy didn't put in a request that his meals were to be found inside three-foot cafes. He didn't pray to God, 'please let me be poor.'"

Lynne looked about. Surprise jacked her eyes wide open. Dirt, filth, and human casualties occupied the streets. Yet it was despair hanging about like days old smog that defined the scene. It had a presence that was all encompassing, yet impossible to touch.

"We spend our whole lives pretending none of this exists." Kerry wheeled his stare back at Lynne. Its intensity sent chills hurling up her spine. "You will again. Once we find your daughter, you'll return to your virtual world, and all of this will become a bad dream."

Lynne wanted to deny Kerry's statement. At the same time, she desperately needed to hold onto the positive part about finding her daughter. There was also something else—something that delivered a truckload of burning coal. Truth was a cruel mistress. She realized that part of Kerry's statement was untrue. It was all a lame attempt to cushion the reality that Kerry was hinting at. "Except for my daughter. That's not a dream. That won't reset, will it?"

"Except for your daughter," Kerry concurred, as gently as he could. Lynne needed to prepare herself for what they would find. The time for evasions and half-truths was behind her now.

It was now out in the open for her to see. For her to acknowledge, and deal with. Her daughter was mentally ill. No denial would change that. One road was being left behind. Now a fork was before her. Before both of them. Which road would she take? Which would her daughter? Would they take separate paths? Or would they reunite to continue the journey of life together? The truth may be hard, but at least it was the *truth*. It was real; so unlike the fog that she had been beating her head against. Delusions and polite lies were now gone. And with that reality, a great sense of relief came over her. The pressure that had been squeezing her heart like a vise had vanished.

"Then, you'll help me find her?" Lynne asked, behind a hesitant smile, knowing where love was propelling her.

Kerry smiled. "But of course! After all, you're my intern, are you not?"

"That would be me." She made no attempt to hide the waterworks flooding her eyes. Instead of the usual tears of sadness, they were now ones of relief. Hope. Real hope had been given birth to.

CHAPTER FORTY

A very long day. Ten hours feeling like twenty. Looking up at the weakened daylight, Kerry realized it was also the time of year clouding his mood. The shortened days always seemed to steal time. More work had to be compressed into shorter and shorter time spans. He sometimes felt that even nature conspired against the poor and homeless. And if time was relative, what was its relationship to the pain that surrounded those poor citizens of Santa Barbara, those calling the streets their home?

He was exhausted by the search for Lynne's daughter. It had taken all day, and no one they had run into knew anything about her. This was a bad sign. She was obviously hiding. He knew they would find her eventually. Santa Barbara wasn't that big of a city. And once he set out to find a homie, he was always successful. Without failure. But the recognition that he was seeking someone, a mentally ill someone who was actively hiding, brought a hard frown to his face. He looked over to Charlene who was staring intently at him.

"Pretty quiet."

The comment drew Kerry's gaze over to Lynne. The day had been especially hard on her. A fine crow's line burrowed into the corners of her eyes. But she gave him a warm smile in return.

"Wait till next week," Charlene offered.

"Next week? What's so special about next week?" Lynne asked.

"Remember all those beds we made?" Kerry said.

"Yes?" Lynne's response was tentative. She wasn't sure she really wanted to know.

"Next week our winter emergency shelter opens," Charlene began. "Instead of sixty beds, we'll be serving three hundred."

Before Lynne could register her shock, and question how three hundred homeless could possibly be housed, served and fed, Rusty came bouncing in through the front door. Briskly, he bounced up to the counter, wearing the same black sweatshirt as before. His was head still trapped inside its hood. "We gotta talk," he boldly informed Kerry.

"So talk," Kerry shot back. He was too tired to engage.

He was looking suspiciously. At least, Kerry thought so. It was hard to read much of Rusty's face, confined within the head cave of the sweatshirt. "No way man! Not here. Gotta show you."

The forced staccato was a warning to Kerry. It had been a long time since he had heard Rusty speak like that. "Okay. So show me already."

Rusty pulled up. He took a step back, like Kerry was

challenging him. Silence ensued. An internal battle raged. Then Rusty's face softened. "Please."

Kerry looked at him hard before coming out from behind the reception cubicle. Stepping rapidly to the door, he grabbed it and swung it open. "Well? What are we waiting for?"

CHAPTER FORTY ONE

The street in front of the alley was dark. It was downright scary. The hairs on Kerry's neck stood rigid. He was grateful for the weak illumination of the streetlight down the block. But even its yellow hue cast an eerie warning.

"First, we need to talk," Kerry said. He grabbed Rusty by the arm, stopping him just as he was about to enter the alley.

"Let go!" Rusty demanded. He spun away from Kerry.

The two men stood frozen. They were appraising each other on the deserted street. "Nothing's going to change," Kerry began. His voice hushed against the ears of the night.

"I, I don't know what you mean." The voice was weak.

"Yes you do, Rusty. My war was over thirty years ago. But it seems like yesterday to me. Yours was yesterday. And unless you deal with it better than I did, you'll be in the same place thirty years from now as you are today. Either that, or dead." Both men looked around, knowing hidden ghosts from their respective wars were in the crevices of the dark.

Rusty was clearly uncomfortable. His tight body language all but screamed it. His head hung low as he thrust his hands deep into his pockets. He was more like smudge than a man standing in the darkness of the night.

"Look, Rusty, at least let me get you into the shelter on a V.A. bed. Do yourself a favor, and give the streets a rest."

"I don't want nothing from the V.A. Nothing from the government! Nothing!" He turned to leave Kerry in the dust of his hasty retreat. Suddenly, he stopped. It was like his legs were encased in the soft sands of the desert, the desert of his war. Kerry began to reach out for him, then he thought better of it. He stopped. Rusty needed to do this of his own volition. *Let the silence work its magic,* Kerry thought to himself.

"How come that mortar drifted?" The voice came from the other end of a deep tunnel, hidden within the confines of the hooded sweatshirt. "Or, did it?" The hood turned to look over the shoulder. "Was it my fault? Did I calibrate it wrong?" His shoulders slumped further, as if grappling hooks had sprung from the hard street surface and were now pulling him down.

"Look, Rusty. It isn't going to do any good beating yourself up over what happened. Or what might have happened. Only thing you got to realize is that shit happens in war. Bad shit. People die. No good reason why. They are slaughtered with, or without your participation. And of course friendlies are going to die with all that firepower. We both know there's no such thing as precision munitions. Weapons are made to kill people. Meant to kill lots and lots of people. Bad guys. Good guys. But mostly the innocent. Isn't your fault. Wasn't my fault. Only fault lies with them jerks who get their jollies sending us off to die for a dime, while they sit safely in Washington, or behind their corporate desks. War isn't about death, Rusty. *War is Death*." Kerry's voice was stone cold.

The silence of the night cut a cold blade into the two men. Both cocked their heads sidewise, listening to the echoes of the clash-of-arms. Rusty's sight again drifted to the shadows. His eyes squinted when he realized they were staring back. They, being his buddies who died, when the mortar had landed at the wrong location. *Had they felt pain? Had they heard the low thump of the mortar as it left the tube? Did they know that they were about to die? Had they looked up to see the lazy mortar wobble before plunging down to the earth? Did they think of wives and girlfriends? Of sons and daughters? Or had the instrument of death stole into their consciousness only at the moment of explosion? Had their existence simply ceased before any thought processes could become involved?* He looked closer, feeling the ghostly stares that were located there. Tears blurred his sight. He turned to leave.

"Wait!" Kerry called out.

Rusty stood frozen by the voice that demanded obedience.

"Why did you bring me here?"

Without turning, without looking back, Rusty raised

his arm scarecrow-like and pointed down the darkened alley. His arm slowly dropped. Rusty walked zombie-like into the embracing arms of the night shadows.

Kerry moved slowly over to the entrance of the alley. He leaned forward. He peered in. "Shit!" he told the black emptiness before him. Sucking up courage, and acting against his better judgment, he cautiously entered the unknown.

CHAPTER FORTY TWO

From within, the alley was even darker than it had appeared. It forced Kerry to feel his way forward, hands on the brick walls that fed into it. As his eyesight adjusted to the faint, cast off streetlight, the landscape turned clay-gray. He pulled up abruptly. He was at the end of the alley. Another brick wall in front of him. He stood frozen. *Had he been played?* No. Rusty was not that kind of man. *Then what,* he questioned. The answer came from a soft rustling of cardboard from behind, a trashcan being shoved off to one side. From the smell of rotting food, Kerry guessed it had been awhile since the trash had been emptied. "Who's there?" he asked.

"Who wants to know? I ain't alone you know. There's three of us here, so don't be messing with me. Ah, I mean us."

Of course, the voice was young. It was not even close to that of a man. And the lie had been told badly.

"Jeffrey? Is that you?"

"Kerry?" Jeffrey answered one question with another.

"I won't speak to a trashcan. Come on out."

"You mean into the night?" The voice was lighter now, having found a sense of safety knowing that it was Kerry who was in the alley. A note of humor could be detected.

"What are you doing here?" Kerry asked, when Jeffrey scooted out from behind the metal monster. "How come you aren't with your mom?"

"She got rolled up. We were going back to camp—you know the tunnels? Anyway," Jeffrey continued without waiting for an answer. "She was pushing her shopping cart. Bad wheel. I told her about that wheel a thousand times, but she wouldn't listen. Loud enough to be heard clear down in Ventura."

"Does this train have a caboose?" Kerry asked anxiously. "Could we move this story along?"

"Yeah. Right. Anyways, I was lagging behind when the black and white rolled up. Of course, they had been drinking, so they took them in. I ran. That was three days ago. They didn't get us though."

If Kerry had been more on the ball, he would had questioned the, "us." But even for him, the conversation was already in the heart of absurdity. Besides, the walls were closing in. The feeling of being trapped was taking over. When only one exit was present, the memories of Vietnam, of survival kicked in. It wasn't something that he wanted. It was just something that was a part of him.

"Come on. We're getting out of here," Kerry said.

"Where?" the thin voice asked.

"Never mind where! We're just leaving," Kerry snapped back. "Sorry. Just come with me. Please," he asked, hating himself for talking that way to a child. Besides, the kid was right. He had no idea what he was going to do with Jeffrey. He remembered all too well the kid's last threat to run if Child Services was contacted.

CHAPTER FORTY THREE

Finding Lynne still at the shelter was unexpected. But after a moment's thought, he realized it wasn't far-fetched. She was full of surprises, Kerry thought to himself. Charlene, who sat next to Lynne, refused to drop her sight from Kerry. His gaze drifted over to Jeffrey, already asleep in the chair he had deposited him. The boy slept fitfully, as if the demons of the night had followed him into his dreams. Kerry had quietly made his way behind the counter to inform Charlene of the status of his current street rescue. She poured her concerned stare into him. "What!" he finally cried out. Charlene just glared at him.

"I just couldn't leave him there, could I?"

"No. Kerry you couldn't. Others could. But not you."

Kerry grunted in response. He was not the type of man to take a compliment easily.

"How about his mom? Or that old guy who was hanging around with him?" Lynne asked.

"Said the police rolled them up. Busted everyone in camp except..."

"Is that what Rusty wanted to show you?" Charlene asked, interrupting him.

"You know, Kerry, it looked to me like he wanted to talk to you about something," Lynne added.

Kerry bolted out of the chair. He flew over to Lynne and gave her a quick kiss on the cheek. "You're a genius!"

"I am?" she questioned.

"Of course you are," Charlene quickly added.

"Why?" both women asked in unison.

"Jeff goes into one of those empty V.A. beds."

"Is he a vet?" Lynne asked in confusion.

"No. He's only..." Charlene began. Kerry cut her off.

"He's a veteran of the streets, and that's good enough for me!"

"Dear Lord," Charlene quietly cried out, knowing where it would likely end up.

"What about repercussions? The rules? Simon?" Lynne nervously questioned.

"Remember Simon? The Boss man? Our Boss man? The man who signs your paycheck?" Charlene quickly inserted.

"He may sign my checks, but I work for my clients. Not for him. And last time I looked, Jeffrey is *my* client. And he's in need."

All three turned their collective stare to the child, forced to grow up too fast.

"As we used to say in Vietnam: Let tomorrow take care of itself, for we may not live to see it."

Kerry's words, carrying embedded icicles, chilled Lynne's and Charlene's hearts, forbidding further conversation.

Who knew? Maybe they would be lucky, and the world would end that night.

CHAPTER FORTY FOUR

Lynne exited the shelter. Across the street, a man sat in a darkened car. She never saw him. Lynne had learned a lot from Kerry. But she had yet to develop Kerry's sixth sense of danger. The man tightened his deadly grip on the steering wheel with leather-gloved hands.

Lynne was tired. More tired and emotionally exhausted than she had been in a long time. She had felt about as useful as a fifth wheel, while Kerry had busily prepared an empty cot for Jeffrey. But she stood by, adding whatever emotional support she could under the circumstances. After all, *isn't that what friends did?* This recognition obsessed her racing thoughts. *Was Kerry becoming more than her mentor? More than a friend?*

Lynne did not hear her hidden observer leave his car. Her powers of observation were not only dented by her busy mind, but also partially focused on a homeless drunk staggering her way. She tried to prepare herself, should the man succumb to a gravity attack. She smiled. She was even beginning to think in Kerry's language.

It was not until she had begun to unlock the car door

that she became aware of the potential danger. Her scream was throttled in her throat. She jumped and turned. She held the keys out in front of her as a defensive weapon. "Jesus, Duncan. You scared the hell out of me!"

"So I see." Even by the poor illumination of the late night street scene, she could see the disappointment that chiseled his face in question. With lightning insight, she realized that the last week had also been hard on others.

"I left a message on your phone. You never returned it. I was worried."

"I'm sorry. So very sorry. It's just, I left for work so early this morning. And, it's been one hell of a day."

"I think there's more than just that, Lynne. You're distant. You've always had a measure of that in you, but more so now. And frankly, I expected a measure of gratitude from you. After all, I did leave my business to come up here and find you."

"I know. And I appreciate it. I really do." Reaching out, she ran her hand alongside Duncan's face. "It's just," she began by dropping her hand, "it's all so different. It's nothing like what I expected."

"What's that? What's so different?" Duncan cautiously asked. Lynne flinched. If he was trying to keep the bitterness from his voice, he was doing a poor job. As if he was the answer to Duncan Smithe's question, the homeless drunk that Lynne had spotted earlier staggered up to them and stopped.

"Got spare change for food?" the man asked. He swayed back and forth, buffeted by a breeze only he could feel.

He was in his late fifties. Old for the streets. He had a days' old beard and long black hair that fell in lazy curls to his shoulders. A mid-western twang added an element of charm. At least in Lynne's book.

"You mean for a drink, don't you?" Duncan savagely spat out. He obviously did not share Lynne's feelings towards the man.

"Okay. For a drink." The man strived for a light voice, trying to chuck off the hurtful comment. But his voice was too tight, too scratchy for that. Lynne heard the hurt. She closed her eyes. *What was the point in dishing out pain? Or as Duncan would say: Where was the payout?*

"Have some pride, man! Get yourself sober! Get a job for God's sakes."

He staggered off with his head bent low. His voice trailing behind, he responded, "Okay. Okay mister. Just asking."

"That's what so different!" Duncan's voice tore high into the quiet night, passing judgment not only on the homeless drunk, but on the whole world of the streets. Surprisingly, Lynne felt part of the equation. Obviously the wrong part of Duncan's view. It was like she was being blamed. Condemned. She was also highly offended for the man who had just been insulted.

"You didn't have to be so brutal."

"That's what's so different?" Duncan repeated. "Losers like him!" His voice still registered incredulous disbelief.

"He's not a loser, Duncan." Lynne's voice was clipped. It was also tightly controlled. Each word was being spoken precisely and slowly. "There's a whole other side of life out here that I'm just beginning to understand. True. They're different than us. And they don't have all the material things that we possess."

"Look," Duncan began. His voice was at its soothing best, realizing from Lynne's tightly controlled response that he had blown it big time. "I understand that's what happened with your daughter, Tracy. It was a shock, a very big shock. And, I—I'm sure that all of this is too." He stammered. He searched desperately for the right words. What he did not want to do was dig himself further into a hole, one that had no retreat. No payoff. "We can call all this a culture clash, but you can't let your judgment be clouded. You have to use your intellect. Not rely on your emotions. What I'm saying is, put all of this into proper perspective."

Duncan felt good. He was smug. He was on his game. He had framed the problem precisely. And he had stayed away from emotionally charged words. Or so he thought.

"Perspective, Duncan? For God's sake, she's my daughter! What perspective would you have me put her in?"

Duncan's face fell hard. And it was not only from the meaning of the words. The voice; Lynne's voice was cold as a frozen margarita.

Suddenly, bright floodlights stole the night from them. Lynne and Duncan looked down the street to the source: Ted Tucker's used car lot. Ted came half-stumbling, half-running from his business trailer, screaming inarticulate words, like an animal gone berserk. He made his lurching way over to a car. He threw the car door open. Reaching in, he roughly pulled out a bag lady. He pushed her violently towards the street. She scurried from the lot like a hunted animal.

"What an ass!" Lynne spat out.

"Him? What about her? It's his car she's sleeping in. She's trespassing. Actually, more like breaking and entering."

"He'd shut us down in a heartbeat if he could figure out how," Lynne mumbled to herself. Unfortunately, not low enough.

"Us! For God's sake, Lynne, listen to yourself."

"Breaking and entering? Isn't that a bit like a hungry peasant stealing bread, and being thrown into prison just before the French Revolution? Is that what we've become?"

"What!" Duncan shot back, before launching into his perspective on crime and punishment. But it was lost on Lynne. Within the shadows of the night, she saw another drama playing out.

Halfway between where she talked with Duncan and Ted Tucker's used car lot, Kerry stood. He was on the curb, on the opposite side of the street. Silhouetted for the most part. But Ted's bright lights caught the edge of his face. She was just able to make out the pain that contorted his features. He had witnessed Ted's inhumanity to the bag lady. He took one step forward and balanced himself on the curb. He was now fully exposed by the lights.

Intermediate traffic rushed by. Hurtling cars bathing

the night with the hushing sound of tires upon the blacktop. Their headlights providing a light show, as their illumination suddenly appeared and then disappeared. The cars were like lonely beasts on the hunt for prey. Which was exactly what Kerry was about to become.

In astonishment, Lynne watched. With his eyes closed, and his head cocked to one side, he calmly and deliberately stepped off the curb. Ted Tucker's lights shut off. Darkness. He walked into the street. "Oh my God!" Lynne shrieked. Leaving Duncan in the dust, she launched herself into the street.

What the driver of the black Ford truck thought when he hurled by them, she would never know. Did he see that Kerry's eyes were closed? Or the frantic fire in her own? Forcefully, she shoved Kerry. Together they both stumbled backwards until they were safely on the curb.

"What the hell's the matter with you?" Lynne cried out. She tried desperately to stop her heart from beating free of her chest.

"Nothing." The reply was meek.

Lynne had never heard him sound so sheepish. So ashamed. "You could have been killed."

"But, I wasn't." *Was he disappointed that he hadn't?* "Besides, it don't mean nothin'."

"What is that, some profound philosophical saying from the war? It's bullshit and you know it. Everything means something, even if you don't want it to. It means something."

Lynne shook her head hard, trying to clear the wet

cotton that her consciousness had become. *Was this how mental illness felt,* she wondered? Did her daughter feel the lack of grounding that was nipping at her mind just now? Of a life lived without rules? How alone. How alone and frightened the mentally ill must feel. Her daughter must feel. Tears sprang to her eyes. Thankfully, they were hidden by the night. She swallowed her hurt.

But Kerry was the person in front of her. He was the one with the immediate need. "Does this have anything to do with the boy?" she asked, trying to do the right thing. "Or something Rusty told you?"

"Do not go there." The voice was as dark as the night was.

"Then?" she asked. She tried to see Kerry better, to somehow read him. He sighed heavily.

"Okay. It was something I used to do when I first got back to the world. With my eyes closed, I'd listen for traffic. When I didn't hear any, I'd cross the street."

"Are you nuts?"

"Maybe. Probably," Kerry responded. A little boy's mischievous smile followed, like he had been caught sneaking a look at Christmas presents hidden under the bed. Then, the smile didn't so much die. It became frozen. Unreal. It deeply troubled Lynne. "You see, over there. Noise was different. It was the difference between life and death. On a trail, there could be noise to the front of you. Or noise behind you. But noise to the sides? You died. And then there was the noise of a mortar dropping down a tube: A soft pop. Long distance artillery being fired had a sound all its own. It was like thunder skipping atop the land. The sharp crack of an AK-47 cutting loose sounded like a god cracking his knuckles. The scream of rockets... now, there was a sound to end all sounds. You'd swear they were going right through your head." His voice dropping to a mere whisper, Kerry continued, "The quietness of death. So quiet—so unnatural. It was more than the mere absence of noise. More like a vacuum had sucked sound down a rabbit hole. Noise meant everything over there. Especially the difference between life and death."

"So? What are you saying? Why not here? Why not throw your life away on what you do or don't hear? On a silly game?"

"Obviously I have good hearing."

"Or just good luck."

"That, I don't have." The voice was heavy. Devoid of hope. "Think we'll ever stop sending boys to die for the arrogance of others?"

"Can't you just leave Vietnam behind?" Her voice was a plea, in response to the heartache she heard tearing Kerry in two. She couldn't understand. She didn't want to understand how something so long ago could cast such a long and dark shadow. Then, with chilling insight, it came to her: She was afraid. Afraid that someday she could find herself in his position. Suffer like he now suffered, if things should turn out badly with her daughter. She shut her eyes. Pain clawed at her heart.

"Sorry if all that blood and hurt is raining on your parade!" Kerry replied savagely.

Lynne's eyes snapped open. A weary smiled followed. Kerry never rolled over. Not for anyone. Anything. He met every opposition, perceived or real, with fire. So unlike the men in her life. *Speaking of which.* She looked across the street to where she had left Duncan. Kerry followed suit. The black night was wrapped snugly around him. He was staring at them. Ted Tucker again exited the trailer-office. Ted Tucker stared at Duncan. Duncan Smithe with an e, switched his sight from Lynne and Kerry, to him. Ted Tucker's stare never wavered. Lynne and Kerry continued to stare at Duncan. It was a cluster-fuck of stare downs.

CHAPTER FORTY FIVE

Again, Kerry's night was fitful. He had left Lynne soon after last night's confrontation. Three decades after the war, and he still didn't know how to talk about it. Despair sat like a hairball in his throat. Maybe he should simply learn to keep his mouth shut. Just pretend none of it ever happened. After all, wasn't that what everybody wanted? Wasn't the country getting good at pretending they didn't live in a state of constant war? Pretending that the blood was *always* someone else's fault? That nobody made financial killings off of people like himself? Men and women who had always answered their country's call to arms, and would do so into the twilight of history, unless they learned to just say no?

His jaws clamped tight. He crossed the street in front of the shelter without paying attention to the traffic. He knew that was the higher powers wanted his silence, along with every other combat veteran. That way, they could continue to rewrite history, and cast themselves as the good guys (or as victims depending on the need), rather than the war criminals that they were. That way, the killing could continue.

He grunted early morning greetings to the homeless, the ones who had the courage to linger in front of the shelter in defiance of the new policies of the Boss man. Simon West's tag, that Charlene had given him, brought the first hint of warmth to an otherwise cool, overcast morning. She was one of the finest ladies that he had ever known. Without her, he would have been toast years ago. In more ways than he could count, she was the anchor that allowed him to navigate the craziness of his job, while keeping his own sanity intact.

With his self-musing in full swing, Kerry did not at first see Simon West when he walked in, standing next to Charlene in the reception station. His greeting to her was forestalled. Abruptly turning, she began to walk past him. Her lips were pressed shut, her eyes made small with suppressed fury. "Wait," Kerry said. He had a sinking feeling, like he was on a free fall ride at *Magic Mountain*.

"It's all yours," Charlene hissed in reply.

"What's all mine?" Kerry reached out, stopping Charlene from flying past him. "What do you mean? Where are you going? You're scheduled to work with me today." Kerry was rambling. He knew that. He was playing the game of a thousand questions. Postponing the inevitable. Yet there was no alternative. Deep down, he knew he was losing Charlene. There was nothing he could do about it, except to find out why.

"Not today. Not ever!" Charlene stated, throwing off his restraining arm. She tried to move past him.

"Charlene. This is me. What's going on? At least tell me that." He begged. He beseeched. He shot a hard stare at Simon West, knowing he was the answer to the riddle.

Charlene stopped. She couldn't look Kerry in the eye. She let her sight slip to the chipped linoleum floor. In a small voice, distorted through tears, she began. "Boss man here tried to put me on Leave without Pay. I've got a kid to feed." Her brown, liquid filled eyes moved up to Kerry. For justice, they pleaded. "What does my daughter have to do with any of this? Why should she have to pay because of this scumbag? No. I quit. Ain't no way. I need to find me a job that pays real money, *and* shows me some real respect. I deserve better than this. Better than him."

Kerry turned for a confrontation. Simon stood impassive. It was as if he was watching the clean-up from a traffic accident.

"Why?" Kerry's voice was small. It had been pounded down with disbelief.

"Don't play dumb with me! A child as a vet? Please!" Simon's voice rang bitter with hurt pride.

Lynne walked in. No attention was paid to her. She was invisible. *Now what the hell have I walked into,* she questioned.

"What did you do?!" Kerry found his sense of injustice.

"Me?" Simon laughed. "How about that boy? I called Protective Services. This shelter is no place for an unsupervised child."

"You didn't..." The question, the protest came not from Kerry, but from Lynne. Everyone was caught off guard, especially Simon West.

"You too?" He was unsure of this new adversary. He had no power over her. "He's corrupted even you." Shaking his head for effect. Directing his remarks to Kerry he continued, "It should have been you I put on leave without pay. But it was Charlene's shift. Her responsibility."

The front door banging open drew their attention. Charlene. She had walked out of the shelter. The sound of the softly closing door reverberated throughout the quiet shelter. It reminded Kerry of a claymore detonating.

"Know that you cost her the job. Perhaps that's punishment enough." Simon's voice was haughty and downright mean. Kerry suddenly wheeled around. He was immediately in his face. Simon took a quick step back.

"Swift move, Boss man! Did you happen to think that tomorrow that woman and I are to open the emergency winter shelter?"

The corner of Simon's mouth quivered. "Are you going to help me?" Kerry demanded to know.

"Me?" Simon replied. The voice was torn high, like Kerry had just asked him to volunteer for a firing squad. He licked the first hint of sweat that appeared on his upper lip. "Of course not." He looked first at Kerry, then over to Lynne. "I'm, I'm administration. Not line staff. Besides. I ah, don't have time. I'm working on the Conditional Use Permit. We, I mean I, need to submit it before the Review Board day after tomorrow. I know it's a mere formality. But without it, we can't open the Winter

Shelter. Or for that matter, even stay open. And, um...our next door neighbor has been poisoning the political well."

"Even though you've done all that he's requested of you," Kerry shot back fast. "Didn't all that groveling help?"

"How did you know?" Simon responded. His color fled south.

"It ain't rocket science," Kerry replied.

"I don't have the spare time. I've got enough on my plate as it is. I can't help you."

"Then what do you suggest? There's no way I can operate the whole Winter Shelter without help. And it sure as hell isn't going to run itself. Charlene's irreplaceable, especially under such short notice. If only you hadn't been so stupid!"

"You've got to!" Simon West pleaded. The magnitude of his mistake was growing exponentially.

Lynne was surprised by how crestfallen Simon looked. Also, by the rapidity of his transformation. She had thought that she would never feel sorry for this man. But his pain was so intense. He looked like one of those pictures an animal rights group had sent her once: A coyote had gnawed off his own leg, cruelly caught in a steel trap.

"Use the homeless, your volunteers..."

"Don't even go there." Kerry's interruption was sharp. "They're good for setting up the beds. Keeping the place clean and working the kitchen. But social workers they aren't. We're going to have three hundred cold and hungry people. Many, if not most, with severe substance abuse problems, or mental health issues. I ask again. Are you going to come and nurse a Bi-Polar who's off his or her meds, and in the middle of a severe manic run in the middle of the night? Are you going to help talk down a schizophrenic suffering from terrifying hallucinations? Or hold the hand of an alcoholic suffering seizures? You think they're going to simply take care of themselves?"

"If you didn't coddle those winos so much in the first place!"

Again, Lynne was whiplashed. Opposing feelings warred. Simon West's sudden transformations were mind-boggling. The meanness that leaped out from the man replaced any compassion she had felt moments before. He had said the word, "wino" with such vehemence. She questioned just where all that hatred came from. But it was Kerry who challenged the prejudice of the man.

"They happen to be the people we serve." His voice was controlled. "You can dehumanize them all you want. Even demonize them. But they're still human."

A glaze settled over Simon's eyes. This was not the reaction he expected.

"I'll help you," Lynne gently offered, breaking through their confrontation.

"What?" Kerry's was taken aback. This lady never stopped surprising him. She was a woman of great depth, and capable of the one thing most adults didn't have the strength or the courage to do: change.

"Why not?" she challenged.

"Because, ah, you're not even paid staff. You're a volunteer. An intern! My intern."

"That, I can take care of," Simon replied.

"No way! Charlene you aren't." Kerry protested, mostly out of loyalty to his former partner.

"That, she may not be. But she *is* our new employee. And now your partner. Make the best of it."

"But I need a true Assistant. Someone I can rely on. Someone who won't add to the drama of the streets, but help defuse it."

"That would be me," Lynne said. She winked at Kerry. At the same time, a hard stance to her body added backbone to her statement.

Yes, Kerry thought to himself. *That would be you.* A slow smile came and went. "Still, we aren't done with Charlene. You are going to make that right."

"No. She's the one that quit. She's history," Simon West interrupted.

"You either agree to find a way to bring her back.... or you run the show by yourself tomorrow."

"But!" Simon West began. He cut a desperate glance to Lynne.

"Don't look at me. I'm with Kerry on this. Besides, you know there is no way I can do this without him."

Lynne was worried. From the amount of blood that rushed from Simon's face, he looked like he had entered heart attack territory.

"Okay! Okay! Just give me time to work it out."

"With a bump in salary. She's got a kid to worry about. The last time we saw an increase around here, gas was still a buck a gallon."

"Are you serious?"

"You're a smart man. You'll figure it out."

"For the love of God!" Simon West cried. Turning, he beat a hasty retreat.

CHAPTER FORTY SIX

Nothing out of the ordinary transpired during the rest of the morning. Rounds were conducted. That meant parks, beaches, streets, and back alleys of paradise were combed for the disabled homeless. A million miles walked. A thousand stories shared with nomads.

At noon, Kerry and Lynne went back to the shelter to help with the lunch crowd. That was the thing about social work: One moment you could be calling the cops to have someone 5150: Forced hospitalized because of severe mental disabilities that were, "a threat to self or others." The next moment, you might be serving that same person lunch because the Mental Health Dept. didn't have beds available for them in the locked psychiatric facility.

Of course, they never stated the actual reason: Lawsuit. Instead the party line was: Criteria. As in, the mentally ill person didn't meet it. Bureaucratic bullshit. Doublespeak. As if living outside in the filth and cold wasn't proof enough. Existing on a starvation diet from what they found in trashcans didn't prove diminished capacity. Again, the party line was that it was a "Life style." Freely formed choice. Same sorry story. It was a "right" of a mentally ill person, to die of neglect, in the wealthiest city, in the wealthiest country that the world had ever known. Kerry had seen scores of mentally ill homeless die every year with this "right."

Hours later, Kerry and Lynne exited the shelter. Looking up, Kerry frowned. Dark menacing clouds, billowing towards the heavens like seized towers under construction spilled over, from the Pacific less than a mile away. "It would appear that even Mother Nature is against the poor."

Looking up, Lynne saw the threat and frowned. Motherly instincts stabbed her soul. *Did her daughter have warm clothes? Was she staying in a place that offered shelter from the storm? God forbid, was she even alive?* Concern turned her face deathly gray. She was playing the "what might happen" game that every parent tormented himself or herself with.

"Just hold off the rains till after tomorrow," Kerry begged the clouds. At that moment, Susie came barreling around the corner. When she reached them, she came to an abrupt halt. Loudly sucking in air. Her eyes were jacked wide open. It was as if the devil himself had been chasing her.

"What's wrong?" Kerry asked.

"It's...its Rusty! You gotta help him!"

"Slow down. What's wrong with Rusty?" Kerry's voice was barely above a whisper. A tactic he used, to calm hyper people on the verge of panic down.

"I don't know." Susie's voice had a strange echo to it. She had begun drifting. She was being tugged from—and to—the other side of sanity.

"Susie. Where's Rusty?" Kerry calmly demanded. He took hold of her by the shoulders, forcing her to look up into his eyes. "Where is he?" He needed an answer, and he knew he needed it fast, before she was lost.

"The Hole." An ironic smile followed when she finished the simple answer.

"Susie. Please. Tell us, what's wrong?" Kerry repeated. Hopefully, it was for the last time.

"I was sent for...told he was in trouble. But I was afraid to go." The words were slow in coming. She was slipping further and further into the other side. Her other world beckoned, enticing her. True, it was often one of terror. But it was also familiar. It was an escape from the cruelties of the real world.

Slowly, she raised her sight back to Kerry. One last valiant effort needed to be made. "Please, Kerry. You're the one we trust. You're the only one we can count on. You gotta help him." With that said, she relaxed, fully embracing the other side. She whistled softly, gently calling forth kindred spirits. For Lynne and Kerry, it sounded grotesque. Like fingernails on chalkboard.

CHAPTER FORTY SEVEN

Dusk was falling fast. Cautiously, they approached the general area of the drainage pipes that ran under the 101 Freeway. Winter shortened the day, which was stolen by threatening grays. The storm rapidly approached. A macabre atmosphere laid heavily on the land.

They finally turned the corner. Susie decided that she would go no further. Lynne and Kerry found the area flooded with cops. Paramedic cars. One ambulance. Against her will, Lynne found herself slowly propelled forward. She was being sucked into the vortex of the lightshow that danced before her. It was a concert, a riot of colors. Swirling reds. Bursts of bright blues. It was as surreal a scene as Lynne could ever imagine. She could feel sanity slowly slipping away. It was all too much. She found herself even afraid to speak her daughter's name. She was afraid that if she did so, she would be calling up images and fears that would be so gut wrenching, she would be unable to handle it.

Breaking points. Everyone had them.

Suddenly, she felt Susie materialize alongside her.

Susie took her hand in hers, giving her a connection to someone else and helping her sturdy herself. Silently, she gave thanks for the saving gesture. Susie had instinctively known the danger she was in. Was it a gift the mentally ill acquired? And if so, at what price? Or, were they mentally ill because they could feel the pain, hopelessness and fears of others?

Hanging back with Susie, Lynne's frightening thoughts and painful feelings continued their assault. But now she could handle them without the panic. Still...she felt like she was standing on someone's grave.

Kerry left her side. Her legs weakened, further. He moved to the ambulance. A gurney stood next to it. He knew it had to be Rusty. Lynne squeezed Susie's hand harder. She was not so sure. And she deeply feared an alternative.

Kerry couldn't remember ever having seen Rusty without his face hidden inside the hood of a sweatshirt. He looked so young and vulnerable. Even in the weird lighting, his skin had such a deathly pale to it. The boy had obviously lost quantities of blood, enough that life itself was now threatened.

"What did you do?" Kerry's voice sounded like chunks of living tissue had been torn from his throat. He took Rusty's hand. It was cold.

Rusty grimaced. Pain trolled his body. "I thought that if I made peace with God, the nightmares would stop." His voice was harsh. Brittle.

"How?" Kerry asked. He was lost as to how the

attempt—whatever it was—had landed the young man on the gurney.

His mouth pinched tightly shut, a useless attempt to deal with the pain. "My grandfather was Jewish. My father wasn't. He strayed. I followed in his footsteps. So I thought that maybe—just maybe that was why God was so upset with me. That maybe that was why he was angry with me. Maybe that was why he made me do those things. See things. That, if I returned to faith then everything would be all right." His voice slowed with the effort.

Kerry squeezed Rusty's hand tighter. "Don't put the crimes of men upon God, Rusty. *And do not* put the crimes of the puppet masters upon the puppets. You did not start that crazy war. You are not responsible."

"We're all responsible," Rusty stated. His eyes closed. Opening them, he asked, "You were in Vietnam. Do the memories ever let go?"

"No. Rusty. They don't."

"Then how?"

"You just learn to live with them." It pained him to be so honest. But Kerry knew that lies had a shelf life. And when that time was up, the exposed lies led to the harshest levels of hell itself. Besides, the young man had already paid a steep price from the lies of others. He wouldn't contribute.

Kerry's body was robbed of strength. A paramedic stepped forward and pushed Kerry aside. She began to rapidly move the boy-man towards the rear of the ambulance. Rusty slipped by Kerry. The sweat smell of blood filled his nostrils. Kerry's stomach rumbled. His eyes riveted onto the white sheet that covered Rusty. His midsection was satiated with blood, like someone had dumped a gallon of red paint on him. "What in the name of God did he do?"

The paramedic slammed the door shut. She paused in fearful wonder, just long enough to say, "Dumb kid circumcised himself."

CHAPTER FORTY EIGHT

The early winter evening brought frosty breath to those huddled at the outdoor coffee shop. Regardless of the sharpness of the weather, a feisty and boisterous crowd was to be found sipping a variety of house specialties. Unlike the other crowded tables, with bountiful youth and joyous laughter, the one occupied by Kerry, Lynne, and Susie was quiet. It was as silent as a cemetery. No youth were found in their collective, just aged souls. With two hands, Susie brought the steaming cup of coffee to her lips. They shook violently. Fearing the scolding liquid, she quickly set it down.

"Caffeine jitters without caffeine." Kerry's lame attempt at humor was stillborn upon delivery.

"You've got to help me find my daughter." Lynne said suddenly, catching both Kerry and Susie off guard. "She's been out here way too long already. And after all this..." Lynne's voice trailed off, threatening to break. "Please! You have to," she pleaded. "I don't know how much more I can take—she can take. Back there, for a moment...I thought. I mean, I knew it wasn't my daughter. At least intellectually. But emotionally, for the briefest of moments—I almost lost it. If it wasn't for Susie." Her voice turned liquid.

The image of Rusty—all that blood. It would stay with her for the rest of her life. However short that might be.

"Look, Susie," Kerry began. He was compelled to address her needs first. "That's what these streets will do to you. You've been out here too long already by yourself. Unfortunately for you, you know how to play the game too well. Well enough to avoid getting help."

Slowly, Susie lifted her sight to Kerry. With Herculean effort, she held his stare. Ever so slightly, she nodded her head, yes. "You must allow us to help you. If you don't, you won't be too far behind Rusty."

Susie' mouth contorted. It was a creepy smile. Definitely not pleasant. It communicated no happiness of any kind.

"If the men I've tricked knew how many times I've fantasized about cutting off his penis. It would shrivel up and die on its own."

Kerry reached across the table. He took Susie's hand into his. "I'm going to make you an appointment with Mental Health Services. *And,* I expect you to keep it. *And,* I want you to do whatever they say. Do whatever it takes to get well." Sternness steeled his voice. But one did not have to listen too closely to hear the concern that poured forth from his soul. Even Susie, in the borderlands of her delusional world, couldn't help but be moved.

"Okay, Kerry," she replied, squeezing his hand. "But

only if you go with me."

"It's a deal." Tension drained from his face, letting go of the stress that had crippled it.

Susie's eyes softened.

"You know, in some ways, in many ways, you're very old fashioned."

"Don't let that get out. It would destroy my persona."

"Persona!" Susie stated joyfully. Her eyebrows rose playfully. Standing abruptly, she threw back her head. She laughed.

Kerry was amazed. He had never heard her laugh before. He smiled. It was the most beautiful sound he had heard in ages. Lynne did not follow his smile.

"Susie? You said, 'his," earlier instead of they. Whose, ah..."

"Whose dick did I want to cut off?"

Kerry braced for the answer. He was pretty sure whose it was.

"Yes," Lynne replied. Immediately, she was sorry that she had asked. She had a dreaded feeling in her gut that she really didn't want to know. She had seen, and heard enough horror stories over the last few days. Enough to last a lifetime.

"My dad's." The voice was devoid of emotions. It was stated so casually, as if it was just a simple statement of fact. As if the concept had been considered so many times that it had lost its horror. It was a simple reality, like a painful toothache that grew into a dull ache with familiarity. Slowly, she got up. Susie turned and walked away.

They watched her walk down the block. She disappeared into the darkness. "You reached her. I mean you *really* reached her."

"I know." Kerry's soft voice reflected his own surprise.

"Something's changed in you." Lynne looked to Kerry with a warm gaze, over the edge of her coffee cup. She held it up to her mouth, more as a prop than anything else.

"And what is that?"

"You know. You reached her because you dropped that macho hard edge that surrounds you all the time. And in turn, she's given you her heart."

Lynne realized that there were two sides to the work: On one hand, there was the pain. But on the other hand, there was the ability to help those in need. The real question was, *would that outweigh the heartache? Would she have courage like Kerry to accept that trade off?*

Kerry looked out into the dark before answering. "That's because you were right. I've spent enough time hiding out here. Hopefully, I've done some good."

"From what I see around here, you've done a world of good."

"But I could do more. If I quit pushing people away." He looked off again, then back to her. "I will stop pushing others away. That's what I have to do. That's what I will do."

Lynne reached over. She placed her hand over his. "Does that include me?"

Kerry turned his hand over. He took hers into his. Looking deep into her eyes, he recognized the feeling that was twisting his stomach into knots: Fear. He was not just afraid of trusting someone. He was also afraid of getting hurt. Maybe in the end, the fears were one and the same. He closed his eyes. Destruction of the ability to trust was the ultimate casualty of war. He'd told others that truth a thousand times. Opening his eyes, he was surprised to find Duncan Smithe standing by the table.

"Duncan," Kerry said matter-of-factly. Withdrawing his hand from Lynne's, he stood. If he was hoping that Duncan Smithe hadn't noticed, he was sorely mistaken. The man's eyes rapidly narrowed into mere slits. Duncan Smithe nodded stiffly. Apparently, he didn't trust his voice.

Lynne, thinking of nothing that would add to the situation, decided to keep quiet. It was up to Kerry to break the deadly deadlock.

"Ah, yes. Well, it's late. I must get going."

Duncan Smithe nodded gravely.

"Since you're my new assistant for the emergency shelter," Kerry began, turning to Lynne, "I expect you to meet me tonight at seven. So, you have just enough time to grab dinner."

"Why tonight?" Duncan managed to articulate.

"We need to start our outreach, to tell the homeless to come to our shelter tomorrow morning for intake. We need a count. Some idea of how many to expect the first day. Collect as much information as we can."

"Information? What information?" Duncan Smithe asked skeptically.

"You know..." Kerry began, before he was sharply cut off.

"Actually, I don't have the faintest idea." Duncan Smithe's voice was dismissive, like the rabble couldn't possibly possess anything of value. Or more likely, anything that he cared to know.

"Like social security numbers. Dates of birth. Mental and physical health." Kerry replied through clenched teeth. The man was really beginning to get on his nerves. "And then," he continued, with his comments directed to Lynne. "We need to start looking for your daughter. If we're lucky...very lucky, she will come to us to sign up for a bed. But we can't count on that."

"Thank you," Lynne managed to squeak out. She had begun to question whether she would ever find her daughter. And she knew that without Kerry's help, finding her would be impossible. The streets were his, as much as a top stockbroker could claim ownership of an insider-trading source on Wall Street. Sitting up straighter, confidence entered her every breath. A feeling she hadn't felt in some time. "I'll be there. I'll meet you at the shelter."

"See ya," Kerry tossed over his shoulder, as he turned. Walking down the street, he tried hard not to imagine Lynne and Duncan Smithe having dinner together. *And why shouldn't she?* He had no claims on her. In fact, he had probably allowed his imagination to run wild. Duncan Smithe, as well as being the jerk of the century, came from her social group. Her class. He had money. Status.

What did he, Kerry, have to offer her? The pain and hopelessness of the streets? The depths of hell that men and women too often became trapped in? An up close and personal encounter with mental illness and drug addiction? *A personal relationship with Death?* No. He was sure he had entertained delusional hope, and now he was paying the price. But he was a survivor. A few more blocks later, his knotted stomach robbed him of breath, then it relented. His breathing returned. The scalding pain in his heart would take longer.

CHAPTER FORTY NINE

Throwing himself into the seat that Kerry had vacated, Duncan Smithe lashed out. "You have to stop this!" The sound of the scraping chair drew questioning looks; the tone of his voice—disapproving stares.

"Stop what?" Lynne demanded in turn. She was not used to having anybody talk to her this way. She was not a child. And she didn't appreciate that his demeanor was creating an audience.

"Your infatuation with these people."

"These people? And what people would that be?"

"You know." Duncan Smithe reply was weak. His voice was now in full retreat. She was not the only one not accustomed to being talked to in such a way. Again, he had forgotten how headstrong Lynne could be.

"Putting aside for the moment 'these people,' you mean Kerry."

"Yes." *Wrong answer*, Duncan Smithe realized, as Lynne's eyes shot wide open. "No, I mean all of this." A flushed feeling of heat rolled down his neck and face. "Look. Let's just go home. We'll work all this out. I promise."

Her voice dived lower. "Without my daughter?"

"Ah, yes, your daughter. I'll tell you what. We'll hire, I mean, *I'll* hire a professional private detective. We'll get the best that money can buy."

"Someone that knows these streets as well as Kerry? I doubt it. I think I already have the best that money can buy. But money can't buy him."

"Then what can buy him?" The cattiness could not be kept from Duncan Smithe's voice. Nor the implication. One that Lynne found highly offensive.

"Maybe love," she challenged back.

"Love!" Duncan Smithe's voice rang loud. He couldn't believe she was admitting it. "You've just met him!"

"I don't mean me." She tried ignoring the burning part within her, where the insinuation had struck truth. "I mean his love for the street people, especially the mentally ill homeless. All of them—however you want to label them."

"One can't love those people!" Duncan Smithe protested. "You can't be serious." He shook his head like he was casting off a very bad mental image. It was a picture that he found to be excruciatingly painful. "They're scum. Bums. Nothing but winos!"

"You don't know him," Lynne replied calmly. A frown rippled across her forehead. "And, you don't know them." She grabbed her empty coffee cup. How had she not seen this side of him before? *Or had she?* Had she simply chosen to ignore it? Even more humiliating, had it not been important to her before?

Lynne was shamed by her insight; also her question. But something else was present: A dawning sense of pride. She had changed in the last few days. She could feel it. She was seeing the world with new eyes. Preconceived notions were melting away.

"And you do? You know these people?" Duncan Smithe's voice was harsh, no longer caring if he sounded judgmental.

"Yes. I think I do. Or at least, I'm beginning to."

"Think about it. We can hire the best. Not only a private investigator, but doctors, therapists. Like I said. The best money can buy." Duncan Smithe was repeating himself, losing the debate. He was at a loss on how to turn it around. His hard face softened. It was becoming readily apparent that he was losing more than that.

"Maybe she doesn't need the best money can buy." Lynne's voice was soft. The tone a parent would take talking to a hardheaded child, explaining things as simply as possible. "Maybe she needs me. Needs my acceptance of who she is. What she is. She needs love. My love. Unconditional."

"What's that supposed to mean?" For Duncan Smithe, unconditional love was a foreign and weird concept. Everything had conditions on it. It was the way of the world. His world. And it was a particularly dangerous one at that.

Lynne sat up straighter. She was now talking as much to herself, as she was to Duncan. "That maybe, just maybe, I need to accept her for what she is. Accept her *as* she is. That maybe she is mentally ill. And that maybe that's something that can't be changed."

"That's a whole lot of maybes."

"Yes. I've discovered that life is full of shades of gray. There's very little black and white out here."

Lynne sucked up her courage. She found it exhilarating— that she really didn't care what he thought anymore. "You know. I've learned a lot out here on these streets."

"Like what?"

"Like maybe, there will be no cure. And that by pretending there is one, I'm forcing her to hide her condition behind a screen. Mentally ill or not, she is *my* daughter, and I love her. All of her."

"But we can buy her a cure!" Duncan Smithe protested.

"Maybe. Probably not." Lynne hunched her shoulders up. "But that's no longer the priority. She is. And my love for her is. We're a family."

"That's crazy talk, and I won't hear more of it! I want you to come home with me immediately!"

"You know me better than that," Lynne stated sharply. Through a forced a smile she continued, "Look, Duncan, I know this is hard on you too. Just let me get through the next couple of days. If nothing turns up, well... maybe we'll go home. I promise you, I'll consider it. And I am really sorry for what I've put you through."

If Duncan detected the falsehood of the feelings behind her statement, he hid it well. She detested the fact that she was unable to draw a proverbial line in the sand and stand by it. But she was emotionally drained. It was a decision she would soon come to regret.

CHAPTER FIFTY

Five of seven, Kerry's pocket watch read. He should know. He had taken it out ten times in the last five minutes. Dark thoughts had terrorized him all evening. They followed him to the shelter. Eating had been an impossible dream. Would Lynne return to L.A. with Duncan Smithe? Had she already? Denial smothered his mind the same way that smudgy L.A. smog, dulled by industrial chemicals, sometimes smothered Santa Barbara. And for the tenth time, his attention was distracted by a giggle of youthful, high-pitched voices. Ones untouched by the pain and hopelessness of the streets.

He knew the girls helping to serve the dinner line at the shelter were around twelve, some thirteen. He worked with enough street kids to recognize the different ages of youth. But they were different than those twelve-year-old street kids. For them, life was still full of wonder and promise. Not defeat, and surely not terror. Tomorrow still held a better future. Not just another new camp, or for the lucky few, shelter. Simon West paced behind the girls like an overprotective peacock, tense and ready for a fight. Kerry turned when he heard a rushing of feet, pounding the old wooden stairs behind him.

"What's this about?" Lynne asked, drawing to a sudden stop next to Kerry. Her eyes widened. She stared at the youthful volunteers. She did not detect the soft sigh escaping Kerry's lips, acknowledging that he was putting to rest his worst nightmare. She had not left with Duncan Smithe. *At least not yet,* percolated just inside his consciousness.

"It's his idea," Kerry replied, indicating Simon West with his chin. "Got a church youth group to volunteer to serve dinner."

"Not a bad idea," Lynne added.

"It's a crazy idea."

"Don't sound so down. They seem to be enjoying it."

"A crazy idea. But not a bad idea," Kerry finally admitted. He had to give the Boss man credit. Judging from the faces of those waiting, a measure of warmth was found. "The homies could use a little morale booster right about now."

"They do seem to stand a little taller. Have a little more pride in their eyes."

Kerry's attention was drawn to Ted Pells. He was an old man of twenty. He was just a few years older, but a reality removed from the girls. He wore his long, thick red hair wild, allowing it to fall into his face. He was also skinny. Black jeans. A black tee shirt under a ratty, black, pseudo leather jacket rounded out his attire. His face was drawn tight with weariness. He slumped low in his chair. He began to take off the jacket. Kerry dragged his attention back to Lynne.

"So, tell me again why we're going out tonight? Besides looking for my daughter that is?" She finished the statement with a voice raised in hope.

"Because most seriously mentally ill street people won't come to be sheltered unless we coax them."

"Even with the winter storms around the corner?" she asked, still not quite believing the norms of the streets.

"Every winter, we lose about a dozen to the Angel of Death. We don't call it the killing season without good reason."

A chill ran down Lynne's spine. She shuddered. It was due partly to the words. Also, to the bitter finality in Kerry's voice. She didn't even want to know where her daughter fit into the equation.

Catching her shocked look, Kerry tried to cushion the harsh reality of the streets with a reassuring smile. He also reproached himself for his careless choice of words. He had to remember that all this was new to her, and that she carried a heavy emotional burden as well. Gentleness was the key. Sadness wrinkled his eyes. It fled in a millisecond. She was confused by his clashing reactions to her. "We also need to do a screening on each and every homie who wants to use the shelter. We do that either tonight or tomorrow."

"Why?" The question popped out. Lynne could think of no good reasons that would forbid entry into the shelter.

"All must be TB tested and have flu inoculations before

they can stay with us, according to the city. Tomorrow will be busy enough. In fact, it's going to be one hell of a day. So anything we can accomplish tonight makes it that much easier tomorrow." Kerry's eyes clouded over. He had entered another dimension of winters past. It took real effort for him to literally shake it off. "Only thing worse..." Kerry began, before Lynne cut him off.

"Would be if there was no shelter here for them," she said completing his statement for him.

He gave her a warm smile. "Careful. You're beginning to think like a social worker."

"That would be you," she replied.

"Yes. That would be me."

A blood-curdling scream broke through their conversation. Kerry reached out, and Lynne slipped easily within his protective grasp. They both looked over to the young girls. They huddled together, casting quick, sharp glances to Ted Pells.

Following the girls' line of sight, they looked over at the young man. He was covered with bright red blood. Letting go of Lynne, Kerry grabbed a drying towel and rushed over to Ted, who was holding a box cutter loosely in his hand. He was staring at the tattered skin that he had sliced open, from elbow to wrist on his left arm. The look in his eyes was that of an observer, not someone who had just let his life flow freely from his body.

"Call 911!" Kerry yelled loudly. He took the box cutter from the boy's hand. Covering the multiple cuts with the towel, he pressed down hard.

For Lynne, the room began to spin. It was suddenly oppressively hot. The hot, thick air made breathing almost impossible. She looked over. The girls had stopped looking. Forming a tight circle, they held their heads down. Prayers were mumbled. Tears fell. She sat heavily down on the nearest chair she could find, and waited for reality to let go of her chaotic soul.

CHAPTER FIFTY ONE

For the second time in her life, Lynne found herself standing next to an ambulance. Again, she witnessed a young soul, damaged beyond belief, being lifted into it. *Who would believe this?* Nothing she had ever seen on so-called "reality TV" even came close to it. All television, film, and books paled in comparison. *How had all of this been so hidden from her all her life?* Lowering her head, she knew. She hadn't wanted to see it. She now knew that she had wanted others to tidy up the dark side of life. Keep her world sanitized. What had she read once? *Evil only needs good people's indifference to succeed.* She had certainly given evil plenty of playing room.

She looked over to Kerry. Realization of just how lonely and painful his life was slammed into her. *How had he kept himself from going insane?* The ambulance pulled away. Adding a sour note to her musings, Ted Tucker swaggered up.

"The city's finest in need of service?"

Kerry spun around. "Why don't you go play tag on the freeway?" Kerry stated savagely.

"A bit testy, aren't you?" Ted Tucker asked. Lynne noticed that the man involuntarily backed away from Kerry. Apparently, he had just realized how stressed Kerry was.

Trying to find a center of calmness, Kerry gulped down air before speaking. "Is there something you want, or are you just having your slime moment of the evening?"

"Just being a good neighbor," Ted Tucker replied. His voice was twisted with mockery. "Save your friends the trouble. Tell them *not* to show up tomorrow."

"I know I'm going to be sorry for asking, but here it goes. Why would I do that?" Kerry winced. A sinking feeling in his stomach burned. Acid was being poured into it. If there was a way to sabotage the shelter, this slime bucket certainly had the savage heartlessness to do it. Kerry's eyes lowered to half-mast. He didn't have the brains. Hadn't, in fact, all the years he had caused the shelter trouble. It had always been petty stuff, more along the lines of nuisance than anything else.

"I looked up your C.U.P." The arrogance of the man's voice grated on Kerry's soul.

"Cup?" Lynne asked. Puzzled.

"Not cup," Kerry responded. Capital C. Capital U. P. Short for: Conditional Use Permit. City rules and regulations that..."

"That tells you under what circumstances you can open the emergency winter shelter," Ted Tucker said, interrupting Kerry rudely. "Also what conditions you can operate it," Ted Tucker added boastfully, as if he had been given the inside number for the Lotto.

"And we'll be in compliance. Always have." Kerry's voice sounded guarded. He was unsure where the conversation was going.

"Not if you let your friends in without proper I.D. Proper forms completed, T.B. tested, etc. The list is actually quite extensive. I never realized just how extensive it was."

"We know all that! So what? We always do what needs to be done."

"No. Actually not."

The pause that followed was for effect. Ted Tucker allowed the silence to drag on. The dead time enabled Kerry to catch a strong whiff of whiskey off the man's breathe. Ted Tucker continued. "You always have that scum loitering outside for days while you process them. And according to the law, more than three people standing together at one time, on a public thoroughfare, is an infraction, I believe it's obstructing the free flow of traffic. Foot traffic included. Ain't the law a bitch?"

"So?" Lynne asked, confused as hell. The two men were speaking a totally alien dialect.

"So," Kerry began. His voice was dark with insight. He knew where this was going. He was unsure if there was a damn thing he could do about it. "You plan on having the police here to issue those citations and run them off. Don't you, Mr. Ted Tucker?"

"Smart boy!"

Kerry took a hard step forward. Ted Tucker stumbled backwards. He spun and hurried off. "Don't say I didn't warn you," came the muffled voice from the dark.

Lynne followed Ted Tucker with a questioning stare. Lurking amongst the used cars, a familiar figure stood.

"I wonder where the hell he came up with all of that. Way too sophisticated for a man who gets his courage from a bottle. He never hit us with that in years past. And believe me he would have, if he had been smart enough to think it up."

"I've got a pretty good idea," Lynne responded. Her voice was as hard as tempered steel. Her eyes were still upon the figure in the lot.

"Huh?"

"Never mind," Lynne dropped her stare. "We've got more important things to worry about. "Now what are we going to do?"

Kerry's shrugged. "We're going out to find our people and invite them in, and we're going to pray like hell for a miracle tomorrow. Not sure how many will have the strength to cross a police line. Just their mere presence will scare off many. And the infractions...court date. Fines. It's too much to expect..." his voice trailed off and died without completing the rapidly expanding horror show of what might be.

Looking up, Kerry saw clouds drift in front of a crescent moon. A chilly breeze kicked up, cooling his feverish skin. "Looks like we're opening just in time."

"Only question is: In time for what?"

Kerry was surprised by the question. It wasn't like Lynne to ask such a hard question. That was what separated the middle and upper classes from the poor. Their belief, and their knowledge, that tomorrow always offered the fulfillment of better times. The poor had no such delusions. Or luxury.

CHAPTER FIFTY TWO

Without the long, heavy-duty flashlight that he carried, they would have been totally lost. Lynne was having a hard time keeping up. But she was strong and on a mission.

They trudged onwards through the broad, empty field. Darkness surrounded them. Threats percolated from the unseen. It was like a pack of predators was waiting in the blackness to pounce and devour them. Only the hazy crescent moon's low illumination, and the narrow beam of the flashlight kept the sinister blackness at bay. The darkness—alive with malevolent intent, reached out and brushed her face. Lynne tried brushing it away like it was a pesky fly. But it wasn't. And she knew it. Ice crystals formed in her veins.

"Be careful where you put your feet," Kerry cautioned her when she stumbled.

Careful of what? Lynne wanted to ask. But she was afraid to know, so the question went unarticulated. Some things were best-left unknown, she decided. This was the third field they had visited. Each one was spookier than the one before in its own unique way. Kerry abruptly stopped. Lynne bumped into him. He shone the flashlight onto a series of discarded and broken shopping carts. They were roughly spaced and formed a semi-circle in front of them.

"I don't understand." Though she whispered it, her voice sounded like a cannon firing off a round. A sound Kerry had grown accustomed to, but never comfortable with in Vietnam.

He tried to command his hijacked blood pressure down. His heart beat to a slow pace. He began to inch forward. His movement constricted with an overabundance of caution. Next, his light snagged on string, stretched from one cart to the next. Cans hung from the string. Lynne reached out, touching the string. Pebbles clanked around inside empty cans. She jumped.

"I don't understand." she repeated.

"Password," The darkness spoke. "Or so help me, I'll blow you away. I'll light you up like the Fourth of July."

Lynne's heart rate accelerated like a racing Porsche. She felt like she was living inside a Hollywood slasher movie, with some psycho about to cut her to pieces. Shame suddenly flamed her face. Deleterious thoughts against the mentally ill came so easy to mind. Kerry was right about the prejudicial conditioning of Hollywood and mass culture. She had to remind herself that her daughter was mentally ill.

"Calm down, Murphy. It's me. Kerry." He swung his flashlight around. Its beam highlighted a man emerging from the night. Murphy was a small man, with long hair that was greased down and combed back. His attire was a World War I army khaki uniform, with knee high black boots worn on the outside of his pants. A neatly trimmed black beard was proudly worn.

"Shelter opens tomorrow. I, I mean we, want you there," Kerry began. He looked back to Lynne. Her stern features relaxed. It was not lost on her that he had used the plural in his stated want. Looking up to a cloud that had moved in front of the moon, he continued, "Looks like a storm's moving in."

"Why you go and walk into my warning system for? My perimeter's well-guarded. You of all people know that." Murphy's speech was clipped. Formal. He cast an accusing stare at Lynne. "You're lucky I hadn't set out my claymores yet."

Lynne wanted to ask what she had done wrong. But she knew better. She leaned in to get a better view. His voice had taken on a hurt quality. It sounded like a little boy rather than a man.

"Yeah. Sorry about that. Got a cherry with me. You know, new. Just in-country from the world."

Claymore? Cherry? In-country? World? What the hell were these guys talking about? Lynne wondered. Again, she marveled at the strange new reality that she had stumbled into.

"By the way," Kerry continued. His voice had a more authoritative tone to it. One that firmly announced he would not take no for an answer. "That's an order about tomorrow. Not a request."

"Don't care much for orders," Murphy responded in opposition.

"I know. But we're calling in a B-52 strike first thing tomorrow morning. The whole place will be subject to an ARC Light, and after that, PUFF will work over what's left. It won't be pretty."

"ARC Light, you say?" his voice solemn.

"'Fraid so."

Again, Lynne was impressed. She may not have the slightest idea what Kerry was talking about, but the foreign words: PUFF, ARC Light and all the rest, seemed to work like magic. For Kyle and the other veterans from that war, these terms were written in blood on their souls.

"Then I guess I don't have much choice do I?"

"Nope," Kerry agreed.

"Okay then. See you first thing tomorrow."

"Okay, then," Kerry confirmed.

They made their way back to the truck. Exhausted, they crawled in "Think we did any good?" Lynne asked. It was just past the witching hour. Stumbling around in the dark, god-forsaken fields had been emotionally trying. Physically challenging.

"Only tomorrow will tell." Kerry's sight was hijacked by the darkness in front of the truck. He shuddered. Shaking off a bad nightmare.

"You mean, this morning?" she teased.

"Yeah. Right."

"We through?"

"No. One more stop."

"Dare I ask where?" Lynne asked.

"Where it all started. At least for you."

Lynne shot a sharp look over to Kerry. *Now what was he talking about?* Then one word came to mind, triggering an avalanche of raging emotions: Daughter.

CHAPTER FIFTY THREE

Kerry was right. This was where it had all started. Lynne tried to peel back the night for a better look at Kerry. But the coming and going of the car lights either blinded her with their strobes, or robbed her of night vision. *Did he think the answer to the whereabouts of her daughter was to be found here?* She pulled her hooded sweatshirt tighter about her. The temperature was falling. The storm front was rapidly moving in. Or at least that was what she tried to convince herself.

"Anyone home?" Kerry's booming voice rang out. The tin walls of the pipe amplified where he had pitched it, startling her in the process. The dead silence that followed was creepy. Threatening.

Kerry shined the flashlight into the tunnel. Lynne followed the light beam until it was drowned out by a sea of blackness. Nothing was there. Nothing stirred. What was beyond the light? What is ever beyond light?

"Should we go in?" Lynne asked. She cautiously leaned into the pipe. Her voice was torn with hesitancy. She was strong enough to admit that she was scared.

"Not unless you got a death wish." Kerry turned, sweeping the outside area with his flashlight. "We don't know what to expect if we go in there. Night time is not good for exploring the unknown."

What did he expect to find? She wondered. She looked up at him. "Besides, you respect the fact that in there— it's someone's home. You wouldn't want someone to go trooping through your home if you weren't there. Would you?" Again, Kerry stabbed at the darkness within with his flashlight.

"Why did you bring me here?"

"I'm not really sure. We've covered a great deal of territory. Your daughter has yet to turn up. These pipes, and others like it—hold the answers to a lot of mysteries. And the last time we were here..." Kerry's voice grew weary. "I don't know." He lowered the flashlight until it illuminated the dirt and trash that covered the floor of the pipe.

"You mean there are more?"

"Yes. And even though we've visited a lot of the camps, there are still so many more. I guess I was hoping for a lucky strike."

"These camps?" The lump in her throat cut her voice high.

"Like the foothills. And the caves."

"Caves? People living in caves?" Lynne had a hard time imagining her daughter living in one. She peered into the pipe, seeking clues in the inky blackness that was beyond the illumination of their flashlight.

In unison they turned to leave. Then Lynne's hesitancy brought them both to a quick halt. "Something wrong?" Kerry asked.

"I don't know." She cut a quick glance over her shoulder. The pipe seemed to shiver. "Now it's my turn. A funny feeling."

"Funny feeling, you say?" Kerry snorted like a wild boar. "Just wait till tomorrow."

CHAPTER FIFTY FOUR

Standing in front of her hotel with Kerry, she suddenly realized just how exhausted she was. *Did Kerry feel likewise?*

"Tired?" Kerry asked. *Had he read her thoughts?* She was glad he couldn't see her face. The lighting was poor. She didn't want him to see the flush that flashed across her face. If he could read that thought, what else had he been able to?

"I know I should be. And I know tomorrow, I mean later—it'll be a long day and all." She stammered. She knew she wasn't making any sense.

"But?"

"But. I'm wide-awake. Tired. Yet pretty sure sleep will come hard."

Kerry grabbed her by the hand, spun her around and headed back to his truck.

"What? Where are we going?" Kerry didn't reply. "Boss's orders?"

"Doctor's orders," Kerry corrected her.

Soon they stood on the ocean floor. It was the same beach where Kerry had taken her before. Yet, it was so different. The beach was embraced by the lover's gentle mantle of soft darkness, cutting them off, and isolating them from the rest of the world. Freeing them from their stressors. The smooth lapping of the gently breaking waves was soothing to both man and beast. From distant bonfires came the musky smell of smoky driftwood, seasoned with salt and seaweed. The smells combined into a heady scent that perfumed the beach and transported them in the process. Lynne inhaled deep. Tension melted away like an ice cube in the desert. Kerry relaxed, letting go of the day's events.

"The best medicine in the world," Kerry stated. He looked out over the water, surrendering to its hypnotic rhythms. "It may not be the Ritz or Club Med..."

"It's merely the whole Pacific Ocean," Lynne interjected. Her voice was lowered in awe.

"That would be my ocean."

"Your ocean?" she asked in surprise.

"Yup. My ocean!" came back the possessively hard answer.

"Yeah. That would be your ocean," Lynne concurred.

Looking into the waves, they were captured by the moon's reflection within the curls. It was enchanting.

"What do you see?" Lynne asked off of a strangely serene look on Kerry's face.

"Without sounding too religious, I see God's face. Why is there beauty? Why cover the fields in the brilliance of spring flowers, or the mountains in the harsh beauty of crystalline snow in winter? Why the radiance of colors in a spectacular sunset? Or the velveteen softness of a moonless sky? Surely all these things can be accomplished in a strictly scientific need without beauty. Yet, they come gifted, wrapped in beauty. Why? Still, we shouldn't look for the footprint of God."

"We shouldn't? But I thought you just said..."

"No. Instead we should look for his or her smile."

Kerry smiled awkwardly. In turn, Lynne smiled gently. "This coming from the world's hardest, street-wise social worker? The angry vet?" she questioned.

"Hard to believe, isn't it?"

"No. Not really." Looking about she added, "You know we don't have bathing suits?"

Taking her into his arms, Kerry's husky voice asked, "Do we really need them?"

"Who says the best things in life aren't free?"

"Nothing's free in life, Lynne. I think I'm falling for you. Something that I haven't done in a long time."

"It's something that I haven't really done in a long time either. I think I let someone in only if he is safely contained within boundaries. I've been too busy chasing other things, *and* keeping my personal life safe and predictable." Lynne's voice was throaty with desire, yet low with vulnerability. Reaching up, her hand played with loose strains of Kerry's hair that the wind teased.

"Love only comes when you stop the chase and allow it to come to you," Kerry said, his own hand gently caressing the side of Lynne's face. "And when you're willing to open your heart to both its joys and pains. I think that is something that I've come to realize lately. Because of you."

"Then come here," Lynne replied, pulling Kerry's lips into hers. Suddenly, she was no longer cold.

CHAPTER FIFTY FIVE

The next morning broke cold. Dark clouds hung low like suspended teardrops—holding whispers of rain within. They looked to Kerry like part of a canvas that was draped in front of the shelter when he and Lynne drove up. The world had grown gray, and more foreboding overnight. Trouble lay upon the street like yesterday's wind, displacing newspapers that were scattered about. Winter's bite rushed them like starving junkyard dogs pouncing on raw meat. Kerry opened his truck's door and climbed out. His jaws clamped to a hard set. He turned his jacket collar up. His eyes screwed down.

Across the street, a line of police cars were parked directly in front of the shelter. Lynne joined him with her hands buried deep into her fur-lined coat. Her face was drawn tight with confusion. She had never seen so many police cars in one location before.

"I don't understand," she began. Kerry was staring intensely at a police car. A tall cop with a hard-set face was leaning over Ted Tucker while talking down to him. Ted Tucker looked worse for wear. She could almost smell the stale booze from where she stood.

"All that outreach last night? Did it do no good?" she asked. Lynne fought hard to quell a sinking feeling of defeat. It tightened her stomach muscles into a sharp pain.

"You mean like, where are the homeless?" Kerry's voice was as raw as the brewing storm. Hopelessness bled out with each word spoken. He knew that the homeless were accustomed to defeat. That in too many instances, they looked for any sign of it, even before it was inflicted upon them. They walked, if even a mere hint was detected. Kerry didn't judge them. He knew it was a way of protecting fragile and beaten down egos. He also knew that particular survival skill, all too soon, became a self-defeating bad habit. If they had somehow gotten wind of the resistance being thrown up around the winter emergency shelter... or merely beheld the sight of the police cars...there were just too many reasons for failure, and damn few for success.

It was a full on, full body contact sport, with Death as the referee. It was the struggle for survival of the homeless against all odds. His conjuring, pleading and begging to them to stand firm in opposition, to a myriad of attempts to run them out of town—or better yet, out of existence—stood little chance against the harsh reality of the battle for survival.

Kerry knew that without the winter emergency shelter opening up, Death would have a field day with the onset of the dying season. He looked about, desperate for a reason to believe—a reason that all was not lost. A wry smile broke onto Kerry's face. That reason was marching down the street.

Erect, proud, and with his head held high, Murphy smartly turned the corner, duffle bag in hand. There was a hard-set cadence to his feet. Behind him came Susie, dressed in a high school cheerleader outfit. She was literally dancing down the street. From behind, in ones, twos and threes, came the walking wounded. In some instances, the walking dead. Up from the beaches, and down from the parks, from hidden camps, and abandoned store fronts, the survivors of America's Diaspora struggled in.

Julie looking like Julie.

Eileen Swartz and her three daughters, aged twelve, six and four, with their waist long blond hair tied back into braids. All wearing the same long, velvet granny dresses. The three girls were holding hands, the youngest trying hard to hide her fear. Their mother struggled with two heavy suitcases. All that remained of the family's life possessions.

A ragged homeless man pushing two shopping carts. They were piled high with recyclables and junk, including a three-legged plastic chair.

An old alcoholic woman pulling behind her a traveler's bag on wheels, like she was late catching the redeye to New York.

Two middle-age women slowed with early old-age, courtesy of a lifetime on the streets. Each pushing a baby stroller cramped with so much stuff that it was obvious no babies were on board.

Following closely behind the mothers-not-to-be was a young boy and girl. Their skateboards, adding a rickety racket to the dawning noise of the morning, followed.

Dorothy and Sam. Alone. Walking with heads down, and shoulders slumped. Sadness nipping at their slow moving heals.

A drunk, staggering down the street came next. He was carrying a singular broken ski.

Four homeless men walked in a straight row. Each pushing a shopping cart. Again, it reminded Kerry of a wagon train from years gone past: A lost wagon train.

Stern. Sheepishly wearing his white bandages on his head and hands like medals, from a war long past, walked quietly alone.

And then came Charlene. She tore around the corner with a large purse, swinging wildly from side to side like a deadly weapon. "Did you think you could have all your fun without me?" she asked. Her voice turned liquid with emotion. She threw herself into Kerry's outstretched arms.

Kerry blinked back his tears and hung on for dear life. "Thanks." His reply came out low.

You know I received a very strange call last night?" she whispered into his ear.

"Really? From whom?"

"Boss man. Says I've been reinstated. You wouldn't know anything about that, would you?"

"Nope!"

"Yeah, right. You're a bad liar."

"So I've been told. Did he by any chance happen to

mention a raise?"

"As a matter-of-fact, he did."

"Imagine that."

"Is there anything I can do?" she asked, pulling back.

"There's nothing any of us can do, unless you brought a miracle in that handbag of yours."

He looked back to the police car and locked stares with Ted Tucker. Happy anticipation radiated from the man's eyes. *But of course!* This was what he wanted, Kerry realized too late. Not only did he not want the winter shelter to open, he wanted this defeat of the homeless witnessed by them, with their noses rubbed in it. Again, Kerry was surprised by just how much hatred for the homeless Ted Tucker had.

Nearing defeat filled his stomach with cold stones. Kerry knew that only half the miracle had been delivered with the appearance of the homeless. Without divine intervention of some kind, Ted Tucker would get his wish.

But the unexpected happened. Snake eyes rolled. Chaos— the norm of the universe. God's will, or perhaps because of the grace of good people. Maybe both. Maybe neither. Maybe it was ingrained in the collective unconsciousness of the human race to take care of the wounded among us. Or, as Kerry silently hoped, and had bet his life's career on: a spiritual need to do so. All that Kerry knew was that his rusty prayers were about to be answered.

A van that had gone unnoticed slowly pulled up. The church girls from before, the ones who had volunteered for the soup kitchen and witnessed Ted Pells cutting himself, tumbled out. Sleep was rubbed from innocent eyes. High pitched shrieks and giggles, clashing with the self-enforced quietness of the self-conscious homeless. Ted Tucker's face collapsed into a mask of purple rage.

"Thank you," Kerry meekly said. He wiped away a tear. He turned to Lynne. It would take a ton of tissues to wipe her eyes dry.

A highly agitated Ted Tucker pranced angrily about. The man was incensed by the appearance of the girls. His kind of hatred, as is most, is best conducted without pure of heart witnesses about. Busy noise caught Kerry's attention. He turned back to the line of police cars. The cops had begun to break out their riot gear. They were replacing soft caps with hard helmets; unsheathing belly clubs. The morning suddenly became tinged with the threat of violence.

Two of the young girls spotted Eileen Swartz's family coming to a halt. The mother could no longer handle the heavy suitcases. They rushed over to her. One of them took hold of one of the suitcases. With great effort that threatened to topple her, she lifted it. The other church girl took the hand of the youngest Swartz, and led them towards the shelter. Another girl ran over to the man with two shopping carts. She began to push one for him. Still another hurried over to the two hippies with skateboards, and began walking with them. The rest of the girls, in ones and twos, peeled off from the van and scattered themselves amongst the homeless, who now walked a little taller. A little prouder.

The driver of the van, a chaplain, if the word printed across his baseball cap was to be believed, joined Kerry, Lynne and Charlene. Also rushing over to join them was Ted Tucker. A weary looking cop, Sgt. Hall, accompanied him.

"This is low, even for you!" Tucker yelled at Kerry. A fine spray of spittle accompanied his words.

"He had nothing to do with this," the sheepish chaplain answered before Kerry could.

"I don't understand," Lynne tossed in.

"Well. I'm not sure that I do either. At least not entirely," the chaplain stated. Finding himself under the collective gun stare from the small group, he continued. "We had a meeting with the girls and their parents after the incident at the soup kitchen."

"Incident? Incident! That psycho bastard tried to kill himself in front of your girls!" Tucker yelled.

"As I was saying," the chaplain continued, after looking at Tucker, as one would upon an unknown insect species. "We were meeting with the girls *and their parents* to make sure everyone was okay after what they had witnessed. One of the parents brought up a rumor that he heard about the emergency winter shelter running into problems. Word gets around," the chaplain explained off a bewildered look from Tucker. "Anyway, the girls insisted that we do something. It was their idea to come down here this morning."

"You should know better than to expose them to this scum! It's dangerous. They're dangerous!"

"I don't see much danger here. Nor do I believe they were in much danger the other day. I do see a lot of love though."

"But..." Tucker began, before the man of the cloth cut him off.

"I do see a place where Christ would be. He did walk with the lepers of his day. And I'd say these people are the new lepers of our day. But you are right. There is a danger here."

"See! I told you," Tucker said to the sergeant.

"I see a danger to the girls' humanity. To their spiritual wellbeing, if they don't follow their hearts. If they were to merely stand aside while this travesty of justice was allowed to play out."

"I'm telling you, they're scum! They're as dangerous a bunch as you're ever likely to run into! There's not a decent man amongst them!" Tucker's voice had brought the volume down, pronouncing his judgment as a historic truth that none could contest.

"Oh, really?" the chaplain said. "How about women? Any decent women about? Or children?" he asked, looking over to Eileen Swartz and her girls.

"I didn't mean them," Tucker stammered, having followed the chaplain's line of sight.

"Christ was homeless. Mary also. You including them in your judgment?"

"Of course not!' Tucker yelled in protest. He looked about. His panicky eyes finally landed on Sgt. Hall. "I demand that you do your job," he began. He tried to match Hall's height by standing up straighter.

"Like how?" the cop asked, taking off his helmet and wiping frustration from his brow.

"How? By arresting somebody!"

"Would you like me to start with the church girls?"

When no answer was given, Sgt. Hall turned to another cop who had just joined them. "Arrest the girls. All of them," he ordered. All of the adults were stunned. But none more than the sergeant's fellow cop.

"Sir?"

"You can't be serious? Are you?" Lynne asked weakly. Her voice was barely audible.

"Of course not!" Sgt. Hall said, speaking loud and clear. A sigh of relief escaped the cop who had been given the order. "I am not going to have my officers arrest those girls, or anyone else. It is not my job to destroy their humanity."

Ted Tucker stood slack jawed, like he was experiencing the first tremors of a powerful earthquake. Finally recovering his voice, he shouted, "You can't do this! I know people." His quick look from the cop to his car lot drew Lynne's stare that way. There amongst the cars stood Duncan Smithe. He was watching the unfolding drama with intense interest. Ted Tucker, drawing strength from Duncan Smithe, turned back to them. His vigor for combat renewed. But before he could say anything, the cop cut him off.

"Remember Tiananmen Square? When the Chinese Government suppressed their democratic uprising?" Of course no one answered the question. He continued, "The man who impressed me the most was not the one who stood before the tank with his briefcase. It was the lead tank driver who refused to run him over. He must have been under intense pressure to do so. But he refused. He stood firm for *his—or because of his*—humanity. And because he did so, he brought the whole damn tank column to a standstill. I've often thought about him. What was he was thinking? I ask myself. What would I have done in his situation? He was a brave man. A decent man." The cop's eyes clouded over. He was lost to the deepest reaches of his mind, where spiritual values are kept.

"And what was your conclusion?" Kerry asked, respectfully.

"He did what he did because he remembered that he had put on a uniform to protect people. Not crush their dreams, nor kill them. In my book, he stood tall as he sat in that tank. He was, and is, a courageous example for every man everywhere who puts on a uniform to help and protect."

"What?" Ted yelled. "I'll have your job for this. Those people are breaking the law. I demand that you arrest them."

Sgt. Hall turned his attention back onto Ted Tucker. "I've been standing here all morning listening to you whine. That, and smelling gin on your breath. And I have to tell you, I really hate the smell of booze first thing in the morning."

Sgt. Hall looked about, finding himself surrounded by the homeless and their new guides. A soft smile spread to his eyes. His quiet words, directed at Ted Tucker were anything but. "If my men catch you so much as a foot off your dealership today, they'll do a field sobriety test. And I think we both know you'll blow numbers so high that you'll be in violation of the public intoxication laws. I'm not kidding." He swung hard eyes upon Ted Tucker. "The ball's in your court. What's it to be?"

Ted Tucker looked about. Panic collapsed his face. The pores of his skin opened wider, allowing another wave of stale alcohol to permeate his immediate environment. Kerry and the cop knew that smell. Kerry studied the practicing alcoholic in front of him. His judgment of the man shifted. He was a victim waiting to join those who struggled unsuccessfully with the disease of alcoholism.

Ted Tucker suddenly realized that he had become the center of attention to the dreaded homeless. He turned abruptly, and hurried across the street, back to the safety of his car lot. More than one homeless person smiled, realizing what had just happened.

"Does that mean we won?" Lynne asked, her voice scratchy with confusion.

"We won one battle," Kerry replied. He knew better than to place too much value on what had just happened. He had seen too many temporary victories turn into bitter defeat. Still...looking around at the homeless and their helpers, and at the cops who placed humanity above blind orders—he knew that he had never witnessed before what he was seeing now. Even blinking hard failed to dislodge the scene before him.

Still...

Turning his head left to right, he scanned the streets. With quivering lips, he said, "There's so many who aren't here. I'm afraid our *friend* has scared off many. We'll have to spend days beating the streets to bring them all in."

A downdraft of winter's breath forced Kerry's head back. He frowned at the menacingly drifting clouds. The promise of rain was in them. Looking over to the car lot, he saw Ted Tucker and Duncan Smithe deep in conspiratorial conversation. "What we don't need is more interference."

"That I can take care of," Lynne replied with bite, having followed Kerry's line of sight.

Lynne approached Duncan Smithe. Ted Tucker quickly retreated to hide behind a yellow 1998 VW Rabbit. "Now, don't go jumping to conclusions. It's not necessarily what it looks like." Duncan Smithe's excuse was lame as they came.

"Oh. Really? Then what is it Duncan?"

"I, ah..."

"Tell me how it can be anything but?"

Duncan Smithe cleared his throat before replying. "It's time to go home, Lynne, ah, honey." A real bad call.

"Honey! Don't you dare honey me! I want you out of my life! Period. And if I so much as see one inch of your ass around, I'll call the firm and have you dropped as a client."

"You can't do that." The reply came courtesy of a breaking voice.

"Take my advice. I wouldn't try me if I were you."

"What does he have to offer you that I can't? This?" He expanded his hands to include not only Kerry, but the entire street before them.

"Yes," she affirmed strongly. "And an ocean, too."

"An ocean? Him?" Duncan Smithe looked over to Kerry. "I bet he doesn't even own a Jacuzzi! And you're telling me he owns an ocean?"

"Yes. That would be him."

To the day he died, Duncan Smithe never did understand the sly smile that Lynne gave him that morning. It was a side of her he had never seen—an expression that intrigued and seduced him to the end of his days.

CHAPTER
FIFTY
SIX

For the hundredth time, Lynne looked at the milling crowd in front of her. For the hundredth time, she pondered, *just where had all those people been hiding?* She cast her eyes over to Kerry and smiled. He was in his element. A glow glistened in his eyes. It was a magical connection. One that was life affirming and profoundly deep. The word that sprung to her mind was love. Sure, it was corny. Overused. Trite. But not today. On that day, it had a meaning, a real and living presence. She knew better than to try and define the word, and its connection to all those diverse people. That if she tried to over-analyze the word, or the present experience, she would merely end up destroying the magical moment.

Now was the time to simply experience what was happening, without expectations or preconceived notions. To tuck it away in her memory bank for a future when troubled times would try to break her. It was a reserve of pure and precious energy that she would savor for years to come. Her smile broadened. Even the cops had showed courage, and a depth of humanity that she had found profoundly moving. She made a mental note to look up that Chinese man who had stood in front of the tanks. She felt guilty that she couldn't remember the incident. But then again, there was a whole world that had suddenly come to life for her.

Lynne's introspective mood came to a screeching halt with the sudden reappearance of Charlene, who had gone into the interior of the shelter on a mission. "Problem?" Kerry asked her.

"And then some!" Charlene responded. "You'd best hurry."

"I wonder...?" Lynne began to ask Kerry. He raised his hand to still her question. They stood before Simon West's office. It was highly unusual for Simon West to ever have his door shut. In fact, she had never seen it that way before. She knew his logic. It would be hard for him to oversee his staff if it was.

"Let's not play the guessing game. Let's just see," Kerry said, before turning the doorknob. Hesitating, he looked back to Lynne over his shoulder. "Just be prepared." The door lazily swung open.

Simon West sat behind his desk. He was disconcerting to both of them. From the wrinkles of his jacket, they guessed he had slept in it. From the day old growth of whiskers, he obviously had neither bathed, nor groomed that morning. Blood shot eyes and the stale smell of rotgut booze told them the rest of the story. The unanswered question was the picture of a woman with gray eyes that he held in his hand. Her mouth was a straight line of despair. The corners of the picture were frayed like he had handled it a thousand times. Kerry stared at the picture. He looked over to the one of a family that Simon had said was his, and he came to a realization.

"Come to gloat?" Simon West asked. Surprisingly, his words weren't slurred. But his voice was hoarse, like it had been burnt raw by a ton of cheap booze. Unfortunately for him, no amount of booze could make his brain, or his memory, inoperable. "To say, 'I told you so?'"

"I don't understand. What's he talking about?" Lynne asked.

"The suicide attempt?" Kerry put out.

"You think?" came back the wounded man's savage reply.

"You're also feeling bad about the young church girls—the volunteers seeing it." This time, there was no question to Kerry's words. It was merely a statement of fact, one without doubt of any kind. Gently, he reached for the picture in Simon West's hands. He struggled to steady his hands when he did so. He needed all his strength to keep them from shaking. "Your wife? Your real wife?"

Simon answer was blinking back his tears.

"I don't understand," Lynne stated. Her voice was rough. Like it had been her, rather than Simon, who had been throwing down whiskey all night. "If that's your wife, then who is this?" she asked, picking up the framed picture of the suburban wife and soccer son.

"*That* picture came with the frame. Didn't it?" Kerry offered.

"Smart boy," Simon responded.

Brittle seconds passed. Finally, the deadly silence was broken. "So. What are you waiting for," Simon began. "Call the cops. Even better, call the newspapers. You've got a 'page one' lead story. I'm sure there's more than one person in this city who would love to read that story. See me this way."

Simon cocked his head sidewise in question. "Maybe no one has more right than you."

A deep sigh followed. Simon eased himself back, deep into the groaning chair which threatened to swallow him. "Those poor girls. That poor boy. Why would someone want to kill themselves? Doesn't she know the pain she leaves those who are left behind?"

Kerry's eyes crinkled. He heard the shift from masculine to feminine. "Your wife? Is it she you're talking about?"

Simon's eyes shot upward. He obviously had no idea what he had just revealed. He tensed. Then, accepting defeat, he slid back further into the chair and into his state of despair. "My wife shot herself as we slept—as I slept next to her. I was only inches away from her."

Kerry's jaws became a spring loaded steel trap. They were set so hard against each other that his teeth threatened to shatter. As to Lynne, she tried as hard as she could not to vomit. She had never heard something so sad, and so terrifying in her life.

"How could she do such a thing? How much hatred for me must she have felt to do such a thing? How did I fail her so utterly?" Simon's eyes danced from Kerry to Lynne, and then back to Kerry. Finally accepting defeat, they slumped down until their gaze was directed inwards.

"Look, West...Simon," Kerry began. "Severe depression, like all mental illness, is a disease. It's not something that anyone would ever will upon themselves. It's a disease that sucks your soul dry. I know some say it's an act of aggression. But I don't buy that. I think that the pain of it just becomes so overwhelming that they don't think of anything else except stopping it. It may be selfish. Probably is. But who are we to judge? All I know is, we all have a breaking point. A finite capacity of pain we can carry before it just gets too much—becomes so overwhelming that death becomes an acceptable option." Kerry was no longer merely talking about Simon's wife.

"The only option?" Simon West's voice was small with uncertainty, which was a good thing in Kerry's point of view. Uncertainty was the best he could hope for at the moment. Anything was better than the tragic road that he saw Simon walking down.

"You done good the other day..." Kerry began before Simon cut him off.

"Yeah, right. By bringing those poor girls..."

"Exactly!" Kerry interrupted. "By bringing them in, you brought an element of humanity and dignity to our people. To troubled souls in a whole lot of pain of their own."

"And your act of compassion gave us our miracle this morning," Lynne interjected.

"Huh?" Simon responded again, tilting his head sidewise.

"Come on. I'll explain on the way," Kerry stated. Simon sat frozen. Kerry walked around the desk. He took Simon by the elbow and gently stood him up.

"You're not going to turn me in?" Simon asked, more confused than ever.

"I'm not exactly into dropping dimes on people."

"Dropping dimes?" Lynne asked. Her turn at confusion.

"I don't understand. I thought that was what you wanted," Simon stated.

"Not unless you make me wear those stupid work shirts. Even with the sleeves cut off, they're a bit much." Kerry's smile reinforced the tone of his voice, and the meaning of his words.

Reluctantly, Simon followed Kerry's lead. "Exactly where are we going?"

"First we're going to show you the miracle you're partially responsible for," Kerry said through a smile.

"And then?" Simon asked.

"And then we're going to visit a friend of mine. Trust me."

"Without meaning to, I think I already have," Simon replied.

Simon was still reeling from seeing the church girls mingling so easily, and being so helpful to the homeless as they were processed for the winter shelter. Finally, something positive was contesting the bitter mood of depression that he had fallen into. With dawning realization, he was beginning to understand just how much pain his wife's deep depression had subjected her to. *If it was anything like he had been feeling since her death*...maybe, just maybe, her death had more to do with that, than it did with him. *Dear God, he hoped so.*

Being too deep in thought, Simon hadn't paid much attention when Kerry walked him a half a dozen blocks over from the shelter. It wasn't until they stopped in front of an old stone church that he became nervous. The air was tinged with salt, and heavy with the smell of diesel fuel from the harbor down the block. Across the street, an old hotel stood abandoned, waiting for earthquake retrofitting, or more likely, tax cuts for the rich investors and the wrecker's ball.

"You don't strike me as the religious type," Simon said to Kerry, after clearing the fear of the unknown from his throat.

"I'm not. I won't try to interpret what should be between a man or woman and their beliefs, nor will I dictate those beliefs to others. I am the spiritual type though. I've seen enough unexplainable mysteries in life to know that there's more to it than bricks and mortars."

The journey continued. They entered the church. They walked into the cavernous interior of the building. They came upon a circle of wooden folding chairs where a group of twelve men and women sat. A few were homeless. A few others were obviously businessmen. The rest were office and blue-collar workers. All present thanks to the leveler of drugs and alcohol. A portly priest walked up to Kerry. He bear hugged him. "It's good seeing you. It's been a long time!"

"Too long," Kerry admitted. "I brought you somebody."

"You mean again?" the priest said. Taking a step back, he gave Simon a quick once over. Stepping up to him, he stuck out his hand. "Hi. I'm Bob. And I'm an alcoholic."

CHAPTER FIFTY SEVEN

It was deep in the night by the time Kerry and Lynne found themselves back at his truck. The street was deserted. The homeless were finally tucked snuggly and safely within their new cots at the shelter. The threat of rain was still that. Just a threat. But the cold was real enough, and with a sharper bite. Lynne wrapped her arms around herself. She was reluctant to call it an evening, regardless of the cold and time of night. Kerry was pleasantly exhausted, but also shying away from ending the day.

"That was quite a day...again," Lynne offered.

"And then some," Kerry agreed.

"About my daughter?"

"I promise. Tomorrow we scour this town from high to low 'til we find her," Kerry stated.

"Will we? Find her that is?" Lynne questioned. Again, fear was crushing her heart, causing her voice to wobble.

"In this business you have to have faith—faith and willpower. Without them, nothing gets accomplished. Okay?"

"Okay," Lynne confirmed. She felt lighter, with the weight lifting from her chest. Soaking up the silence,

Kerry looked up and down the street.

"Is your life always so full of drama?" Lynne asked.

In response, he gave her a mischievous smile. "Actually I've been thinking of finding the right person. Slowing down long enough to smell the roses. You know, like maybe I don't have to be mad at the world all the time."

"Like maybe just some of the time?" Lynne teased.

"Yeah. Just some of the time," Kerry agreed. His smile broadened. "I'm not getting any younger you know."

"Oh, really!"

"I know it's hard to believe. And I hear that falling in love is the ultimate fountain of youth. According to leading scientific thought that is."

"So? You got anyone in mind?" Lynne asked. She moved easily into Kerry's outstretched arms.

"Yeah. That would be you."

Their lips melted together in passion, with their hearts beating against each other as if they were joined. At first, the touching of their lips was tentative. Probing. Then it became more soulful, deep and long, only breaking when breathing became a necessity.

Then, noise from the shadowy night reminded Kerry of the very real dangers of the world. He whirled around and went into a modified fighting stance. "Who's there?"

Susie hesitantly stepped forward, from a wall that had blended around her, as if she had been a part of it all along. Kerry wondered how long she had been standing there. "You scared the hell out of me!"

"Sorry," Susie said. She looked upon Lynne like a

hound dog would stare at an intriguing find. Several seconds dragged by. A shudder rolled through Susie, bringing her back to the present. Turning her attention again to Kerry, she continued, "I need to talk to you."

"I, ah, can grab a taxi," Lynne offered.

"No!" Susie's unexpected and definitive response startled them.

"What?" Lynne asked. Her voice was skittish.

"Why?" Kerry asked. His own, sturdy.

"Because it involves her." Susie moved forward. Again, she cast a strange gaze at Lynne. While not exactly friendly, neither was it hostile. It was just downright spooky. Lynne reached deep down inside herself for untested strength and smiled. Susie reply was a sly smile. "Just give me a minute alone with Kerry. Please."

"Sure," Lynne replied. She moved a few feet away. Susie stood on tiptoes, and Kerry bent low to allow her to whisper into his ear. Whatever Susie said brought a stern frown from Kerry. Again, that goofy smile came to Susie's face, just before she turned, and walked away like an ethereal fairy.

"Thanks," Kerry's voice barked out after the retreating figure.

"What was that all about?" Lynne asked, when Kerry rejoined her.

"We have one more stop," Kerry informed her.

"I'd like nothing better. But it was a very long night last night. And today was even longer. I'm exhausted."

"It's your daughter." The words were spoken in English.

But at first, they failed to register with Lynne. When they did, a stone logged in her throat. Being unable to talk, she walked over to the truck and got in. Kerry quietly followed suit.

CHAPTER FIFTY EIGHT

Tracy sat hunched by a dying fire. A thread-worn blanket that did little to hinder the invasive cold, was draped over her thin shoulders. Her feet, tucked under her, were caked with dirt and encumbered by neither shoes nor socks. Her stringy hair was patted down with body oil and dirt. It hung down into her face. Petting the rat in her lap, she asked wistfully, "Why did you die for?" She looked about at the empty space that surrounded her. She felt imprisoned behind iron bars. "Why did everyone leave me?" Her words bounced off the drainage pipe, mockingly tossed back at her in spitefulness.

Aloneness collapsed about her like a cave-in, with tons of rocks robbing her of breath. Sitting became too taxing. Hunger. Real, life-defying hunger and crushing despair was taking its toll. Laying into a collapsing state, she curled into a ball to await her fate.

The air was oppressively still. Laced with the smell of rotting food. Human waste. Dorothy and Sam had abandoned the hellhole a few mornings back. *Or had it been weeks?* Since then, she had had nothing to eat, nor companionship of any kind. That is, except for the rat. Her friend. And now it had gone and died on her. *Maybe it was time for her to die also.*

"What is time," she asked. It had both elongated and truncated. First, turning into an instrument of confusion, then into nonexistence. Maybe she had always been crazy. Maybe she had been that way for a thousand years and she had lived in the cave for all that time. Maybe, this state—this mental illness was real, and everything else was an illusion. After all, what is a shadow? There's no substance to it. You can neither touch nor smell it. But it is real. You can observe it. And you can kill it.

"No!" the sound that shot out of her throat was scratchy. An image of her mother had come to mind. It was soft and kind. So unlike "them."

The voices in her head had become increasingly savage in their condemnation of her. Lately, they had added loud screeching noises, like birds being tortured. Also the sound of squealing pigs, which she was positive were being slaughtered. Maybe even right outside her tin house. And just last night—or was it last week, they had teased her that help had come. She thought that she had heard her mom and a man come to the entrance of the pipe, and call out her name. She had heard their discussion. Or at least she thought she had. But then the voices laughed at her. They mocked her. They told her that no one cared about her. They convinced her that in reality the man who had hurt her had come back to do those bad things to her again, if she dared respond to the voices outside in the other world—the rapidly fading, real one.

She sighed. Life was simply becoming too much for a fifteen year old to endure. And she missed her mom so much. But she couldn't leave. The voices wanted her to stay—alone and isolated in the metal tomb that her new home had become. She decided she would simply lay her head down, and wait for the shadowy figure in black to come and claim her hurting soul. She looked about for him. She knew that he lived in the darkest corners of her abode. He no longer scared her. In fact, she had had increasingly long and deep conversations with him over the last few days. And in a way he had become her confidant. The one entity with whom she could share just how terrifying her mental break had been. To lose one's mind—one's sense of identity, was to lose the ability to cope. It was even worse than that. Her mind had become an enemy full of vile, hopelessness and cruelty of unbelievable dimensions.

Sounds from the entrance told her that her real life tormentors had returned. Running her hand over the bruise on her face, she cringed further into the dirt.

"Please don't hurt me again," she whimpered. Then the floodgates opened, and tears cut rivers through the grime on her face. "Please," she softly pleaded again.

"It's okay. I'm here to help."

The first thing she saw of Kerry were his cowboy boots, as he gingerly made his way to her through the accumulated trash in the pipe.

"Please! Not again. Don't hurt me!" This time, her voice was louder. But not stronger. Panic ate away at its edges, until it twisted and folded back into itself with fright. She dared a quick look and saw that the man was too tall for the pipe, forcing him to walk stooped over. A sudden rustling sound behind him caused Tracy to scoot back.

"Tracy! Tracy! It's okay. He's with me!" Lynne stated, voice hammered raw like she had just had throat surgery. With watery eyes blurring the already dimly lit environment, she rushed over to her daughter.

"That you, Mom?" The voice was small. Tracy's eyes squinted, trying to see past the hallucinations that she now lived in. After all, it wouldn't be the first time that the demons of her mind had screwed with her.

"Oh, Tracy. It's me. Of course it's me!"

Lynne instinctively drew up short. Her daughter looked so different. She was several pounds skinnier, her body was encased in dirt, and her voice and body language had changed. Tracy lay tense. She tried to shift her legs so she could jump up and run for it. She wouldn't let those "others" hurt her again. She had been trapped by them, and if she had anything to do with it, she wouldn't be again.

All was quiet while reality, hallucinations, love and motherly instincts, battled for supremacy. Tracy had to know. "I mean like for real. Or, you know, are you just inside my head?"

Blinking back tears, and struggling with pain, Lynne calmly replied, "It's me, hon. it's me." She was surprised by the strength she heard in her voice. She was ready to do battle. She was prepared to vanquish any foe to protect her daughter. To reclaim what was rightfully hers. She was also willing to accept her daughter as she was. It no longer mattered what disease of the mind she may have had. The only thing that mattered lay cowering before her.

"Mother?"

"That would be me," Lynne responded. Her voice was soft and caring. She bent down and kneeled by her daughter.

"You gonna send me away?"

Brushing back hair that had fallen into Tracy's eyes, Lynne looked over to Kerry, who was using his cell to call for help.

"No, honey. I'm not." Lynne smiled. "We're going to get you help first. But you belong at home. With me."

"Even if I'm different from others? Different from who I used to be?"

Lynne took her daughter's face into her hands. "Listen Tracy. Listen close. We're all different from whom we used to be. Especially me."

"You?"

"Definitely me."

"But...?" Tracy began only to be reassured by her mother.

"Let's just start with that acknowledgement. Accept whoever we are. Whoever we've become. We've both been changed by this experience. But we're still family, Tracy, and that's all that counts."

CHAPTER FIFTY NINE

Kerry felt totally useless. He willed himself to relax. He stood silently off to the side while Lynne comforted her daughter in the back of the ambulance. After tucking the blanket about her, just as she had done a thousand times before, when Tracy was a child, Lynne climbed down. The only illumination was the yellow light that crept towards them from a streetlamp down the block. It was like a hideous monster, stretching menacing tentacles towards them. The only sound was the soft crunching of gravel under the ambulance tires when it drove slowly away. Lynne turned to Kerry. She fell into his outstretched arms, burying her face into his chest. Gently, he stroked her hair.

"God. That was the hardest thing I've ever experienced." Pulling back, Lynne looked deeply into Kerry's eyes, searching for answers. She was looking for human connection in a time of need. "Now what? Where will they take her? What will they do?"

"They'll take her to the hospital. Clean her up. She'll stay there for a couple of days for observations. Try out different meds. Give her a proper work up. A diagnosis."

"She so young, Kerry—my baby."

"And you need to be strong for her. I need to be honest with you. You need honesty now more than ever to help her."

"I know. I want to help. I will help."

"Yes you will. But you need to realize that meds don't always work. Sometimes they actually make the situation worse. You need to be there for her through it all. Through all the ups and the downs. You need to be there. That's the most important thing. Be there."

"I will, Kerry." Lynne stood straighter. She had grit in her eyes. A steel edge to her voice. "I'm her mother."

Kerry smiled in acknowledgement of the strong lady standing before him. "That would be you."

"And you?"

"I'll be there for you through it all. That is, if that's what you want."

Her answer was to once again melt into Kerry's arms. But then her attention was averted—to a young boy of eighteen, walking by them. His unmoving stare was glued to the ground. "And what about them?"

Kerry looked over to the figure of the retreating boy. "It's about survival. How to help reduce the pain. Or, as it's known in the profession: Harm reduction. We do what we can to help them survive with less pain in their lives. A few times we even manage to turn a life around—save a life...but that alone cannot be our measure of success."

"Survival? Pain reduction? I guess I can learn to live with that."

"The question is, can they?"

Again, they leaned into each other, until they realized that the boy had stopped a few feet away and he was now staring at them. Pulling back, Kerry turned to him and said. "Can we talk to you for a minute?"

"What about?" came the reply. His voice was a mixture of the brashness of youth. Insolence.

"Listen." Lynne's voice matched her warm smile. "We have this sweet deal on the Presidential Suite at this outrageous shelter..."

"What are you? Like guardian angels or something?"

Turning to each other, they replied in unison, "That would be us."

EPILOGUE

Hard gray clouds painted the sky. They were draped low, just above the crashing surf. A stiff sea breeze that rode in on the backs of the roaring waves broadcasted a spray of salt water towards shore. The strong winds whipped into the faces of Lynne, sending her hair into her face. She pushed it back to no avail. Seagulls added a cacophony of harsh cries, perhaps protesting the approaching storm, or Kerry and Lynne's intrusion. Kerry held an urn with reverence in his arm. Lynne stood next to him.

"I think she would like this day," Kerry said, looking into the threatening sky.

"Yes. I think she would have," Lynne agreed. "Should we, you know, say a few words?"

"Yes. I think that would be appropriate," Kerry agreed.

The cold wind sent chills throughout Lynne's body. The hard quietness that was Kerry only added to it. "Well?" she finally said.

"Maybe you should be the one," Kerry said. Clearly, he was uncomfortable with the task at hand.

"No," Lynne began. "It's better if you do it."

"Thanks." Kerry tried, shrugging the importance off with an ironic voice, but it was too tortured to be successful.

Kerry stepped into the surf with the urn held out before him. *But of course,* Lynne thought. She quickly followed suit. The freezing water that washed into her shoes sent knives of icy pain slicing up her legs.

"Skitty. May you find the peace in the hereafter that eluded you here on Earth." With the words softly embraced by the musical rendition of the ocean, he opened the urn and poured the ashes out. "And may Tracy find peace in the here and now—along with the love of her mother," Kerry added. He turned to Lynne. Suddenly, she no longer felt the cold.

"And may you find the peace that has eluded you all these years." Lynne looked deeply into the troubled eyes of the man who stood before her. He turned towards the ocean, and heaved the empty urn into the waves. Turning again, Kerry took Lynne into his arms. A warmness that was more than merely two bodies huddled together— embraced them.

Peace. As was justice—was allusive and fleeting. He knew that. But he would take this moment with this woman, as is. One day at a time never seemed more appropriate. That's, after all, how you build for the future.

One day at a time.

OTHER BOOKS *by* KEN WILLIAMS

CHINA WHITE

SHATTERED DREAMS, A STORY OF THE STREETS

THERE MUST BE HONOR

ABOUT *the* AUTHOR

In one of the world's most beautiful places, amid
swaying palms and ocean breezes, Ken Williams battled
death and hopelessness. For over thirty years he worked
for the homeless in Santa Barbara as a Social Worker.
His clients included the mentally ill, alcoholic/drug
addicts, war veterans, the infirmed, people with AIDS,
the neglected, survivors of sexual violence, and the aged.
During that time, over three hundred of his clients and
friends died on those unforgiving streets.

In an attempt to keep Death at bay he helped establish
homeless shelters, soup kitchens and halfway houses.
His most cherished projects were Casa Rosa, a recovery
home and rescue for pregnant homeless women battling
addiction or mental illness, and **Maritza's Cocina**, a
children's soup kitchen. For his struggles he won many
awards, including being recognized as Public Citizen of
the Year for California by the National Association of

Social Workers. He was also given the 2010 Civil Rights Award by the Santa Barbara Chapter of the A.C.L.U.

Like many of his clients, Ken Williams was a combat veteran. He served with the Ninth Marines in Vietnam, who are better known as "The Walking Dead" of the Vietnam War.

Ken is the author of ten novels, seven screenplays, and numerous articles. Along with actor Paul Walker and movie producer Brandon Birtell, Ken helped produce and starred in "Shelter," a documentary about his work with the homeless. He was also featured in "Streets of Paradise," another documentary filmed in Santa Barbara.